Smok

Philip Michael Cooper

This is a work of fiction. Similarities to real people, places, or events are entirely coincidental.

SMOKESCREEN

First edition. April 16, 2023.

ISBN: 979-8223508571

Written by Philip Cooper.

Also by Philip Cooper

Alex Kalfas Series
The Gladio Protocol
Smokescreen

Dedications

To all my family and friends who supported me during the writing of this book. The many friends who undertook editing and proofing duties but particularly Chris Horsman, who used his magic proofing to give the book its final polish. Finally, to my understanding and beautiful partner Pauline who put up with my long absences to the study. Without all these lovely people I could never have finished this book.

Chapter 1

15th August 2013 – Kifissia Athens – 10:30

The man entered Venetia walking purposefully past the rows of pastry display cabinets towards the back of the pastry shop where the area serving pastries, snacks and beverages was located. Anyone observing the man would have found it rather odd that he did not stop to look at the pastries, for Venetia had the reputation for baking the most delicious pastries in all of Athens. Established in 1875 in the rich northern suburb of Kifissia by two brothers, the shop and its excellent standing had withstood two world wars, a civil war, and a German invasion, in its one hundred and thirty seven years of existence.

The display cases were full of traditional Greek pastries, baklava, kadaifi, galaktoboureko and many more, plus ice creams and beautiful cake creations, which on a weekend day would be empty by the time Venetia ushered its last customer out. Today the fifteenth of August 2013, was one of the most celebrated of Greek festivals, the day of the Assumption of the Virgin Mary.

'There won't be any pastries left by two o'clock' thought one of the sales ladies as she watched throngs of people buying boxes of pastries as gifts to give to anyone, they knew who was named Mary or Maria or any combination of that name in typical Greek name day tradition.

She noticed the man as he strode passed the displays, groups of people stepping aside as if realising he would not give way himself. She thought him rather handsome in a swarthy sort of way despite that he had several days of stubble on his face which was the modern style, as was his completely shaved head. The white suit he wore fit like a glove, and she noticed that he was well proportioned without an ounce of fat on him. The suit looked expensive, as did his brogues, his blue shirt, his yellow tie, and the briefcase he was carrying in his right hand. It was already thirty degrees centigrade outside at a few minutes before eleven in the morning but there was not a bead of sweat on the man's face.

The sales lady pinned the man as a businessman, probably an entrepreneur. He had that entrepreneurial look about him, devil may care, confident and street smart. She watched him, her eyes boring into his back as he entered the seating area and disappeared from her sight.

The man headed for the far corner of the seating area and sat down at an empty table carefully placing his briefcase on the floor next to his chair. Before he had hardly settled into his seat a waiter was at his side.

'Καλιμερα σας κυριε, τι μπορω να σας φερω,' said the waiter with a slight bow of deference, asking the man what he would like.

'A double Greek coffee please,' said the man in Greek.

While the waiter was getting his coffee, the man looked around him. He noted that all the waiters looked as though they should be retired but they all looked smart in their traditional white jackets which were the trademark of Venetia. He smiled with satisfaction as he observed that all the tables, of which there were fifteen arranged in three rows of five, were made of oak, as were their plush chairs, dutifully covered in expensive fabric. The walls of the eating area were also clad in wood as were the wooden pillars of which there were five that he could see. In the centre of the wall facing him was a set of French windows which opened out onto a huge patio area filled with awfully expensive bamboo furniture and huge canvas sun canopies over every table. The French windows were closed to allow the air-conditioning to do its work. The man was surprised that so many of the outside tables were occupied considering it was now over thirty degrees centigrade. He was grateful that the air-conditioning was working efficiently as he didn't relish the heat.

The waiter approached with his coffee and set it down in front of him together with a gold clip which held the till receipt.

'Ευχαριστω,' said the man, thanking the waiter and giving him the faintest of smiles as he inserted a five euro note into the clip. The waiter on seeing that the five euros covered the cost of the coffee and a nice tip smiled back and touched his brow before making his way to the cash desk.

The man sat drinking his coffee watching as both the indoor and outdoor tables began to fill up as lunchtime approached. 'It's time,' he thought to himself. He reached for his mobile and pressed a speed dial button.

'I'm ready,' he said when the phone was answered.

'We'll pick you up outside in one minute,' said a voice. The man disconnected the call, then picking up his briefcase without getting up he slid it onto the chair which had its back towards the open area of the room. Unless someone actually came over to the chair, they would never see it lying there. He looked around making sure none of the waiters were looking in his direction, then sliding out from his chair he walked quickly but calmly towards the entrance which he had entered Venetia twenty minutes earlier.

As he passed through the area where the pastries were on display the sales lady who had watched him when he had entered the premises noticed that he was not holding his briefcase. Instead of going into the area where the tables were, she decided to catch up with him and ask him if he had forgotten it. This probably saved her life as by the time she was near enough to call him she was outside in the street. She called out to him but either he didn't hear her above the noise of the busy street, or he ignored her, crossed the street, and got into the waiting white convertible C-class Mercedes, which immediately accelerated away at speed expertly driven by a raven haired young woman.

The sales lady turned back towards the entrance to Venetia and stepped into the shop area. As she did events seemed to move in slow motion. The first thing she noticed was the warm air rushing engulfing her and tearing at her clothes almost forcing her backwards. Then she saw the wall of fire surging towards her consuming and atomizing everything in its path. She dived to her right hitting the ground just outside the open doors of the entrance and curled herself into a ball. Then she heard a demonic roar and felt an unbearable heat, as the wall of fire screamed out of the doors into the street. Without any material to devour, except for a passing cyclist and a car, leaving both severely burned, the wall of fire simply extinguished itself and stopped existing.

The sales lady was severely burned, in unbearable pain but alive and later she was able to tell the authorities her account of the events including an accurate description of the man.

Later that same evening the news programmes updated their viewers on the casualties suffered; twenty-five people had died; another forty in hospital and of those eighteen were critical; Venetia itself was just a shell of a building, the fireball having consumed or melted everything in its path. They then broadcast a taped speech of Prime Minister Alex Kalfas, who had earlier visited the scene of the incident.

'Fellow Greeks,' began the Prime Minister. 'Today we have witnessed a horrendous crime against the Greek people and against democracy. I know you will join me in sending our condolences to the families and loved ones of the victims of this tragedy. My promise to them and all Greeks is that we will find the people that committed this horrific deed and bring them to justice. God bless our great nation,' finished Alex. The camera followed him as he spoke to the members of rescue teams, medical teams and forensic experts giving them his appreciation of their hard work.

In a living room in an apartment in a southern suburb of Athens the man now dressed in scruffy jeans instead of his white suit, was watching the newscast with a detached air. Smiling in satisfaction he looked down at the raven haired girl who had her head against his bare chest and murmured 'A job well done darling.'

Chapter 2

16th August 2013 – Athens – 08:00

In the Mega Maximo, the Greek Prime Ministers' official residence and office, seven people sat round the oval mahogany table which was positioned in the middle of the conference room atop a plush thick-piled Turkish carpet. This fact invariably raised the eyebrows of those who knew of the long standing bitter relations between Greece and Turkey over the years. Around the walls of the conference room were portraits of previous Prime Ministers all seemingly staring down over the cabinet ministers who had participated in cabinet meetings in years gone by, perhaps daring them never to say anything against the national interest of their beloved country.

Alex Kalfas cast his eyes around the table attempting to catch the eye of each of the six cabinet ministers who were present. He found that catching everyone's eye before the meeting started, focused them on the agenda at hand and allowed him to start the meeting before their minds started to wander.

He had convened the National Security and Anti-terrorist Council in response to the incident in the pastry shop in Kifissia the previous day.

'Good morning everyone,' said Alex. A general murmur of greetings rippled round the table. 'We have a big agenda today, not least the terrible events of yesterday, so we will start with that. Have we got any further with identifying the responsible party or parties?' asked Alex of his Home Secretary Kaliope Vlachos.

Kaliope casually flicked her fringe away from her green eyes and glanced down at her notes.

'The police have nothing yet unfortunately. We still don't know whether this was a terrorist attack or some domestic extremist group with some sort of grudge. We have over one hundred officers scanning traffic- cam footage but nothing as yet.'

'Isn't there a traffic-cam on the street where the incident took place?' asked Achilles Nikolaou, the finance minister, staring intently at Kaliope.

'No,' replied Kaliope. 'Neither are there traffic cams at the crossroads at the top of the street.' Kaliope let a rueful smile play on her lips as she turned towards the finance minister. 'You realise of course it's your cutbacks to our budget that you imposed at the last budget, otherwise we would have had traffic cams in the area.' The nearest cams to the incident are almost two kilometres down the road and they could have turned anywhere off the main thoroughfares before being picked or even hidden the car,' finished Kaliope suddenly realising her voice had gone up an octave.

'Alright Kaliope calm down,' said Alex. He liked Kaliope despite the fact that she tended to raise her voice when she felt her abilities were threatened. She was intelligent, highly intelligent, being a member of Mensa rather proved it. Kaliope studied at Athens University where she achieved a doctorate in economics and at Princeton in New Jersey, on the back of her admittance to Mensa, where she achieved a doctorate in astrophysics. All done and dusted by the time she was thirty years old. Why she then chose a career in politics Alex could not fathom. Mind you, he was glad she had because at the age of thirty-six she had become the youngest cabinet member ever and now she was probably the best and most respected Home Secretary for a long time. Both the Chief of Police and the Director of Customs and Excise adored as well as respected her. In fact, everyone adored her, she was a typical Greek beauty, long dark hair, piercing green eyes set against an olive skin that did not seem to have a single blemish.

'Any increase in chatter on the internet?' said Leonidas Papadakis, the Industry and Business Minister, unknowingly interrupting Alex's train of thought.

'Nothing obvious,' replied Kaliope. 'Of course, daily chatter is not static at one level all the time, it generally mirrors a wave-like pattern, however it's the spikes that alert us that something may be brewing. We haven't observed any spikes for some time now.' Kaliope looked at each of her peers in turn as if daring them to question what she had said. Then her green eyes settled on Jasonas Makris, the Health Secretary.

'What have forensics come up with Jasonas?' she asked, giving him her sweetest smile. 'Thorough investigation at the scene of the bombing could go a long way towards finding the guilty parties. Evidence must be collected in a professional manner. Are you satisfied that you have the resources to accomplish a positive result?' continued Kaliope.

'I have every confidence in my men,' replied Jasonas. Then smiling at Achilles Nikolaou who was sitting directly opposite him, he said. 'Thanks to Treasury funding, my teams have everything they need to conduct a professional operation. We have all the necessary safety gear, crime scene tools, technical equipment, evidence collecting equipment, and specialized equipment to support our endeavours,' finished Jasonas, looking Kaliope straight in the eye as if to emphasise that he had all the necessary support from the Treasury, and she didn't.

'But do you have anything to report?' pushed Alex feeling decidedly frustrated at the obvious infighting taking place before his eyes.

'Yes,' said Jasonas, switching his gaze in Alex's direction. 'The first responders did a fantastic job in treating the injured and securing the integrity of the scene. Then, the investigators did a walk through before assigning documentation, photographic and videotaping duties to the appropriate persons.'

'Interviews?' asked Alex.

'Joint effort between Kaliope's people and mine,' replied Jasonas. 'We are collecting the evidence at the moment and transporting it to a secure location where it is being processed.'

'Anything I can work with?' asked Kaliope.

'We have had one significant breakthrough,' replied Jasonas looking down at his notes. 'We found a piece of the detonator early on in the evidence collection and our forensic scientists have identified its origin.'

'Fantastic!' exclaimed Alex.

'Its origin seems to be eastern Europe.'

'Can you point to a country?' asked Kaliope.

'The scientists believe it's either Kosovo or North Macedonia.'

'That doesn't mean that the bomb was made in either one of those countries does it?' asked Argi who was the Foreign Minister; another of Alex's prodigies, and the first female foreign minister that Greece had ever appointed.

'No,' cut in Kaliope.

Jasonas glared at her. 'Thank you, Kaliope,' he said sarcastically. 'No, it doesn't Argi, but my scientists are confident that by morning they will have narrowed it down to one of those two countries.'

'Are we suggesting that the bomber is either a Kosovan or a Macedonian?' questioned Leonidas the Industry and Business Minister, of no-one in particular.

'Not at all,' said Jasonas. 'Being made in that area has no bearing on who the bomber might be. Don't forget we only identified the detonator as coming from those countries. It could be that the bomb was made here in Greece and the bomber used a detonator or even other components of the bomb from other countries.'

No-one spoke for a few seconds while they digested this latest information. Everyone comprehended that the good news of where the detonator was manufactured was dampened by the realisation that the origin of the bomb and bomber was still not within their grasp.

'If we can capture the bomber, we will be nearer the answers we need,' said Alex breaking the silence. 'Let's....

Alex was interrupted by the sound of Kaliope's mobile phone vibrating and dancing across the table. She grabbed it impatiently and put it to her ear at the same time standing up and moving over to a window. She listened spellbound for a minute seemingly hanging on every word, then she said. 'Go ahead but I want him or her alive, I have not issued a 'Crimson' order for this operation. Do you understand?' After a couple of seconds Kaliope spoke again. 'Good luck, I'm on my way down to the command centre.'

She returned to her seat; her face flushed with excitement.

'We've had a breakthrough,' she said elatedly. 'We've picked up the Mercedes on traffic cam and managed to follow its journey through Athens to the southern suburb of Kalithea, even though its registration plate changed three times.'

'How did you know it was the same car?' asked Alex quizzically.

'We were lucky it was daylight. If it had been during the night, we would never had spotted the blemish on the windscreen in the top left hand corner to the left of the driver. Apparently, it looks like stone damage. We have two units of the elite EKAM counter terrorist squad heading for that area.'

'Have you identified the apartment building where they are hiding yet?' asked Leonidas.

'The undercover unit we sent down there has pinpointed two buildings as possibilities where the parking bays under the buildings show a white Mercedes parked. As yet they haven't identified either of them as the car we were tailing.'

Kaliope stood up eager to get to the command centre and follow the operation. 'I have to go to the command centre to support my teams. Sorry for ducking out of the meeting sir,' apologised Kaliope.

'Of course,' said Alex. 'There is nothing more to say here today. Keep me informed Kaliope and that goes for you Jasonas too.'

Turning to Achilles he said. 'I want to know how the stock exchange is doing too,' and without waiting for an answer he left the room.

Ten minutes after the meeting had broken up a burner phone rang in a third floor apartment in the suburb adjacent to that of Kalithea.

'Yes,' answered a man who was known as 'the fixer.' His real name was Alkis Eleftheradou, a married man with three young kids. Several months later when his neighbours and friends were asked what sort of person he was, they described him with words such as accommodating, amiable, easy-going, and obliging.

'Are you alone?' asked a voice at the other end of the line.

'No, but I am alone in this room. No-one can hear me,' replied Alkis.

'EKAM are about to find our friend. They have already traced his Mercedes so there is not a lot of time left,' said the voice.

'What do you want me to do?' asked Alkis.

'Go to ground zero and make sure he won't talk if he is arrested. He mustn't be taken alive, the girl too and get rid of the phone after this call.'

'I'm on it,' confirmed Alkis, then without waiting for a response he opened the battery department, took out the SIM card, bent it in two and dropped it into the toilet and flushed.

Two minutes later he wheeled his Harley Road King out from his parking bay below his apartment block, turned the key, gunned the engine, then headed towards ground zero.

Alkis glided through the backstreets in the direction of Kalithea thankful that he had chosen a Harley as his mode of transport. A Harley did not announce its presence, it was quiet and unobtrusive as it glided smoothly through the morning traffic. Its twin saddlebags filled with the tools of his trade. With those, Alkis said to himself half smiling, he could 'fix' anyone or anything.

Chapter 3
16th August 2013 – Athens – 10:30

It didn't matter how many times Kaliope entered the Command Centre her heart always seemed to speed up from the excitement and the adrenalin rush. Today was no different, perhaps her excitement was heightened even more by the potential capture of the bomber.

The Command Centre was state of the art, with high tech tools which mirrored some of the more sophisticated command centres around the world. When Alex had brokered the deal two years earlier, with the Americans and the British, which gave them sole rights to the oil and gas under the Aegean Sea, he had insisted that part of the package would be a sophisticated control and command centre including the mandatory spy satellites, drones, and communication equipment. Kaliope knew that Greece could never have afforded such modern and sophisticated equipment and was grateful to Alex for having the vision to make such an agreement.

She sat down in her usual place at the apex of a huge thirty seater circular mahogany table and surveyed the room. The wall directly opposite her had six seventy-two inch video screens in two vertical banks of three. In between them a gigantic video screen, about a third of the size of a cinema screen, on which could be displayed a video feed from any one of its six satellite screens.

To her left and her right were banks of computers attended by men and women whose fingers were dancing like whirling dervishes over their keyboards, as they manipulated the video feeds or controlled the satellites and drones at their disposal. Above the computer banks on the left were digital clocks showing the time in several key capitals of the world, while on the right hand wall was a huge interactive map of Greece.

At the table were the Chief of Police, Commander Takis Stomatou and his aides, and the head of the Counter Terrorist Squad Commander Thomas Davanellos and his team. Everyone at the table was watching the large screen which was showing an arial view of the area around an apartment block.

'What are we looking at Takis?' asked Kaliope, staring at the screen.

'This is the apartment block where the target has his apartment.'

'Have we identified which apartment he is in yet?'

'We think he is in the penthouse but due to the bright sunlight we are having difficulty in seeing through the windows,' said Thomas. 'We are in the process of setting up directional listening devices in the building but it's slow going because there are residents going in and out all the time, so we have to be extra careful.'

'Are you certain he has not slipped the net?' queried Kaliope.

'Definitely,' insisted Takis. 'We would have picked him up. Besides if he had decided to leave the area, he would have taken his car but that's still parked in a parking bay under the building.'

'Who is in charge on the ground?' asked Kaliope.

'Colonel Yannis Spanos,' replied Thomas. 'One of our best men. As you can see on the main screen there is no sign of our vehicles near the building or any of the counter terrorism squad or police. There is no way the perpetrator will realise that the apartment block is surrounded. Spanos is one of our most experienced men for this sort of operation.'

'Can I speak to him?' asked Kaliope.

'Yes, no problem. Manos! Patch the Home Secretary over to Spanos will you,' shouted Thomas to a young man manning a computer on the opposite wall.

'Go ahead,' said the young man. 'You're online.'

On the large screen the picture of the overhead view of the apartment block was replaced with a full body video view of Colonel

Spanos standing in the car park below the apartment block. Kaliope's immediate thoughts were that he was an impressive man who even on a video screen radiated authoritative confidence. Kaliope liked him immediately, feeling that he would tell it as it was and not gloss over any detail. She also noted that he was tall, lean, with what seemed like a well-honed body. He was dressed in all black the trademark uniform of the counter terrorism unit but held his black helmet in one hand, leaving his bronzed face framed in the black balaclava, worn under the helmet to protect the head.

'Good morning ma'am,' greeted Spanos staring straight at the camera.

Kaliope took a sharp intake of breath as his piercing blue eyes seemed to be looking directly at her, as if he were sitting just opposite her at the table.

'Good morning Colonel Spanos,' replied Kaliope as she composed herself. 'Would you mind briefing me on the current situation?' she asked trying not to sound or look too friendly or let him know that she found him startlingly attractive.

'Of course, ma'am,' replied Spanos, his face breaking into a wide smile showing Kaliope an even set of teeth. 'We have deployed several bug drones, which our friends from the American military have asked us to test, around the building, and are now extremely certain that the bomber is in the penthouse on the fifth floor with his partner, the woman who was his driver.

'Excuse my innocence,' interrupted Kaliope. 'But what are bug drones?'

'They are miniature listening devices, using nano technology, which are smaller than my palm,' said Spanos holding his hand up with his palm facing the camera. 'They are silent and can hear conversations clearly behind several metres of brick wall or one metre of concrete. Much more efficient than using directional microphones. As you can see the Mercedes they used as their getaway car yesterday, is in the bay behind me and as a precaution we have disabled it. In half an hour at eleven we will raid the apartment and take him into custody.'

'You sound very certain,' said Kaliope.

'Yes, I am certain,' replied Spanos. 'Only something beyond our control will prevent us taking him into custody alive.'

'I like your confidence,' admitted Kaliope allowing herself a smile. 'Good luck Colonel Spanos.'

'Thank you, ma'am, we won't let you down.'

The screen went blank, then returned with the overhead view of the apartment block and the immediate surrounding area.

'Will you stay to watch the action,' asked Thomas.

'I think I will,' confirmed Kaliope.

In the bomber's apartment his burner phone rang. The bomber picked it up.

'Yes,' he said, putting it to his ear.

'You're surrounded by the counter terrorist squad,' said a voice he recognised. Get to the roof. A helicopter will pick you up at ten fifty five in twenty minutes. Don't show yourself too soon.'

'What about the girl?' asked the bomber.

'Take her with you,' said the voice. 'Don't forget to dump the chip in your phone before you board the helicopter. The pilot will have new phone for you.'

'Thanks,' said the bomber and closed the connection. He broke open the phone, retrieved the sim card, snapped it in two, then walked into the bathroom and flushed it down the toilet.

'Get ready, we're leaving. No bags!' he instructed the girl.

At ten fifty, the bomber and the girl made their way to the internal staircase, in the hallway of the apartment, which led up to the roof. The bomber went first, unlocked the trap door, and pushed it on its hinges so it lay flat against the roof, and peered out over the rim.

Lying on the roof of an apartment block three hundred yards down the road Alkis spotted the trap door opening. He adjusted his position making himself more comfortable and looked through the scope of his Steyr SSG 69, one of the most accurate sniper rifles ever made. His crosshairs centred on the bomber's head as he lightly depressed the trigger. He waited for the bomber to ascend onto the roof hoping that the girl would follow him, and he could take them both out.

The bomber heard the sound of the helicopter before he actually saw it. He watched it as it approached, he could see that it was travelling on a parallel course to the apartment but reasoned that it would swing in at the last moment when it was too late for the counter terrorist squad to do anything about it.

'Stay where you are until the helicopter has landed,' instructed the bomber. When he judged that the whirlybird was about five hundred metres away, the bomber ascended the final few steps and stepped out onto the roof.

Back in the command centre Kaliope could see the satellite image showed the bomber stepping onto the roof.

'What the hell,' she exclaimed. 'What's he doing?'

'There's a helicopter heading towards that block of apartments. It looks like it's his ticket out of there,' said Thomas. 'Spanos has ordered his men to break into the apartment but I don't know if they will get there in time.'

Back on the roof the bomber watched the helicopter approach until suddenly as it drew level with the apartment block it veered off and started to climb away. Too late the bomber realised it was a trap. He turned, intending to run back to open trap door but before he had even taken half a step the back of his head exploded with the force of the sniper's bullet, spraying brains, and bone over the horrified head of the girl whose head was above the threshold of the trapdoor. She involuntarily flinched as the concoction of blood, brain and bone hit her full in the face. She lost her footing and started falling down the stairs. This saved her life because the bullet from Alkis's second shot slammed into the side of the trapdoor opening instead of her head and ricocheted downwards penetrating the girl's left thigh.

When the counter terrorist team entered the apartment, they found her in a ragged doll heap at the bottom of the stairs, alive but suffering a broken left arm, two broken legs and a gaping wound in her thigh.

Chapter 4

16th August 2013 – Mega Maximo – Athens – 14:30

The phone on Alex's desk buzzed annoyingly. Oh no, thought Alex, how many times have I told Maria to change that infuriating ring tone. He pressed the intercom button.

'Yes Maria,' he said gruffly.

'I have Kaliope waiting to see you.'

'Send her in and Maria, please change the ring tone on my phone to something more relaxing. It is beginning to annoy me greatly.'

'Yes, Prime Minister, I'll do it this afternoon while you are out.'

'Remind me where I'm going,' said Alex. His brow furrowed as he tried to remember where he was supposed to be.

'Chris Horsman,' replied Maria. 'At the usual place at five o'clock.'

'Thank you, Maria, you can send Kaliope in now please.'

Alex rose from his chair when Kaliope entered his office. He knew that it could be daunting walking into it, even if you had visited before. It was exceptionally large, almost cavernous in shape. Its ceiling was slightly curved and gave the impression to the naked eye that the floor sloped down towards the massive floor-to-ceiling picture window that offered a view of the beautifully manicured gardens. It was bullet proof and access to the patio outside was through the French windows in the outer office where Maria worked.

Alex sat not at a desk, for he was not one into too much formality, but at a large table which could easily seat twelve people. It was positioned in front of the huge window and the only recognition of his position was his chair which was bigger and far more comfortable than the other eleven chairs round the table.

Kaliope walked across the luxurious thick piled carpet towards Alex who had already started to pull out a chair for her to sit.

Alex waited until she was comfortable before he asked her what had happened at the bomber's apartment.

'We're still trying to piece it together,' said Kaliope. 'A forensic team is on the roof still sifting for any evidence.'

'I think I know most of what happened,' said Alex. 'Do we know who shot the bomber?'

'Who told you the news?' asked Kaliope, ignoring Alex's question.

'Leonidas,' replied Alex.

'Yes, I did see him there briefly, but I didn't get a chance to talk to him because he was talking on his cell phone and I was being briefed by Colonel Spanos,' said Kaliope. 'What was he doing there, did he say?'

'He was visiting the head office of one of our biggest export companies, Hellenic Aluminium. Well, if you didn't speak to him where did he get his information from?' questioned Alex.

'I don't know,' said Kaliope. 'He probably spoke to one of the counter terrorist officers, although I'm not sure how they knew all the details.'

'Perhaps I haven't got all the details yet. Why don't you fill me in now?'

Kaliope told Alex that once the apartment had been breached and the bomber's girlfriend found, she had left the command centre and headed to the scene. It was there that Colonel Spanos had given her a briefing on what had happened.

'I don't want to sound paranoid, but it sounds as though there is a leak somewhere,' commented Alex when Kaliope had finished. 'What is your take on it?'

Kaliope sat for a moment gathering her thoughts. She was momentarily distracted by a nagging thought in her head which she couldn't quite put her finger on.

She pushed the thought away. 'Both Colonel Spanos and I believe that it's more than just a leak. It was a precision operation well planned and perfectly executed. They had a helicopter, with Skai News markings on it that acted as a decoy to lure the bomber out onto the roof. Either it was stolen from Skai News, although they haven't reported a missing helicopter yet, or it was hired and liveried to make it look like a Skai helicopter. Whoever they are, they might even actually own the helicopter. None of these options are cheap,' Kaliope paused for a moment.

Secondly, they had a sniper on an apartment roof which was over three hundred metres away. The sniper took an amazing shot, and it would have been two incredible shots, if the bomber's girlfriend hadn't slipped on the ladder, the instant she was covered in the bomber's brains. Snipers of that calibre are hard to find, and they don't come cheap either. '

'Are you starting an investigation?' asked Alex.

'Yes, I'm setting up a team and putting Colonel Spanos in charge of it. He seems a good man and he is well respected by his peers and seniors,' replied Kaliope. She did not mention that part of the reason she was putting Spanos in charge was that she would see more of him. She was quite attracted to him.

'Good girl,' said Alex.

'Prime Minister!' admonished Kaliope, a half-smile playing on her lips. 'I'm not a snowflake, but that was a naughty sexist remark.'

Alex feigned surprise that she had reacted that way to his remark. He knew that although she was an independent woman, who like many Greek women, and despite the fact that she, like the majority of Greek women had attended university obtaining a well-rounded education, culturally valued family more than anything else. Care homes were almost unheard of in Greece. Finding a household comprising grandparents, parents, and married children all under one roof was the norm rather than the exception. Kaliope's Greek background would not allow her to fully join the western 'political correctness' movement, which was running rife in other parts of Europe and the USA.

'You can be such a chauvinist sometimes,' said Kaliope laughing. It wasn't the first time that their banter had centred around politically correct issues.

'Have we learned anything about the girl or indeed the bomber yet?' asked Alex.

'Yes, two North Macedonian passports were found in their respective bags. Before she was operated on, the girl confirmed she and the bomber had come from there.'

'Now that is interesting. But I can't see that the bombing had anything to do with North Macedonia's claim on the Macedonian region of Greece. Can you?'

'I would have thought that if they were planning a bombing campaign they would concentrate on the cities and towns in the Macedonian province of northern Greece,' said Kaliope. 'Mind you it could have been retaliation for us vetoing the name North Macedonia at the United Nations last month.'

'True,' said Alex thoughtfully. 'By the way, the Health Minister confirmed that his forensics team have determined that the Semtex used for the bomb was manufactured in Czech Republic.'

'I'll have my people look at the travel movements of the bomber during the last couple of months. There was something else I wanted to talk to you about other than the bombing.'

'Fire away,' said Alex.

'I was thinking that for operational expediency the terrorist forensic teams should report directly to me rather than Jasonas. I don't see that the Health Ministry should be responsible for that side of forensics. He can keep the crime forensic teams if he likes,' finished Kaliope.

'Actually, I was thinking of taking all forensic activity away from the Health Ministry and giving it lock, stock and barrel to you. I believe it sits better at the Home Office. Most other countries have forensics with their Home Office anyway. Why the hell the previous Prime Minister took it from the Home Office into Health I have no idea.'

'Oh, you mean Xenakis,' said Kaliope. 'Didn't he kill himself after he was disgraced, during that Gladio incident three years ago?'

'Yes, he did,' answered Alex as memories flooded into his head filled with images of Gitta. He pushed them away. 'So, Kaliope are you ready to take the forensic teams under your wing?'

'More than ready,' confirmed Kaliope, afraid that Alex would see the glow of pride in her face as she felt herself flush. With forensics she now had five major departments reporting to her, forensics, police, anti-terrorism, fire, and homeland security.

'Good, I'll talk to Jasonas and then you and he can arrange the handover to your authority. If there is nothing else, I need to get ready for my meeting with Chris Horsman.'

'Thank you, Prime Minister, have a good evening.'

Alex's mind turned to his upcoming meeting with Chris Horsman as Kaliope closed the door gently behind her. He enjoyed Chris's company now, but it hadn't always been that way. After Alex had been invested as Prime Minister in October two thousand and ten, he had been advised by the Americans to meet with Chris at least once a month. He had appreciated being kept in the loop although he had also harboured a little resentment that Chris would have known what Gitta was up to but always insisted he was not in contact because Gitta had taken a sabbatical away from the CIA. Gradually however he got to appreciate more and more the top secret information that Chris was able to share with him and he stopped bringing up Gitta in conversation so regularly.

Alex pressed his intercom button and asked Maria to get his driver to bring his unofficial car round to the side entrance. As with all his meetings with Chris there were no bodyguards and he always drove himself.

Chapter 5
16th August 2013 – Voula Athens – 16:30

Alex had the air conditioning full on as he drove southwards from the centre of Athens towards the coastal suburb of Voula. It was almost five o'clock and the temperature was still in the mid-thirties centigrade, so he was thankful the traffic was light keeping the carbon emissions low.

He was a fast driver usually but today he drove at a measured speed giving him time enough to think through his earlier meeting with Kaliope and the curious text he had received from Chris Horsman just before he had left his office. It had read *-think aluminium-* which was easier said than done as the only two things he knew about aluminium was, one, that it was used on aircraft fuselages because it was lighter and stronger than steel at the same density being one third lighter. And two, Hellenic Aluminium was one of the success stories of Greek industry. The bauxite mines from which aluminium is extracted and refined were all situated in Macedonia, the northernmost county of the Greek mainland, stretching from Salonika to the border with North Macedonia, one of the countries born out of the splitting up of the former Yugoslavian Republic.

These mines produced over half a billion dollars of exports every year and Alex knew from Leonidas that two new mines located just north of the town of Edessa in Macedonia, were coming on-line soon. He recalled that Leonidas had been overly excited about the news, but Alex could not remember what Leonidas had told him about the estimated income from the mines.

Maybe that was why Leonidas was at Hellenic Aluminium earlier today mused Alex. Perhaps he was discussing the new find with them. However, was it Hellenic Aluminium who owned the new mines or was it another Greek company? He made a mental note to ask him the next time they spoke.

Alex had to stop his reverie as the car park for the taverna he was meeting Chris in was a few hundred metres ahead. He pulled in, parked up, then headed for the entrance of the Pasiphae Taverna. The taverna was set in a rocky escarpment which was seven metres high. The typical Greek family taverna which was popular with the elite of Voula and Vouliagmeni, served wholesome home cooked food consisting of the usual Mediterranean fare.

Alex had known the couple Petros and Pavlina since they opened the taverna eighteen years earlier and over the years they had become good friends. This is why for his clandestine meetings with Chris he had chosen their place. He trusted them implicitly never to reveal that he used their premises, and as always, he had requested a reservation on the table at the back of the main area, which was inset into a rocky alcove, out of the way of prying eyes. In the three years since he became Prime Minister not once had anybody recognised him.

Petros met him at the door.

'Καλώς ήρθες Alex,' he enthused as he kissed Alex on both cheeks and hugged him. 'The taverna is empty of customers and your table is ready,' he continued as he bustled around Alex showing him to his table. Petros was short, dumpy with a mop of tousled hair and definitely in need of some gym work. His wife however was quite a contrast to him. Pavlina always appeared radiant and stylish even with an apron around her slim waist. Her jet black hair hanging loose around her shoulders set off her piercing blue eyes perfectly.

'Lovely to see you again Alex,' said Pavlina, greeting him with open arms and a wide smile showing off her beautiful white teeth.

'And you too Pavlina,' said Alex as he sat in the proffered chair pulled out from the table. He had his back to the rock wall and when he looked out into the main taverna area there was only one table in view thanks to the deepness of the rocky alcove.

'Would you mind not seating anyone at that table?' asked Alex indicating the table in his sight line.

'Of course, my friend,' agreed Petros. 'Will Chris be joining you tonight?'

'Yes, he will be.'

'Would you like something while you are waiting for him?'

'Perhaps a few olives, Taramosalata, Tzatziki and some of your warm home-made bread.'

'Drink?' asked Petros. 'I have some beautiful home brewed Tsipouro.'

'Superb,' raved Alex.

While Petros was away ordering the Meze, Alex turned his mind back to the events that had propelled him from obscurity to his current position as the Prime Minister. Three years ago, he had been an ignored junior cabinet minister in the justice department, married to his wife, Marina, and living the quiet life, without a care in the world.

Then, on the morning of 23rd October 2010, five days before Οχι day, he had been summoned in front of Themis Xenakis the then Prime Minister of Greece. He had been blackmailed by Xenakis, who had threatened to publish compromising photographs of Alex, into taking a senior ministerial job that Alex didn't want. Xenakis had explained to him the philosophy of the Gladio protocol, and how it had become the pillar for the execution of the most audacious political scheme in European history. All of which Alex had not particularly cared to hear about. From the moment he had reluctantly accepted the position of Finance Minister, his world had plunged into the abyss of subterfuge, espionage, killing and the threat of the Aegean region going up in flames.

Alex's recall of those five days were indelible in his memory banks, but which, he realised later had turned him into the strong and decisive man he now was. During those days he had been activated from his sleeper role in the CIA and had become an active field agent, taught the agents field craft by Gitta Lehrer, a former Stazi double agent who had been assigned by Langley to be Alex's handler. He had fallen madly in love with her and she, much to his surprise, had reciprocated his passion. Together, with Chris Horsman they had managed to thwart Xenakis's plans and restore peace to the region, albeit it at a price. The price being giving away some of Greece's sovereignty in exchange for protection from Turkey.

Now three years' on, he was divorced, still missing Gitta, who had left him to return to Germany as soon as he had been invested as the Prime Minister of Greece. He had understood her reasons as he had been married at the time and to get embroiled in a scandal during such a sensitive period would have been political suicide.

But, he reasoned, he was doing a decent job as Prime Minister so far. The people loved him, the Americans and British loved him, financially Greece was out of debt and economically sound and he was ahead in the polls for the general election in six months' time. It was all good except for one thing. Yesterday's bombing in Kifissia. Was this, he asked himself, a one off, or was it the start of an operation to destabilize the political arena? Perhaps, Chris had some information on that issue.

As if summoned by magic Chris walked through door into the taverna. He wasn't his usual dishevelled self because he was wearing a nice sand coloured suit today. For most meetings with Alex, he had worn grubby jeans, trainers, and an equally grubby t-shirt. Okay, so today his tie was askew, and his shock of tangled brown hair needed a comb, but his shoes were clean, so he looked almost dapper.

Alex rose from his chair to greet him. 'Hello Chris, good to see you,' said Alex as he gave Chris a hug and a peck on both cheeks.

'Hello Alex,' Chris responded, his face uncontrollably reddening. He still wasn't used to the uninhibited greetings from Greek men.

'Would you like a Meze and a glass of tsipouro?' asked Alex.

'Please,' said Chris as he sat down.

Petros came over to their table to take Chris's order and ask them what they wanted as a main meal.

'What do you recommend tonight Petros?' asked Alex.

'Pavlina has made some delicious keftedes,' said Petros.

Both Alex and Chris nodded in unison; they adored Pavlina's fried meatballs. 'With French fries and a Greek salad with lots of olive oil and feta cheese, with your red barrel wine,' Added Alex.

They ate their Meze and chit-chatted about soccer and basketball while they waited for their main meal. As was their usual habit 'business' would be conducted over a glass of port and a cheese board after they had eaten.

While they ate, little did they know that the second violent act that would shock the nation was about to take place in Macedonia.

Chapter 6
16th August 2013 – Edessa – 18:30

Andonis Papaspiro looked at his watch. It read six-thirty. He was late and it was his daughter's fifth birthday today. They were having a small party at the house, mainly close family, and neighbours. He didn't want to be late, but he was puzzled.

Andonis had been based in the administrative offices of Hellenic Aluminium, located in the beautiful town of Edessa in northern Greece, as Group Financial Officer, for the past five years. The pinnacle of what had been a meteoric rise from trainee accountant to his current position, in a mere ten years. At the age of forty-two he was fit, lean, with a golf handicap of three. Not that he was thinking about golf at the moment. He was thinking about the figures he had just seen on the report in front of him.

The report was the monthly review of the income and expenditure, mining production, and aluminium stocks. But the figures that had him puzzled were in the share capital and movement report. He had noticed that in the last month, that three times a block of shares amounting to 4.8% of the total share capital had been purchased. The financial regulation authorities in most countries including Greece, have a rule which mandates that any individual or company purchasing a block of shares worth 5% or more had to announce the fact to the public. Each subsequent purchase of 2% or more also had to be announced publicly. One block of a 4.8% purchase would not be alarming but three in thirty days was alarming and pointed to a company or individual attempting a silent bid for the company.

Andonis picked up his mobile phone and called the securities officer at Hellenic Aluminium's headquarters in Athens. He was concentrating so hard on his problem that he failed to hear the slight change in the ring tone and a faint click which lasted a split second before reverting back to the original tone. Someone was listening in.

'Yannis Blounas is that you?' inquired Andonis when the phone answered.

'Yes, who is this? Oh, it's you Andonis, how can I help you?' said Yannis.

'Have you got the share register to hand?'

'Yes, I have, what are you after?'

'Could you check the share purchases over the last thirty days and tell me if you have three blocks of share purchases registered, each equivalent to 4.8% please?' asked Andonis knowing that they were probably there but hoping they weren't.

Yannis tapped into his computer, found the register, and scrolled to the relevant page. How could I have missed something like that he thought to himself. He studied the page. Yes, Andonis was right, there were three. 'I've found them. I can't believe I missed them. In fact, I'm perplexed how I did miss them,' he said lamely.

'Have you been away at any time in the last month at all and has anyone else access to that share ledger?'

'I have been away a couple of days but not on the days these shares were registered,' said Yannis, his brow furrowing as he tried hard to remember something – anything that could mitigate his error. 'Apart from myself, only you and the Managing Director, Dimitris, have access.'

'Check which stockbroker made the purchases will you?' requested Andonis, his voice sounding more panicky by the minute. There was silence at the other end of the phone as Yannis checked each share transaction. 'Three different brokers,' he eventually announced.

'Right,' said Andonis. 'I believe you wouldn't have missed them if you had posted all three transactions, I know you Yannis, you are a stickler for detail. I also believe that if, and that is a big if, someone else had posted those transactions, you would still have noticed them. We are missing something here. Any ideas?'

'Thank you for your confidence sir,' answered Yannis, relieved that the blame wasn't going to be on him. He mentally put on his IT hat and thought through the problem. Much to his dismay there was only one other solution he could think of.

'There is something we could check but it's a long shot and if what I'm thinking is correct it means that someone on the outside has access to our systems,' said Yannis.

'You mean a hacker?' said Andonis incredulously.

'Well sort of, but worse than that if I'm right,' said Yannis.

'How can we find out?' asked Andonis.

'I could check the timestamps of the transactions. The share postings are entered with the date that the shares were actually purchased. The broker would electronically transmit the share purchase docket to us overnight and the register would get posted in the morning by me. So, the transaction would be time-stamped one day after the actual date of purchase,' Yannis paused waiting for Andonis to respond.

'Interesting,' said Andonis. 'So, if I understand you correctly, the process is that the share purchases are always posted with the actual date of purchase and not the date of posting. Am I right?' asked Andonis.

'Yes sir,' confirmed Yannis.

'So, following that logic,' continued Andonis. 'If you check the timestamps of those three records and they don't follow the pattern of the other postings, in all probability we have a hacker.'

'Probably,' confirmed Yannis. 'But also, each timestamp is appended by the IP address of the computer that was used for the posting.'

'Brilliant!' exclaimed Andonis. 'Can you check now please?'

'It will take me a couple of minutes. Will you wait?'

'Yes, of course. Get on with it,' said Andonis impatiently. He looked at his watch – it was now six-thirty five. He still had time to get to the party.

'Bingo!' shouted Yannis. 'All three of the postings although the shares were purchased on different days, have been time-stamped as early this morning at two o'clock and they don't have IP addresses appended to them. So, we have been hacked,' finished Yannis triumphantly.

'And that is why the postings were not picked up until I looked at the report, something I don't normally do in detail. But we'll have to go back over the register to check to see if there are any more surprises,' said Andonis. There was thirty seconds of silence while both men thought through the implications of their find. Andonis broke the silence.

'We can't do any more tonight Yannis, but tomorrow morning you must report this to the Financial Services Authority and the fraud squad. I'm going to inform the cabinet office of the Industry and Business minister. Call me in the morning on your progress. Excellent job this evening. Goodnight,' said Andonis, and without waiting for a reply he closed his phone.

As Andonis closed his phone, five hundred yards away in an apartment on the basement floor of an apartment block, the listener took his earphones from his head and picked up his burner phone. He called a number in Athens.

'Yes?' said the voice.

The listener relayed the conversation he had heard between Andonis and Yannis.

'Thank you,' said the voice. 'I'll handle it from here. Stay vigilant.'

Five minutes later in a hotel room in Edessa, the burner phone belonging to Alkis Eleftheradou - also known as the fixer - rang.

'Yes, who is it?' questioned Alkis, although he knew it was the man who went under the codeword *Cyclops*. He was the only person who called him with a suppressed number.

'You know very well who I am,' said *Cyclops* with a hint of annoyance in his voice. Cocky young man, he thought to himself. 'How was your trip?'

'Very smooth,' said Alkis. 'I caught the Olympic midday flight out of Athens airport and was here in my room by two o'clock.'

'That was good shooting this morning. It was unlucky about the girl surviving and being captured. Still, she can't tell the authorities anything much that would help them. Now you have an urgent job. Two employees of Hellenic Aluminium need to be silenced. I'll send their details to your phone,' said *Cyclops*.

'How do you want it done,' asked Alkis.

'It's up to you how you do it, but we want it dirty, so collateral damage is preferable. We want a big statement similar to Athens.'

'Understood,' confirmed Alkis.

Two minutes later Alkis was reading the information that *Cyclops* had sent him. Alkis noted that there was to be a gathering at the home of the Andonis Papaspiro, his first mark. That will be easy, Alkis thought. The second mark might be a little more difficult, but both would require him using his over-the-shoulder rocket launcher. He checked the address with Google maps on his personal mobile phone and saw that Papaspiro lived on the outskirts of Edessa, not much more than ten kilometres from the hotel.

Time to move thought Alkis checking his watch. Papaspiro will have arrived at his house by now.

Ten kilometres away Andonis pulled into his driveway stopping just short of his garage as he waited for the door to become fully open. After parking his Audi Quatro, he walked through the connecting door to the kitchen to be greeted by a cacophony of sound from the gathering that was there.

It was a typical Greek family gathering with everyone talking over everyone else. To a foreigner it would seem as though there were tremendous arguments being played out. But of course they weren't, it was their way of enjoying themselves, being spirited, animated, carefree, and loving, not at all introverted or dull.

Andonis greeted them all with hugs and cheek kisses with a special hug for his birthday girl and wife.

'Xronia polla darling,' enthused Andonis giving his daughter Melita the traditional birthday greeting - many years to come – as well as a big hug. Turning to his wife Voula he kissed her on the lips before saying. 'She will live my love.' Another traditional Greek birthday wish.

'Darling, you have to go out again I'm afraid,' apologised Voula.

'Why?' questioned Andonis.

'We are short of lemons for both drinks and food. Sorry,' said Voula. 'But no need to take the car, the mini mart around the corner has lemons.'

Andonis managed a rueful smile 'No problem darling I'll go now.'

As he left the house Andonis looked back at his daughter laughing as she played with her friends. She turned as she heard her father call her name, smiled, and blew a kiss at him as he left the house. Andonis felt his body give a small shudder as he returned her blown kiss. A fleeting feeling of dread surged through his body. He dismissed the feeling as foolish and set off towards the mini mart. Later, he would recall that feeling and wish that he had taken notice of it.

At the end of his driveway, he turned right and walked the three hundred metres to the corner where he again turned right and immediately spied the mini mart a further one hundred metres in front of him. As he approached his destination, he heard a loud 'whomp' from somewhere behind him. Then a thunderous explosion coming from the direction of his house. The night sky glowed bright orange from the flames reaching for the stars.

With his heart in his mouth Andonis turned and ran back towards his home and as he ran all he could hear were the piercing screams of terrified and injured people.

Chapter 7
16th August 2013 – Voula 19:00

Oblivious to the events taking place in Edessa, Alex sat back, closed his eyes, and savoured the port and cheese he had been consuming. The taverna where he was eating dinner with Chris Horsman was full of the cacophony of animated conversation and the clatter of cutlery and crockery. It amused Alex that the piped bouzouki music was fighting a losing battle against the noise and might as well be turned off, although the few dancers on the small circular dancing area might not have agreed with him.

'So, what is it you want to talk to me about Chris?' asked Alex suddenly.

Chris was leaning back in his chair with one of Petros's famous Cuban cigars in his mouth, was clapping in time to the music's beat, and watching a woman in a noticeably short skirt, bare midriff and a top that obviously had no bra beneath it. She was performing all sorts of gyrations on the dance floor. He tore his eyes from the dance floor and sat up bringing his chair closer to the table.

'Have you heard of Arthur Eckersley Alex?' asked Chris.

'Of course,' said Alex feigning hurt as if Chris was evaluating his business knowledge. 'He is a British industrialist from the North Yorkshire region of England, near Malton I believe, who built a business empire, the flagship of which is Xplore Industries.'

'He also owns bauxite mines on three continents, and he is greedy for more,' said Chris.

'Why invest in bauxite instead of precious metals such as gold or silver?' asked Alex.

'Because from bauxite you can manufacture aluminium and alumina both of which are highly prized metallic compounds. Aluminium is an extremely strong, pliable, and is anti-corrosive and a low density metal. It's used for cladding aeroplane fuselages and wings. Alumina or Aluminium Oxide is used for ceramics, polishing and abrasive products but also body armour and fire resistance materials. Eckersley has invested billions in research and investment and his scientists have developed a metal which has both the properties of aluminium and alumina combined.'

'What are it's uses?' asked Alex.

'Cladding his space and launch vehicles,' said Chris. 'Imagine having a space vehicle that is cladded in a metal that is ultra-strong but lightweight, which is impervious to small space debris collisions and fires.'

'You do know that our existing bauxite mines are worth five hundred and seventy million dollars per year in revenue and the big new one coming on stream in the next few days is estimated at a whopping two billion dollars per annum in revenue?' questioned Alex.

Before Chris could answer him Alex suddenly exclaimed 'Wait a minute! I seem to remember that this Eckersley person was looking for a summer home here in Greece around springtime. In fact, Leonidas Papadakis my Industry and Business Minister asked me if he could show him around unofficially. He thought that it would be good PR to entertain him for a couple of days and might attract some much needed foreign investment into the country.'

'Yes, I do know the numbers Alex,' said Chris. 'I also know about his house search in the spring.'

Alex looked at Chris with a quizzical look on his face. 'Why are you following the house hunting exploits of Eckersley? What's your interest in him? Do you know if he eventually bought a place?' asked Alex. 'Leonidas must have forgotten to tell me the outcome.'

'He did indeed,' confirmed Chris as he took several photographs from his inside jacket pocket and placed them face down in front of Alex. 'Don't look at them yet,' instructed Chris.

Earlier, you rightly said that Harvey Eckersley was a British industrialist. But do you know where he was born?' asked Chris

'I assumed he was born in the UK. Don't tell me he was born in Greece,' laughed Alex.

Chris chuckled at Alex's remark. 'No, he was born in Yugoslavia.'

'I still don't see the relevance,' confessed Alex. 'Chris you are holding something from me, aren't you?'

'I'm just seeing if you can join the dot's,' teased Chris. 'Everything I have told you so far is connected. Bauxite mines; Xplore Industries; holiday homes; Yugoslavia; they are all connected. Take a look at the photographs in front of you.'

Alex turned over the top photograph and saw that it was a view from either a drone or a satellite of what looked like a Greek town. The typed text in the bottom right hand corner has the words Edessa, and a series of numbers which looked like coordinates.

He turned over the second photograph which this time was taken at ground level. It showed a willowy tall man; probably in his sixties, thought Alex. The man had a bountiful head of straw coloured hair, meticulously combed and he was wearing what looked like an awfully expensive blue pin-striped suit, accessorised by a bright yellow tie, light blue shirt combination. He was carrying a burgundy briefcase as he stood in front of what looked like the driveway of house or villa. It was difficult to see what type of property it was because of the high hedging and numerous trees.

Alex saw that there was no indication as to the man's identity, but he noted that the man had a high forehead which indicated eastern European.

'This is Eckersley isn't it?' said Alex in triumph as he waved the photograph at Chris.

Chris chuckled. 'Now you are getting warmer. Look at the third photograph.'

Alex turned it over. Again, it was a drone or satellite view of a large mining complex with numerous open-cast mining scars in the landscape, and administrative buildings seemingly covering many hundreds of square metres of land. What the facility was, Alex could only guess. He looked up at Chris who had an amusing smile on his lips.

'I'll take a stab at this and I'm going to say this is a bauxite mining complex. I'm only saying that because it looks like an open-cast mine.'

'Correct,' said Chris. 'It's one of Hellenic Aluminium's mines.'

'I still don't get it.'

'Perhaps this will help. The photograph wasn't taken by us. It was taken by a foreign power using a drone.'

'How do you know it was a drone and not a satellite?' asked Alex.

'Because a satellite looks straight down but a drone can look ahead. If you check the photograph again you will notice that the images in the picture are slightly ahead of the camera.'

'Do we know who took the pictures?'

'The two overhead shots were taken by the same foreign power and the shot of Eckersley was taken by the CIA,' said Chris.

'Has Eckersley bought the place he is standing in front of?'

'Yes,' said Chris. 'You haven't joined the dots up yet have you Alex? I'll give you another clue. Eckersley bought the property on the outskirts of Edessa.'

Why would the CIA be interested in a businessman buying a property near Edessa, thought Alex? Okay so he is a multi-billionaire and there are many other more fascinating and lovely places in Greece where he could have bought a property. Sure, Edessa is a pretty town famous for its waterfalls and natural hot water spas which attract tourists from Salonika and further afield. The only other activity around Edessa is the open-cast mining.

'That's it!' exclaimed Alex. 'Eckersley bought a property near to the Bauxite mines because he what? He wants to buy their production, or could it be he wants to buy the mines?'

'You got it Alex, but the piece of the puzzle you are missing is the Yugoslavia connection.'

'Hmm,' said Alex pouring himself another glass of port from the carafe Petros had left on the table. 'Belgrade was the capital of Yugoslavia but now it's the capital of Serbia and the rest of what was Yugoslavia is broken up into several other countries.'

Alex reeled of the names one by one. 'Bosnia, Kosovo, Croatia, Slovenia, and North Macedonia.' He looked at Chris who had that smug little smile he used when he had extracted the information, he wanted out of someone. Alex continued.

'Eckersley was born in what is now North Macedonia, a country that lays claims to our own region of Macedonia. He does want to buy our Bauxite mines, doesn't he?'

'Yes, he does,' confirmed Chris. 'He has been buying up Bauxite mines around world and in some cases some very sinister events preceded the sale of the mines to him. He is fanatical about his and his Government's notion that North Macedonia and the Greek region of Macedonia should be one country. Buying up one of Macedonia's and Greece's most valuable assets could be the start of a disturbing campaign to annex Macedonia from Greece.'

'Wait a minute,' said Alex. 'The Athens bomber was from North Macedonia, wasn't he? But why Athens and not Salonika or another city in Macedonia?'

Chris answered by taking a long drag of his cigar and then blowing a long stream of smoke Alex's way.

'A smokescreen to divert our attention in the hope that we won't be vigilant in the area of Edessa. Which by the way as you know is only twenty three kilometres from the North Macedonia border.

Another worry is that North Macedonia has hired a small private army from John Dexter.'

'What!' exclaimed Alex. 'The bastard, he is contracted to keep our borders with Turkey secure. Has he reneged on the contract secured by your country and mine after the Gladio incident three years ago?'

Not at all, that contract is still in place, but he has a huge company and legally he is free to contract out mercenaries to other countries as long as it doesn't compromise his contract with us. But it could become a problem as the North Macedonian border is so close to Edessa.'

'You are not suggesting that North Macedonia is going to invade Greece, are you?' said Alex with the appropriate look of astonishment on his face.

'No of course not. Well not yet anyway, but the mercenaries could be used for incursions into the region around Edessa. We will know their intentions well in advance anyway as we have managed to infiltrate Eckersley's inner circle.'

'That must have been quite a feat. Don't tell me you have a North Macedonian on the CIA's books.'

'No, it's a woman and she has managed to become Eckersley's private assistant. She travels everywhere with him. In fact, when he moves into his new property near Edessa she will be staying there too. She is our best agent in Europe,' said Chris.

Alex who was looking at Chris noticed that he dropped his eyes to the table when he spoke about the woman. Alex gave a slight shiver, and his heart missed a beat. Could it be he thought to himself.

'Chris, tell me the truth is it someone I know?' Alex stared hard at Chris.

Chris looked up with a sheepish smile on his lips. 'Yes, it is Alex. It is Gitta.'

Alex said nothing as memories from three years ago crowded into his mind. His Gitta was back in the CIA and would be in Greece in a few days. His heart raced as the recollections of their affair replayed themselves over and over in his mind. Finally, he said. 'Would I be able to see her?'

'We will try and arrange a meeting, but you must understand it could be dangerous for her.' Before Chris could continue his mobile phone rang. He picked it up. 'Horsman.' Then after a minute of listening he said. 'I'll fly up on the company's jet, see you in a couple of hours.'

Chris turned to Alex. 'I have to go Alex. There has been a mortar attack on the home of Andonis Papaspiro, the Group Financial Officer of Hellenic Aluminium. No survivors as far as my guys can tell. His daughter was celebrating her birthday with a small group of friends and family. No doubt you will be going up to see the devastation in your official capacity as Prime Minister?'

'Of course, I will Chris. Tomorrow I'll go up. In the meantime, keep me abreast of any happenings.'

'I will, get that nice Home Secretary of yours to go with you,' said Chris with a wink as he disappeared into the bustle and noise of the taverna.

Alex sat down trying to take everything in that he had heard from Chris. What a mess he thought and how dangerous was this man Eckersley to Greece. He looked at his watch – eight-thirty – he would have to get his Cabinet together before the hit on the house was all over the news.

After paying the bill and complimenting Petros and Pavlina on once again serving up a scrumptious meal, Alex walked to his car. As he slid into the driver's seat, he noticed a small package on the passenger seat. There was a note in Chris's spidery scrawl beside it.

Sorry for breaking into your car – no damage done but by opening this package you are agreeing to be activated from your CIA sleeper status. Keep smiling – Chris.

Without hesitation Alex opened the package. It was the object inside that made him realise how dangerous the next days and weeks were going to be. He was staring at a Glock pistol.

Chapter 8
16th August 2013 Edessa – 20:00

Alkis Eleftheradou sat in his car two hundred metres from the house of Yannis Blounas. He couldn't be sure if his mark were in the house or not. Certainly, since he had parked up over an hour ago at eight-thirty, nothing had moved in or out of the house. It was still light and even though the attack on Andonis's house earlier had been in broad daylight, he also realised he had been lucky that no-one had seen him, at least that's what he had gleaned from the news broadcasts.

Nothing about the casualties though and until they mentioned that Andonis Papaspiro had been killed he was going to be anxious. Anyway, he had been lucky once and he wasn't about to ride his luck and do anything in daylight, even though the twilight was encroaching over the area. Alkis loved the Greek twilights, the colours were incredible, soft yet sharp, bathing the land and sea with a mauve like haze.

He was getting cramps in his right leg. Γαμοτω! He swore to himself as he got out of the car and stepped onto the pavement. He decided to walk his cramp off and set off towards the house he had been watching. By the time he had reached the front gate his cramp had gone, and he was walking without a limp or pain.

Stopping by one of the trees that lined the payment and keeping in the shadows, he studied the building. He saw that it was not a single house but a two-story property consisting of an apartment on each floor. As with many similar types of property in this part of Greece the ground floor apartment had a front door facing the street and the upper apartment had a front door on the side of the building accessed by a set of cement stairs. There were no lights showing in either of the apartments, at least not at the front. Alkis thought that if there was a light in a back room he probably would not see it without trespassing on the property.

Alkis was just about to step away from the tree and step over the low wall that separated the property from the street and made the gate rather redundant. When the sound of a powerful engine filled the air belonging to a car which was racing down the street full headlight beams lighting up the whole area. Alkis slipped into the shadows of a parked van hoping the occupants of the car had not spotted him. His hand in his pocket holding a small derringer pistol.

A lot of things seemed to happen very quickly. The car screeched to a halt in the middle of the street, music blaring from its open windows. Alkis realised the sound of a powerful car was in fact a car that had drilled a few holes in its exhaust pipe. It sat in the middle of the street making a throbbing sound which reverberated against the walls of the buildings lining the street.

Alkis couldn't see what type of car it was as it was hidden from his view and he hoped he was hidden from the occupants' view. A young woman got out of the car talking on her mobile phone, then she shouted, 'Here he comes.'

Alkis who was concentrating on the car failed to hear the sound of Yannis Blounas running through the front garden and vaulting the low wall. He was out in the middle of the street and had boarded the car before Alkis could decide on a move. The car roared off accelerating away from where Alkis was hiding. Shit he thought, I missed him, and I don't know where he is going. He trotted back to his parked car as he formulated his next move.

Once in the car he called the *listeners* in the basement apartment the other side of Edessa.

'It's the *fixer*,' said Alkis. 'Can you trace where the second mark is located through his cell phone?'

'If the phone is on and we know the cell phone number,' replied a voice at the end of the line.

'You do know the number because it is the other party that the first mark was talking to earlier this evening,' said Alkis.

'Hold on a second,' said the voice. Two minutes later the voice came back. 'Okay we've got it.'

'Right, I'm keeping my phone open so you can relay his location.'

With that Alkis started his car and drove towards the centre of Edessa. It was a small town with an approximate population of eighteen thousand people most of whom either worked at Hellenic Aluminium or in the retail and hospitality sectors. Alkis reasoned that young people would head for one of the many coffee bars or tavernas that lined the only main street that ran through Edessa; that being 25th March Street, the date of Greece's independence from the Turkish occupation. His phone crackled.

'We've tracked the phone to the Coffee Island coffee bar on Monastirou Street,' said the voice.

'Good work, thanks,' acknowledged Alkis.

Good I'm heading in the right direction thought Alkis congratulating himself. Five minutes later he had parked in a side street just two hundred metres from Coffee Island.

He got out of his car and walked the two hundred metres to Coffee Island. He saw it was a typical modern-day Greek coffee place. Metal tables spread out on the pavement in front of the main shop in a five tables wide and four rows in depth formation. The shop front itself was made up of several large glass metal framed bifold doors which had been opened onto one side of the shop front leaving the whole interior open to the outside. Although it was now almost ten o'clock, early by Greek standards, most tables on the pavement still had four people around them in predictably Greek animated conversation. A foreigner would think that there was an argument at every table.

Alkis looked around the tables finally spotting Yannis sitting with his friends and his girlfriend, so he moved towards a table in the far front corner of the table formation. As luck would have it a foursome left the table immediately behind Yannis's party and Alkis lost no time in claiming the table as his own.

He ordered a Mythos beer, as despite the time of day, the temperature was still in the upper twenties, from the waiter who had pounced the moment he had sat down. He then tuned into Yannis and his friends' conversation which was fairly easy as they were talking quite loudly. They were debating movies, deciding which movies they had seen were the most realistic. The girl named Sophie who kept on caressing Yannis as she spoke was talking animatedly about one of the Mission Impossible films where Tom Cruise's character was hacking into a powerful mainframe computer, hanging upside down.

'Talking of hacking,' butted in Yannis. 'I've got a real hacking story to tell you. But before I tell it you must all promise me not to breathe a word to anyone else until I say you can.'

'I promise,' said Sophie.

'Me to,' said the man called Thomas.

'I won't breathe a word,' promised the girl named Maria.

'Thank you, you won't be disappointed,' said Yannis. He started to tell his version of the events and conversation with Andonis earlier that day, blissfully unaware that the man sitting behind him was a cold blooded killer.

Alkis was now thinking hard. In the space of a minute, he had gone from having to eliminate Yannis to having to eliminate everyone at the table. Should he call *Cyclops*? He decided against it on the grounds that he was absolutely convinced that he would be told to finish them all. He actually felt a twinge of sorrow for the two women, they seemed lovely people, beautiful too. Alkis quite fancied both of them. Then chiding himself for almost making it personal rather than a business decision he began to devise a plan.

He only had the small Double Tap .45 ACP Derringer with him and that only chambered two bullets, with an extra two in the grip. Also, the derringer had no silencer so it would be foolhardy to use it in a public place, besides, he could never reload the pistol fast enough to stop the remaining two people running off or screaming and attracting attention. He had his Glock Gen 5, which chambered seventeen rounds, back in the glove department of the car. That had a silencer which would give him a chance of getting away before anyone in the coffee shop noticed anything. Or he could retrieve the howitzer from the car and cause a lot of collateral damage. Not a good idea he thought, senseless collateral damage was not something he favoured. He preferred precision kills whenever possible.

A third option is to wait until they leave the cafe, follow them, and take the first opportunity that presents itself. To Alkis the third option seemed the best. Decision made, Alkis called over the waiter, paid for his beer and continued to sip the last few dregs whilst waiting for the two couples to make a move.

He only had to wait another half-hour before they decided it was time to leave. He followed them at a safe distance some thirty metres back as they turned into the very street where Alkis had parked his car. He was pleasantly surprised when as luck would have it their car was parked just three cars back of his.

Alkis slipped into his car and swiftly retrieved his Glock from the glove department and attached the silencer. He looked around but for the moment the street was deserted except for the one called Thomas who was getting into the driver's side and the last of the four people to board the car.

Alkis moved with speed. He was abreast of their car within seconds and before any of the four realised what was happening he had opened the driver's door and shot Sophie, who was in the passenger seat, in the throat. Maria was sitting behind Sophie so Alkis shot her through the mouth as she was formulating a scream for help. As Alkis had anticipated, the two men instinctively turned to see what had happened to their respective girlfriends, giving Alkis the time he needed to shoot them both before they made any noise which might attract attention. Both were killed instantly with head shots. Alkis saw that the two women were still barely alive but bleeding out fast. He realised that they would be dead within minutes, so he decided not to give them the coup de grace unnecessarily wasting his precious bullets.

The whole operation had taken less than a minute from the time that Alkis had retrieved his Glock from his car to the moment he got back into his own car. He felt pleased with himself, both targets had been eliminated as ordered and it was still only ten-thirty in the evening. As he drove back to his hotel he made a mental note to call *Cyclops* and give him the good news that both missions had been accomplished.

Chapter 9
16th August 2013 – Edessa Airport – 22:30

Edessa Airport is located approximately eighteen kilometres outside of Edessa. Its position nestled as it is between mountains and a lake, makes it one of the more picturesque airport settings in Greece. It has only one runway which runs east to west and a small terminal area which houses one arrivals lounge, a departure lounge, a cosy coffee corner, and one check-in desk.

As with many provincial airports in Greece where there are few flights a day and no international flights, the staff double up into separate roles. Edessa Airport is no exception as in the summer, which is the busiest time of year, except for the Christmas period, the airport handles two incoming flights from Athens and two outgoing flights back to Athens.

The Traffic Manager, Kostas Frekas, when he is not managing the daily traffic information sent to him each morning by Athens Centre, operates the weather station or as he is a traffic controller in his own right, works the radarscope when Babis Varvalas, the aircraft traffic controller, is sick or on vacation. He also on occasions runs the small coffee shop when Maria Tsoukas is busy elsewhere.

Maria operates the quick change jobs. She is ground hostess for arriving flights, check-in desk for departures and in between times serves coffees and snacks in the coffee shop. On occasions she is called upon to be passport control when a private jet comes in from another country. When that happens, invariably a smile crosses passengers' faces when they see Maria change uniforms for her distinct roles. Yellow for ground stewardess, blue for customs officer and white for barista.

The planes that Olympic Airways used for all of Greece's domestic flights are ATR 40-600s which are small turboprop aircraft with a maximum load of twenty-five to thirty passengers and three crew. So, clearing and processing the passengers and crew on arrival or departure is relatively quick and trouble free for Maria. But, more troublesome a job was that of Telis Dalakas who is the baggage handler. There is no carousel at the airport so poor Telis has to cart the luggage from the plane into the arrivals lounge and leave the pieces in a reasonably tidy line on the floor.

At the moment Alkis was entering his hotel room on the west side of Edessa, with the sounds of police sirens filling the balmy night air, Edessa Airport was about to become unusually busy for such a late hour.

Kostas Frekas put down his earphones, then turned to his controller Babis Varvalis and said. 'My god, anyone would think it's Christmas. Babis you can't go home I'm afraid. We have three flights coming in within fifteen minutes of each other around eleven-thirty.'

'What!' exclaimed Babis. 'I thought the Olympic flight down to Athens, which I have just handed over to Salonika Centre was the lot for today.'

'Not today,' said Kostas. 'Athens Centre has just informed me to expect three flights at around eleven-thirty later tonight.'

'Commercial?' asked Babis looking at his watch. 'That's a little over an hour from now. I don't have time to go home and I'm starving.'

'Not commercial, two are private jets, one from Athens and the other from Skopje, North Macedonia. The third flight is the Prime Minister's official plane. According to the passenger manifesto Athens Centre just sent me, the other passengers are his driver, Kaliope Vlachos the Home Secretary, Leonidas Papadakis, the Industry Minister, and Aliki Trakas, the Culture Minister.'

'Quite a distinguished list,' said Babis, and then as an afterthought. 'I'd better warn Maria not to go home, her services as ground hostess and snack bar server, will be required later.'

'Don't forget Telis either, he might be needed later. I have no idea how much luggage needs to be managed,' reiterated Kostas as he checked his watch again. It was ten-fifty and he needed to make sure that Maria had been successful at securing a limousine for the Prime Minister and his entourage and one for Mr. Eckersley and party who are arriving on the plane from North Macedonia.

'I'll be back in ten minutes or so,' said Babis. 'I'm popping down to tell Maria and Telis about the arrivals. I'm starving, so I'm going to get a sandwich from the coffee shop too.'

It'll be a tricky one tonight, thought Babis as he made for the lift which was the only way down the five floors to the terminal level. There was no wind to speak of and that always made landing a little more difficult for the pilot not to hit the runway too hard. With a wind, however light, the landing can be slower and softer than without one.

Babis pressed the lift button for the terminal level and thought about which end of the runway he should use for the threshold. Edessa Airport did not have an Instrument Landing System, which in itself made night landings a little tricky, so Babis liked to give the aircraft a long final approach as possible and that meant bringing the aircraft in from the west over the lake.

The lift doors opened just as Babis had made up his mind that he would bring the aircraft in from the west. He strode to the coffee shop where he could see Maria sitting on a stool a coffee mug clutched with both hands.

She was wearing her ground hostess uniform without the jacket, her white blouse still immaculately pressed as was her yellow skirt which was riding up her tanned long shapely legs giving Babis a glimpse of her thigh as she sat there cross-legged her feet encased in a pair of black high heeled shoes.

He was in love with her and had been for a long time now, ever since she had first started working at the airport. However, because of protocol, he had never let her know how he felt or let himself show it. He smiled as he approached her, and Maria turned her head letting her long dark hair swirl around her head. She smiled at him and his heart missed a beat.

'Hello Babis, going home?' she asked her stunning blue eyes locked onto his. He is so handsome she thought as Babis stopped in front of her. She had often wondered why he had never made a move on her as she knew she was an attractive looking woman. She slid off her stool and purposely mis-stepped so that she almost fell against him.

'Careful,' said Babis with concern in his voice, as he gently held her upper arms to stop her falling. 'I'm not going home, and neither are you.'

'Where are you taking me,' Maria said with a twinkle in her eye, 'somewhere nice?'

Babis let out a soft chuckle. 'I'd love to, but we all have work to do. There are three flights coming in around eleven-thirty, two private jets and the PM's flight.'

'Oh no, that's spoiled our evening out,' said Maria giving Babis a look of feigned disappointment. As she said it her mobile phone which was on the counter in front of her rang. She picked it up and seeing it was Kostas calling said. 'What can I do for you Kostas? Babis has already filled me in on what is happening later.' Kostas told her about the requirements for the limousines and as she listened she nodded her head. Finally she said. 'I'll get on it but are you sure there is no limousine for the other flight from Athens?'

'Certain,' replied Kostas. 'We don't have a passenger manifesto yet anyway for that flight. Only that there are three passengers. Can you tell Babis to come back up as quick as he can we have received the flight progress slips for each flight. Thank you Maria.'

Maria cut the connection and turned to Babis. 'What type of sandwich do you want?' she asked.

'Ham and Cheese will do,' said Babis.

Maria reached across the counter to get the sandwich from the glass enclosed display cabinet. Handing it to Babis she said. 'Not so fresh I'm afraid. You'd better run along; Kostas wants you up there as the flight progress strips have arrived. It looks as though it's going to an interesting night and one not without mystery too.'

She teasingly ran her hand across his curly dark hair. 'Now run along *chriso mou*,' Over emphasising the endearment. 'You're master awaits you. See you later.'

Then before Babis could react she gave him a wink, turned, and marched off towards the administrative office on the other side of the terminal.

Babis headed for the lift that will take him up to the control tower. As after every encounter he had with Maria his heart was racing and he could barely catch a breath. Yes he thought it is going to be a fascinating night.

Chapter 10

Hellenic Airforce One – Greek PM's Flight – 23:05

Hellenic Airforce One is a converted Airbus 321 twin jet engine plane, the workhorse of the Airbus fleet. The conversion entailed that all the passenger seats be ripped out of the whole fuselage and replaced by a thick pile carpet in Greek blue. Within the new space looking back from the cockpit area to the rear of the plane is the refurbished galley area which caters for freshly cooked meals if needed. The four toilets which are near the galley on the original configuration have been turned into two restrooms. Beyond the restrooms are two rows of four extremely plush seats, which fold down into a bed. Attached to each seat is a table, a TV screen, and various electronic sockets for charging phones, laptops, or games consoles.

Beyond the seats towards the back of the plane is an open plan conference room, with a cigar shaped mahogany table set in the centre of the fuselage with eight chairs around it.

Beyond the conference room is a communication area which enables the Prime Minister to speak to anyone in the world wherever or whoever they may be. Beyond that, there is a small bedroom for the Prime Minister's use only, four restrooms, and more galley area, for snacks. The crew on this particular flight are the pilot, the co-pilot, three butlers and one cook.

The plane travelling at seven hundred kilometres an hour, was half an hour out of Athens Airport cruising at twenty-one thousand feet towards Salonika. Alex Kalfas and all the passengers, except for Alex's driver, were sitting around the conference table discussing the earlier events in Edessa.

'We still don't have any confirmation that Andonis Papaspiro is alive or dead,' said Kaliope. 'Until we know it would be foolhardy to allow his name to be mentioned in the press. It's going to take a while to sift through the body parts and make accurate identifications. There were over twenty people in the house when the bomb went off.'

'My god,' said Aliki Traka, 'it's all so tragic.'

'What do we know so far?' asked Alex.

Before Kaliope could answer her mobile phone started chirping.

'Excuse me,' said Kaliope a touch of exasperation in her voice as she opened the text application and started reading the incoming message. The irritation she felt was not for the interruption, it had to do with the fact that everyone wanted answers immediately. They still did not appreciate that forensics is a painstaking exercise and that corners could not be cut for fear of compromising the results.

'It's worse than we thought,' said Kaliope as she put the phone down.

'Why, what has happened now?' said Leonidas, suddenly coming to life, 'Has there been another incident?'

Kaliope looked at him with a quizzical stare. 'At the house you mean?' she asked. 'Or elsewhere in Edessa?'

'Oh, err, sorry, bit of a silly question that. The house was flattened wasn't it, so couldn't be another incident there. Or elsewhere I shouldn't have thought. Too much in one evening. Err, sorry Kaliope do go on,' finished Leonidas tamely. His face had a nice red hue to it and inside he was mad as hell for making a fool of himself. At least, he thought, better that they believe I have been foolish.

Alex was flabbergasted by what Leonidas had just said. Was he drunk? No thought Alex he has hardly touched his gin and tonic. He noticed that both Kaliope and Aliki were also staring at the normally calm and relaxed Leonidas.

'Well,' said Kaliope. 'Something else has happened in the centre of Edessa which seems to be connected to the incident at the house of Andonis Papaspiro.'

'What happened, not another bombing?' asked Alex.

'No not a bombing but what looks like an execution, a professional hit,' said Kaliope.

'In Edessa!' exclaimed Alex. 'What the hell is going on Kaliope?'

'We'll get to the bottom of it sir. We have a good man on the ground there,' said Kaliope with more confidence than she felt inside.

'Who have you got on the ground Kaliope?' asked Leonidas, his voice sounding far more assured than it was a few minutes ago.

'Yannis Spanos, commander of Bravo Two EKAM squad. They flew up to Salonika and drove the ninety odd kilometres to Edessa this evening after the news broke of the bombing. Spanos should be liaising with the local police as we speak,' said Kaliope, failing to mention that she was looking forward to seeing him again. Had it only been this morning when the bomber had been killed in front of their eyes.

'How many men in his squad?' asked Leonidas.

'Ten in Edessa at the moment, the rest of his men remained in Salonika.'

'Why?' asked Alex.

'We had some intelligence that there might be a bomb set off in the city. It's precautionary. We have deployed two reconnaissance drones over the city with sophisticated face recognition software which matches faces against the photograph of the ID card database of cards issued in Salonika,' said Kaliope. 'Quite a sophisticated system thanks to our American benefactors.'

'Good work Kaliope,' praised Alex. 'I would like to meet Yannis Spanos before we head for the hotel tonight. Can you arrange it?'

'I'll arrange it, no problem,' said Kaliope. Bugger! She thought I'm not dressed in the appropriate clothes. What I'm wearing wouldn't complement a shaggy dog, in fact I probably look like a shaggy dog. Oh you silly woman you're acting like a foolish teenager, get a grip, Kaliope chided herself. She left the conference table and went into the communications area to arrange the meeting with Spanos.

At that moment, the pilot's voice came over the intercom. 'Good evening ladies and gentlemen. We've just passed over Salonika and we'll be starting our descent into Edessa in a few minutes. Our route will take us out towards the west before we turn east for a long final into Edessa airport's single runway. Weather on the ground is a balmy twenty-one degrees with clear skies. Estimated time of arrival is eleven eighteen. I recommend you strap in and make yourselves comfortable for the landing. Thank you.'

'I'll just pop to the restroom,' announced Leonidas to no-one in particular, as he rose from the conference table and headed for the restrooms at the back of the plane. Leaving Alex and Aliki to buckle themselves into the plush forward facing seats.

As Hellenic One started its descent Kaliope informed Alex that she had arranged the meeting with Spanos at ground zero. She then sat in a seat and put on her seatbelt.

'Where is Leonidas?' she asked as she suddenly realised he wasn't sitting down.

'Still in the restroom,' said Aliki.

'Perhaps he has fallen asleep,' said Kaliope laughing.

The plane's twin engines had powered down for the descent into Edessa and in the quietness the passengers stopped talking and turned their minds to what was in store for them on the ground in Edessa.

As their collective thoughts were focused on the small town of Edessa, ninety kilometres north of their position in a hotel room in Salonika two men were getting their equipment ready for their assignment in the city. Both men possessed burner phones which had been purchased in Athens earlier that day, before they drove up to Salonika. One of the men's phone rang. He picked it up and put it on speaker.

'Yes,' he said.

'I have a message from *Cyclops*,' said a voice. 'Make sure you keep your heads down and don't wear hats, I know it's high summer but there is no sun at night, and you will stand out like a sore thumb. The authorities have deployed reconnaissance drones which use face recognition software. It's best you use the motorbike you hired, and go to plan B.'

'Understood,' said the man and closed the phone. He turned to his colleague. 'It's a good job we hired the motorbike earlier, they'll never be able to work their software on a face covered in googles and a crash helmet. Come on let's go.'

As the two men left their room to make their way down to the underground hotel garage where their motorbike was parked, back in Edessa Dimitris Moustakas, one of Yannis Spanos's squad members, was idling away time sitting on a wall outside the cordon which had been put around what was left of Andonis Papaspiro's house to prevent neighbours and casual onlookers getting too close to the scene.

He was thinking about the argument that he had with his wife just before he was called for duty that morning in Athens. As usual the argument had been over money. He adored his wife and would never intentionally hurt her, but he was also addicted to gambling. The night before he had got involved in a poker game and had lost three months' salary and now he was thinking how and where he could find money to pay this month's rent and bills.

His rumination was interrupted by the chirping of his mobile phone.

'Who is it?' he said opening the connection.

'Am I talking to Dimitris Moustakas?'

'Yes, who wants to know?'

'Are you alone?'

'Yes. What do you want?'

'I'm sending you a video clip. Watch it!'

Dimitris's phone pinged as the video came in and he opened it immediately, more out of curiosity than anything else because he didn't like the man's tone at all, and it made him uneasy.

Dimitris couldn't believe what he was seeing. His stomach churned as he watched. The video showed what looked like a basement room and in the centre of the room was his wife tied naked to a chair and restrained by two masked men. A third man, also masked, with a cigarette in one hand walk towards his wife and stubbed the cigarette out on the inside of her right thigh. His wife screamed in agony calling out his name.

'You bastards!' yelled Dimitris. 'I'll kill you if you hurt her again.'

The man at the end of the phone sniggered taking no notice of Dimitris outburst.

'My friend has a full pack of cigarettes and each one will be stubbed out on your pretty wife's body if you don't do what we say. Do you understand?' As if to emphasize the point the man switched his phone to facetime mode so Dimitris could see what was going on in real time. The masked man with the cigarette lit up again and took a few drags until the tip was red hot and started towards Dimitris' wife again. Dimitri was in no doubt what he intended.

'Stop!' he yelled. 'Please stop. What do you want me to do? Just don't hurt her anymore, please.'

'If you do what we say we will let her go and as a further incentive we will put fifty thousand euro into your bank account. That should cover your debts. But if you fail to do it we will return your wife to you dead. After we torture her of course.'

'Okay, okay,' sobbed Dimitris utterly dejected. 'I'll do anything you say.'

'It's a simple task for a man of your calibre Dimitris,' said the voice on the phone. 'You have twenty-four hours to kill your commander Yannis Spanos.'

Then the line went dead.

Chapter 11

16th August 2013 - Edessa Airport Control Tower – 23:10

Babis Varvalis sat in front of his radar console watching the blip that was Hellenic One as it slowly edged towards Edessa. He was waiting for the handover from the National Air Traffic Control. A couple of other blips were passing across his console heading south, but those planes were far above Edessa at thirty-seven thousand feet, probably heading for Athens or a country beyond Greece and both also under the control of the NATC centre located just north of Athens.

NATC managed all aircraft that were flying over Greece above ten thousand feet. Once the aircraft was at ten thousand feet from its arrival airport, NATC would hand over the aircraft to an airport controller and similarly once an aircraft had ascended to ten thousand feet from its departure airport, the airport control tower would hand over control to NATC.

Babis spoke into his microphone. 'Gulfstream 323 taxi to gate one via taxiway Alpha.'

Gulfstream 323 was the aircraft with which Chris Horsman had travelled from Athens and which Babis had guided down to the runway five minutes before. The passenger manifest listed the one other passenger as a Mr Ryan Jones, salesman Hellenic Aluminium which of course was a bare faced lie but neither Chris Horsman nor Ryan Jones could own up to being CIA agents.

The speakers on Babis's headset burst into life.

'Edessa Tower approach, good evening, this is Hellenic One descending through one-one thousand for ten thousand feet on heading three forty.'

Babis acknowledged that he had Hellenic One on his radar scope and gave the pilot a new heading and altitude. The pilot of Hellenic

One confirmed he had Zulu, which was the code name for the Automatic Airport Information Systems that informed pilots of the local weather conditions, which runways were open and the direction for landing and departures.

For the next ten minutes Babis gradually guided the plane down to a five mile final heading for runway nine zero which was a landing in an easterly direction. Edessa airport being small had no Instrument Landing System therefore Babis liked to give the pilots as long a final as possible to enable them to see the runway early enough to make good landing.

As Hellenic One touched down another blip which had been on Babis's scope for the last five minutes made a turn from a southerly direction to a south-eastern direction.

That's Eckersley's plane thought Babis. The pilot, with a distinctly Slavic voice, gave Babis his altitude and heading, then confirmed he too had Zulu. Babis rerouted the Gulfstream on a heading and altitude that would bring it down safely to in easterly direction towards Edessa's runway. He waited for the pilot to confirm the instructions and then turned his attention back to Hellenic One which had just landed.

'Hellenic One, taxi to gate two via taxiway Alpha,' said Babis.
'Two down safely and one to go,' said Babis to Kostas.

'Not long now,' replied Kostas. 'I'm going down to greet the Prime Minister and make sure Maria doesn't get into any trouble.' Kostas laughed and Babis laughed with him allowing the tension of the last fifteen minutes to ebb away from his body. It was the first time he had handled three planes in such a short period of time, in the dark too. It wasn't an easy task, but he was thankful that he had only one more to bring home safely.

'Okay,' said Babis. 'I'd better get back to that Gulfstream and start giving it instructions to line it up on final.'

Down below in the main terminal building, Chris Horsman was sitting with Ryan Jones at a table outside the coffee shop, both of them drinking a frappe coffee, a popular cold summer drink in Greece. They were waiting for the car which would take them to the Four Seasons Hotel the only five star hotel in Edessa.

'You realise that we won't be the only official guests at the Four Seasons, the Prime Minister and his entourage will be staying there too,' said Chris. He took his straw into his mouth and started sucking but it encountered air at the bottom of his paper take-away cup, and he made a kind of gurgling noise.

'I guess we'll have to keep a low profile,' said Ryan. 'You and Alex are good friends aren't you?' he asked.

'True,' said Chris. 'But the others in his entourage must not realise that. Too much knowledge could be dangerous. I have a nasty feeling in my gut that some serious stuff is going to happen here.'

'Why is that?' asked Ryan.

'In truth, even if our car turns up in the next few minutes I'd like us to stay until Eckersley has left the airport.'

Ryan nodded his agreement without taking his eyes from Maria's legs that he had been staring at ever since she had greeted them in the arrivals lounge. She was lounging against the counter talking to Telis who hadn't been needed by Chris and Ryan because they were travelling light, both only having a briefcase and a suit carrier with them. He was still hanging around though in case he was needed for the other two incoming flights.

Maria, who had just served both of them a second frappe and was feeling extremely uncomfortable under Ryan's gaze, noticed Kostas leave the lift and enter the arrivals lounge, hurried over to meet him. Any excuse to get away from the stare of the younger of the two men sitting in the coffee shop.

'Do you want me to come with you to greet the Prime Minister?' she asked.

'Yes, why not, you have never met him have you? It will be a good experience for you.'

A minute later Alex Kalfas and his team entered the arrivals lounge. After introductions all round Maria instructed Telis to go out to Hellenic One to pick up the luggage and bring it into the airport building. Alex motioned for the others to sit down while they waited for their transport and Yannis Spanos to turn up.

'Would any of you like something from the coffee shop?' asked Maria to the gathering.

'I'd love a freddo,' said Kaliope. 'And could you direct me to the ladies washrooms please Maria?' Kaliope was determined to make herself more presentable before the arrival of Yannis Spanos. Again a little voice in her head was questioning her teenage-like crush behaviour.

After directing Kaliope, Maria collected the rest of the orders before heading over to the coffee shop to prepare them. Alex looked around at his party. He watched Aliki his Culture Minister, working on her speech in preparation for the unveiling of the new statue of King Philip of Macedonia, scheduled to take place the following day.

Leonidas however was playing with his phone again and had Alex wondering what he was doing spending so long on it. He made a mental note to talk to him about it. Alex could see that it was not his business mobile phone, but his private phone and he feared that Leonidas was using it for business, perhaps not realising that the encryption software used on the business phone was much more robust than his personal one.

His thoughts were interrupted with the sound of the roar of the reverse thrusters slowing Eckersley's plane down as it rushed down the runway, then came the gentle whine of the engines as the plane taxied to its designated stand. Alex began to feel nervous because in a few minutes Gitta would come through the doors to the arrivals lounge, but he could not, must not, give any indication that he knew her. His heart pounded faster as the plane taxied towards the stand and he found himself scarcely able to breath.

A few minutes later the entrance doors to the arrivals lounge glided open seemingly announcing the entrance of Eckersley's party. Firstly, Eckersley stepped through the doors, confidence oozing from him with every stride he took. Alex noted that he was wearing the same blue pinstripe suit that he had seen him sporting in the photograph Chris had shown him earlier. Same light blue shirt and yellow tie, same burgundy briefcase. He seemed taller than he was in the photograph though.

Following behind was his bodyguard who looked at any moment that he was going to burst out of his ill-fitting suit. Not a man to tangle with thought Alex, this guy is just full of muscle. So much so he didn't really need the gun that was plain to see in the shoulder holster underneath his unbuttoned jacket. The bodyguard had a shaven head which tended to highlight his high, typically Slavic featured, forehead.

By now Alex's heart was pounding in his chest as he waited for Gitta to step through the door. It seemed like an age, but she eventually appeared and entered the arrivals lounge. Alex figured that she had obviously wanted to distance herself from Eckersley and the bodyguard and had hung back. He learned later that she had thought that Eckersley and his minder would walk directly to the front entrance of the terminal and give her a little time to be near Alex.

She had planned to drop her handbag in such a way that the unzipped main compartment would spill its contents onto the floor, and that Alex being chivalrous, would have helped her retrieve the contents while at the same time their hands could touch as she passed a note to him. She never expected that Eckersley would stop to talk to Leonidas Papadakis the Industry Minister.

'Good evening. Leonidas. What brings you to Edessa?' asked Eckersley in English, shaking Leonidas's hand in a firm grip.

'The Prime Minister was travelling up tonight so I thought it a good opportunity to come up and meet with you. I knew you were flying in to complete the paperwork on your house purchase,' said Leonidas motioning with his hand towards Alex. 'This is Alex Kalfas our Prime Minister.'

Eckersley extended his right hand and shook Alex's proffered hand. 'I have heard a lot about you of course,' said Alex as he gave Eckersley a firm handshake. 'I understand you have bought a property in our lovely Macedonia?'

'Yes I have and I'm looking forward to spending my summers here,' said Eckersley with a sardonic smile playing on his face. 'After all Macedonia and North Macedonia could almost be the same country they are so alike. Is that not so Prime Minister?'

Alex bristled at the remark but managed to appear calm as he said. 'Similar in landscape I would agree with you sir, but culturally I'm afraid that Macedonia has a far more significant historical past than your adopted country.'

Eckersley didn't say anything for a moment, his eyes narrowing slightly as he continued to stare into Alex's eyes. Then he said rather brusquely. 'It's late we must be going, perhaps we will meet again in more convivial surroundings when we can continue this debate.'

'Nothing to debate,' retorted Alex. 'History is on our side. Enjoy your stay.'

Eckersley said nothing, instead he turned to his bodyguard Bogdan and said, 'Let's go, you too Gitta.'

Gitta started to follow Bogdan but as she passed Alex she stumbled to her knees. She put her right hand out to support herself, placing it next to Alex's shoe. Alex who was leaning forward instinctively trying to help her, suddenly felt her hand sliding, what felt like a folded piece of paper, into his sock. He helped Gitta up as she uttered 'Thank you.' in a soft voice, her wide smile, and bright green eyes moist with emotion lifting Alex's heart. She then turned and followed Bogdan out of the terminal.

Kaliope who had kept a low profile while the verbal exchange was taking place was perplexed as to why Leonidas had not introduced anyone to Eckersley except for Alex.

'I don't trust that man,' announced Kaliope. 'I don't know why, maybe women's intuition.'

'Neither do I. He's an interfering bastard,' agreed Alex. 'What do you think Leonidas? Why the puzzled face?'

'He has never given me any cause to not trust him,' said Leonidas still sporting a puzzled look on his face. 'I'm puzzled that you two do not trust him.' What Leonidas did not tell them was that he had seen Gitta slip something into Alex's sock and that was why he was puzzled.

Alex looked at his watch and saw that it was now ten minutes past twelve in the morning. Yannis should have been here fifteen minutes ago. He felt very tired it had been a long day. He hoped the meeting with Yannis would not take long because he was ready for bed. He decided that he had time to look at whatever Gitta had slipped into his sock and headed for the men's rest room.

The terminal building was now unusually quiet with no conversation with everyone in Alex's party deep in thought. Chris and Ryan had been told by Maria that their car was outside waiting but Chris had decided they should stay to talk to Yannis Spanos.

No one however could imagine that at that moment back in Salonika one of the most valued symbols of Macedonian and Greek culture was about to be heartlessly destroyed.

Chapter 12
17th August 2013 – Salonika – 00:10

The motorbike with two men riding it kept well within the speed limit so as to not attract attention. The time for speed would come later but now stealth was called for. They were heading towards the sea, south of the city, and so it seemed were all the residents of Greece's second city and regional capital of the Macedonia region. It was a balmy July night the temperature still around twenty-six degrees centigrade and the Salonika residents were doing what Greeks like to do in the summer - spending the early morning hours eating and drinking by the sea to try and catch a cool breeze.

The driver of the motorbike expertly weaved in and out of the traffic as he headed down the motorway standard 30th October Avenue. A dual carriageway which wound its way along the Salonika seafront with its hotels on the landward side and restaurants, cafes, and nightclubs on its seaward side. When the bike was opposite the Salonika Performing Arts Theatre, the driver took the slip road that would take the bike into the car park of the theatre.

The theatre is situated in a small park that has a small copse of trees scattered in it with beautifully landscaped borders throughout, amongst magnificently manicured lawns. Every night there are many couples young and old in the park, either sitting on benches of which there were many, or walking hand-in-hand through the park enjoying the romantic atmosphere enhanced by the soft lighting emanating from the thousands of fairy lights amongst the trees and the landscaped shrubbery.

The two men, however, were oblivious to the beauty of the place as having parked their bike, the pillion rider took the sports bag which he had held in his lap throughout the journey. They kept their crash helmets on because they feared for the drones they had been warned about and they afforded extra protection against recognition by passers-by on the ground. They walked quickly towards a small area of open space where the ground was laid in marble and there in the centre of it was their objective. The striking statue of a man sitting astride a prancing stallion, with his cloak flowing out behind him, sword by his side, was the most beloved hero of Greece, especially Macedonia where he was born. Their target, Alexander the Great.

Without hesitation but moving at a casual pace, the two men moved round to the back of the statue hiding from any prying eyes. One of the men opened the sports bag and took out four slabs of C4 explosive and handed two slabs to his partner. The square slabs are about the size of a standard one-ounce gold bar. Being a stable but malleable plastic explosive it can be moulded into corners or around pipe-like surfaces. Each man quickly and deftly moulded a slab of C4 around one of the horse's back legs and one slab into the bottom corner of the square plinth. A detonator with a small receiver was then inserted into the centre of each slab.

It had only taken the two men a couple of minutes to place the explosives. No-one had noticed what they had done, and no-one really took any notice of them as they walked briskly back to the car park where they had left their bike. In the car park they both mounted the bike, the pillion rider taking out a mobile phone.

'Shall I do it?' he said.

'Wait,' said the driver. 'There is a crowd gathering in front of the statue. There is no point in adding to the collateral damage that will occur anyway. Besides, there are a couple of children in the crowd.'

'It only takes one of that crowd to move around to the back of the statue to spot our handiwork. You appreciate that don't you?' said the pillion rider.

Just as he finished they heard a shout from the vicinity of the statue. 'Bomb! There's a bomb! Run!

'Do it!' instructed the driver. The pillion rider entered a four-digit code onto his 'phone and within a nanosecond the radio signal from the 'phone had triggered the detonators on all four C4 explosives simultaneously.

There was an extremely loud boom as the area around the statue became a ball of fire and dust. The plinth bearing the statue exploded into hundreds of pieces of various sized marble missiles, many passing through bodies or decapitating heads as the percussion threw the bloodied limbs of once whole bodies fifty metres into the park. The statue itself seemed to rear up as if taking a jump in an equestrian event, then seemingly in slow motion it shattered into pieces which like bullets travelled at the speed of sound into the park adding to the carnage.

The reconnaissance drones were a couple of kilometres from the park when the explosion occurred. The drone pilots, who were piloting the drones from the Tatoi Air Base just north of Athens, were immediately ordered to move the drones over the roads around the park. A ploy which often led to perpetrators of an incident being spotted, which then, often led to an arrest.

However, although many heads reviewed the video-feed live and later the recording, no-one managed to identify that the two men on the motorcycle were involved in the incident. At least, not until the authorities had interviewed visitors who had been in the carpark and remembered seeing a motorbike with two men on it, and other visitors who remembered two men in crash helmets carrying a sports bag walking through the park towards the area of the statue. But, by the time they had put out an all-points bulletin for the two men it was way too late.

Back in Edessa it was forty-five minutes after midnight and Alex, Kaliope, Yannis Spanos and Chris were sitting in a quiet corner of the bar of the Four Seasons Hotel. They were still in a state of shock having heard the news of the explosion at the statue, some five

minutes earlier from the Chief of Police in Salonika. The news was
not good. Twenty dead including two young children and thirty-five
injured, of which twelve were in intensive care with life-changing
injuries.

Alex checked his watch. He was feeling very tired now. Apart
from the fact it had been a long day, he had been up at six yesterday
morning and he also had been anxious about meeting Gitta for the
first time after three years. It was only his adrenalin keeping him
going, and his elation at seeing Gitta and her note. Some of which he
desperately needed to share with those around the table. He was also
furious because Leonidas had gone AWOL.

Although he was angry, he was also relieved because he didn't
want Leonidas to suspect that Chris was a good friend. He was under
no illusions that Leonidas liked him at all. Someone as ambitious as
Leonidas would have no qualms in sticking a knife in his back. All
the same he thought, it was irresponsible of him not to be joining
them.

'Where the hell has Leonidas got to? He said five minutes, and
it's been twenty minutes,' Alex said showing his annoyance.

'I texted him five minutes ago but as yet he hasn't answered,' said
Kaliope.'

'Has he got a woman up here I wonder, he comes up here quite
regularly, supposedly to visit Hellenic Aluminium. Damn it! Let's
start without him. I need to share with you part of the note which
Gitta slipped into my sock.'

Alex retrieved the note from his pocket. He had considered just
handing it around so everyone could read it for themselves but then
he remembered that Kaliope and Spanos knew nothing of his
relationship with Gitta, so he decided to read the more pertinent
pieces which were relevant to the security of the country.
'*Conversations overheard between Eckersley and another - annex of*

*Macedonia Pella Municipality - No dates - private army - majority
shareholder - thirty percent - Hellenic Aluminium'*

'That's it,' said Alex. 'Do we know that Eckersley is the major
shareholder, surely we would know that?'

'I know somebody who should know,' answered Yannis Spanos, a
wide grin on his face.

'Who?' asked Kaliope.

'Andonis Papaspiro.'

They all turned in unison to look at Yannis, all with a look of
incredulity on their faces. Nobody said anything for a minute as
Yannis just sat there grinning from ear to ear. Kaliope was the first
with the question that was on all their lips.

'Did he survive the attack on his house?' she asked.

'He was not in the house. He was picking up some groceries
from the local supermarket around the corner. When he plucked up
enough courage to leave his hiding place he was picked up by one of
my men. Once we had established that he was who he said he was,
we put him in a safe house. Well not a house exactly. We took the top
floor of the Aigai Hotel just outside of Edessa.'

A lucky break at last thought Alex. We have been on the back
foot since this whole thing started. He recalled the note that Gitta
had slipped to him. She was staying in one of the bungalows in the
grounds of the Aigai Hotel, room number seven, his lucky number.
He couldn't stop himself from smiling.

'You look as though the cat's got the cream,' said Chris with a
chuckle.

'I was just thinking that we were due for a lucky break and we've
got one,' Alex said. 'Has Papaspiro said anything yet?'

'I would say it was a miracle,' proclaimed Yannis. 'From what he
said, he had only just left the house a few minutes before it was blown
up. The forensics have confirmed it was a rocket launcher attack by

the way. He is still shocked by the events, so I think it better that Kaliope waits 'till tomorrow morning to debrief him.'

'I agree,' affirmed Kaliope. My god he looks so ruggedly handsome with five o'clock shadow thought Kaliope. 'Perhaps he can shed some light on that share business. Maybe that is why his family was targeted. He might have discovered something.'

'Yes,' said Chris. 'I have been thinking about this. One of the four people murdered in their car in the centre of Edessa a few hours ago was a Yannis Blounas who worked for Hellenic Aluminium in their operations office. He was the keeper of the securities registry there. One theory is that he spotted something out of the ordinary in the share registry, informed Papaspiro and somehow they, whoever they are, found out and decided to quieten them for good.'

'You could be right,' agreed Yannis Spanos. 'We need to find out how they knew, do they have an inside man, or have they been tapping the phones.'

'I'll get forensics into Hellenic Aluminium's head office and their operations centre right away,' said Kaliope.

'Why would you send forensics there?' said a voice behind them.

They all looked around. Standing there was Leonidas Papadakis.

'Where the hell have you been Leonidas?' asked Alex with a slightly raised voice showing his annoyance.

Leonidas sheepishly apologised profusely saying that he had been suffering from a migraine-type headache when he had returned to his room after he had been dropped off from the airport, and had taken a pill, then fallen asleep before he could let them know he was not in good shape. Alex rolled his eyes upwards grudgingly accepting his apology. Then he asked Kaliope to fill Leonidas in with everything they knew so far.

When Kaliope told him that Andonis was still alive and safe and sound in the Aigai Hotel Leonidas's colour drained from his face. Kaliope didn't seem to notice but both Chris and Yannis did, and they both wondered why he had reacted in that way. As Kaliope continued to relate the rest of the information and summaries of their theories, Leonidas didn't seem to be listening. Both Chris and Yannis were watching him very closely now. It was obvious to them that Leonidas *wasn't* listening to Kaliope, but behind his eyes his brain was whirring.

When Kaliope had finished, Leonidas thanked her and then announced that he was still groggy from the pill he had taken earlier to manage his migraine and needed to sleep. He would join the others at ground-zero in the morning around ten-thirty as agreed; he then bid them all goodnight and left for his room.

The rest of the group broke up soon afterwards and retired for the night, little imagining that the waters were about to get extremely muddied with forces beyond their control unleashed upon them all.

Chapter 13

17th August 2013 – Edessa Four Seasons Hotel – 01:30

Ryan Jones was sitting in the foyer of the Four Seasons hotel ostensibly reading a newspaper but in reality he was observing the entrance to the hotel, the bank of lifts to the upper floors and the entrance into the bar area. After the others had retired to their rooms Chris had brought him up to date with everything they knew and asked him to sit tight observing who was leaving or entering the hotel.

He didn't have to wait long. At first he didn't recognise the tall slim man dressed quite casually in jeans and a blue polo shirt, carrying a man bag over his shoulder. As the man passed him he realised that it was Leonidas Papadakis the Greek Industry and Business Minister. Ryan got out of his chair and sauntered over to the revolving entrance door. He left the hotel just in time to see Papadakis climb into the passenger seat of a car which had pulled up outside the hotel. Unfortunately for Ryan there was not enough light for him to recognise the gender of the driver.

When the taxi was out of sight of the hotel the driver stopped by the side of the road. She removed her cap, shook her head, and let her titian hair fall over her shoulders. She turned towards Leonidas, took his face between her hands, and kissed him full on the lips.

'I love you,' she said.

Leonidas adored that she was always telling him that she loved him. 'Love you too,' he said. He sat for a moment gazing into her sparkling brown eyes marvelling at the amount of love showing in them.

'Let's go Melita,' he said, giving the steering wheel a tap with his hand. Melita put the car into drive, accelerating quickly away from the kerb she headed in the direction of the Aigai Hotel. She was a good driver, although she tended to speed, she handled the BMW 118i with skill. Leonidas had met her eighteen months ago on his first visit to Edessa after Alex Kalfas had promoted him to Industry Minister. He had travelled up to pay a courtesy call to meet with Spyros Emmanuel, the CEO of Hellenic Aluminium at their head office.

After the meeting he had invited the CEO to dinner but as the meeting had been a last minute decision Spyros Emmanuel who had prearranged a dinner party at his home, had to decline the dinner. But in a polite gesture he invited Leonidas to the dinner party which Leonidas gratefully accepted because he hated eating alone.

When Leonidas arrived at the Spyros Emmanuel's home he was pleasantly surprised that there were two other couples and a single woman without an escort, named Melita. Much to Leonidas surprise he and Melita quickly became friends. She seemed much younger than his fifty-five years, he was to find out later that she was forty-two and a widow, her husband having died of cancer two years before. They talked all through the dinner relating stories from their past lives both funny and sad. Too soon the evening ended. Leonidas wanted to see her again, but he didn't know what to say. He had told her that he was married with two children but even so he just had to see her.

His dilemma was solved by Melita who offered to run him back to his hotel. During the journey Melita made it very obvious that she also reciprocated the attraction Leonidas had for her and they agreed that he would come up the following weekend as her house guest. When Melita dropped him off at his hotel she leant over and sealed their arrangement with a lingering kiss on his lips.

Now eighteen months later they were on their way to the Aigai Hotel for a late supper before heading back to Melita's home for what would be left of the night.

'Penny for them darling,' said Melita interrupting his memories.

'I was just recalling when we first met at Spyros's home,' Leonidas replied.

'That was a beautiful evening my love as is every evening with you. Oh, here we are at the hotel,' said Melita pulling into the hotel's forecourt. After handing over the car to the car park attendant they walked hand in hand into the hotel lobby confident that at this time of the morning there would not be anyone in the hotel's supper lounge who would recognise Leonidas. They were sadly mistaken; they were being watched.

Back at the Four Seasons lobby Ryan was wondering where the Minister was going at this time of the morning. Ryan supposed that he might be going out to eat, as there could very well be a taverna open at this time of the morning, or maybe a bar because he didn't want to be recognised drinking in the hotel bar. There seemed no point in supposition, so Ryan returned to his seat back inside the hotel foyer. Another few minutes passed before Ryan had made up his mind to call Chris and wake him up.

'Yes,' said a sleepy voice. 'This had better be good.'

'It's Ryan sir. Leonidas has left the hotel.'

'Did he grab a cab?' asked Chris.

'No sir. A private car picked him up. I didn't manage to get a good look at the driver.'

'Did you recognise the gender?'

'No sir, sorry sir, it was too dark outside,' apologised Ryan.

'Don't worry it's not your fault. Call me the moment he gets back. I'm going to check his room. Something wasn't right about him tonight.'

'Will do sir,' said Ryan, closing the connection.

Ryan wondered how long Leonidas would be out. He realised that he could be out all night and so he wouldn't be getting any sleep. It was going to be a long night. Ryan stretched his long legs out so he was lying back in the chair and started playing with his mobile phone. He had downloaded a game called Mini-Metro which he had found quite addictive. It was a simple game but also hard to survive and he hadn't survived it yet. The whole idea was to make sure no station got overloaded with passengers, if one did that was it, game over.

Ryan heard footsteps on the marble tiles coming from the bank of lifts, he looked up. He immediately picked up a newspaper to hide his face. Too late!

'Hello Ryan,' said Alex, grinning from ear to ear at Ryan's attempt at hiding his face.

'Good evening Prime Minister,' said Ryan sheepishly. He stood up and walked towards Alex at a loss as to what to say to a leader of a country who was going out by himself at two-thirty in the morning. Just before he reached Alex, Ryan said. 'Enjoy your drink sir.' Thinking that only a bar would be open at this time of the morning.

'Thank you, but I'm not going out for a drink I'm visiting a friend. Has Chris finished his search of Papadakis's room do you know?'

'Not yet,' replied Ryan, but he shouldn't be long now.'

'Alright, I don't need to speak to him if you can give him a message.'

'Of course sir, what's the message?'

'Tell Chris that I'll be at the Aigai Hotel. He'll know who I'm meeting.'

'No problem.'

'Thank you,' said Alex.

Ryan watched Alex walk out of the hotel and get into a taxi that had obviously been waiting for him. Before he could call Chris he felt a vibration coming from his trouser pocket. His burner phone was vibrating. A feeling of dread came over Ryan as he pulled the phone from his pocket. He looked around furtively which he then realised was silly as nobody would comprehend he was using a burner.

'Yes,' said Ryan.

'It's Cyclops,' said a voice. 'We've heard a rumour that Papaspiro survived the attack on his house. Is that true?'

Ryan hesitated. He could say no but if they found out later that he had lied they would certainly go through with their threat. 'I believe so,' said Ryan.

'You believe so or you know so. Don't play around with us Mr Jones, you know what we can do.'

'I know so.'

'Where?' asked Cyclops.

'Top floor Aigai Hotel,' answered Ryan. 'They have taken the whole floor.'

'Thank you Mr Jones. I wouldn't go to that hotel tonight if I were you. Goodnight.'

The phone in Ryan's hand went dead as Cyclops disconnected. He was now in a quandary. Could he take a chance and conveniently forget the call to Chris. If he didn't call Chris, both Chris and Alex would definitely find out. He couldn't take that chance because he would almost definitely be taken off the case, risking the wrath of Cyclops. If only I hadn't gone to that infernal club, he berated himself with the thought.

Two years ago soon after Ryan had graduated from the CIA academy at Camp Perry he was assigned to the CIA station in Greece under Chris Horsman. He was over the moon at getting an overseas assignment so quickly. After his arrival in Greece he began looking around for a suitable place to live for himself and his pregnant wife, a lawyer, who had stayed back in the States, to finish an important case before she joined him.

One night he ventured into one of the sleazier areas of Athens to experience for himself the traditional bouzouki music not the music played for the tourists ears. What he didn't know was that the area was controlled by the supporters of the extreme right wing party The Golden Dawn. He hadn't entered the area more than five minutes before his presence as a stranger and an obvious American was on the jungle drums.

By the time he had settled at the table of the Oneira Club, through contacts in both Greece and America, The Golden Dawn knew that they had in their midst someone worth exploiting. They had set a honey trap for him in the form of a beautiful young woman who had gone to his table asking for a light and engaging him in conversation. He had been weak, he knew that now, but he could not resist her charm and intense sexuality. Later that evening he had gone with her to her apartment and during one of their energetic and enthusiastic bouts of sex, three men had entered the apartment.

They had video and sound recordings of the whole evening including his sexual cavorting. Ryan realised that he had been well and truly snaffled. They told him that everything would be put on social media and his wife would get a special package if he didn't do as they asked whenever they asked. They gave him a burner phone telling him to keep it on his person at all times as this was the way they would contact him. Then they let him go.

For fifteen months Ryan heard nothing and he had almost forgotten about the incident, but when the North Macedonia diplomatic row with Greece became more emotive, they had contacted him. Just snippets of information at first, nothing that made him feel like a traitor, until the phone call a few moments ago when they asked him to give up Andonis Papaspiro.

His mind made up, Ryan keyed his mobile called Chris, who immediately answered his phone saying. 'Nothing in Papadakis's room that's out of the ordinary so where the hell is he?' said an exasperated Chris. 'Have you got anything to report?'

'Well, I haven't seen Papadakis since he left but I have seen the Prime Minister. He passed me by on his way out and asked me to tell you that he would be at the Aigai Hotel.'

'What!' exclaimed Chris. 'Not a good idea. We'll have to go to make sure he is safe. Stay where you are Ryan I'll be down in ten minutes.' After hanging up the phone Chris sat on the edge of his bed fuming. Alex's trip to the Aigai Hotel was foolhardy and reckless. Edessa was not a safe place for him, or anyone associated with him at the moment. However, he was obviously seeing Gitta, and she was probably armed, so she can protect him if anything happens. Chris picked up the room phone, dialled the night porter and requested he order a taxi to take him and Ryan to the Aigai Hotel.

Ten minutes later Chris and Ryan were in a cab travelling to the hotel some fifteen minutes away. Ryan was reluctant to accompany Chris after the phone call with Cyclops, but he could not see a way out. He had to come up with something, but what? He was too tired to think, it had been a long day. Ryan thought that maybe after a drink he could get his little grey cells to work. He realised that his life was a mess right now, yet he had to come up with something.

Chapter 14
17th August 2013 – Edessa Aigai Hotel – 03:30

In one of the holiday bungalows in the grounds of the Aigai Hotel the lights were low and the only sounds were the heavy breathing of Gitta as she sat cowboy style on Alex's member, slowly gyrating, letting the movement give her ever heightening intensities of pleasure. Her eyes never left Alex's as she increased her tempo, starting to moan as her orgasm seemed to be emanating from every nerve ending.

Alex too was thrusting upward, keeping in rhythm with Gitta's movements. Rivulets of sweat were running down between Gitta's breasts, then dripping onto Alex's stomach. He moved his hands from her buttocks and took her proffered hands helping her to keep her balance as the force of her thrusts made her lean over Alex's chest.

She sensed that Alex could hold back no longer and thrust even harder. Her orgasm was totally enveloping her whole body, her soft cry signalling to Alex that he could now release. He exploded into Gitta making a guttural sound as his body trembling and shuddering, mingling his fluids with hers. Gitta collapsed on top of Alex totally spent. She lay there for some moments with Alex's arms around her, keeping her close. Then she rolled onto her back turning her head towards Alex, a smile of complete contentment on her face.

'Darling that was wonderful,' she whispered. 'I have missed you so much these past three years.'

'Me too sweetheart,' said Alex smiling, marvelling at her almost perfect body. 'But if it weren't for Chris assuring me that you were alright I would have gone mad.'

'It had to be that way; you know that. You were married, had just become Prime Minister, saved Greece from that tyrant Xenakis, and needed time to steady the ship.'

Alex knew she was right. If they had continued their relationship it would have become a scandal which was the last thing that Greece needed. But now he was divorced things were different. Could they now have a proper relationship? 'I am divorced now; did you know that?' asked Alex.

Gitta knew of course and she felt now was the time to tell him the news about the baby. She rolled onto her stomach so that she was gazing into Alex's eyes. 'I know that you are divorced, daddy,' she giggled as she said it.

'I figured Chris must have told you,' Alex said, at first not picking up on what Gitta had said. Suddenly his eyes widened.

'Oh my god! Did you say daddy?'

Then with more conviction. 'I am aren't I? Boy or girl?' he almost shouted.

'Hush darling,' whispered Gitta, placing a finger on Alex's lips. 'You'll wake up the neighbours. It's a boy.'

Alex laughing said, 'We don't have any neighbours. Have you named him?'

'Of course my love. I named him after you because I didn't really know if I would ever see you again, and I wanted to preserve your memory in him.'

Tears were welling up in Alex's eyes as he looked lovingly at Gitta feeling that he would burst with happiness. He rolled on top of her kissing her deeply and passionately. As they kissed she felt his hardness pressing urgently against her and she opened her legs pulling him deep into her already wet pussy. Losing themselves in their adoring passion they made love once again.

Back in the main building of the hotel in the supper lounge Chris Horsman sat with Ryan Jones listening to the combo of a piano and bouzouki playing classical Greek tunes. They had arrived there an hour ago and after talking to the front desk and finding out that Alex and Gitta were in a bungalow in the grounds, they had decided to stay for a while to make sure Alex would be safe.

Neither of them noticed the man that called himself Cyclops who was sitting partly out of sight in a booth in the far corner of the supper lounge. But they did recognise Leonidas.

'Well, well, well,' said Chris with a smile. 'I guess that explains why he was not concentrating on what we were talking about. Alex guessed correctly that he does have a woman.'

'And what a woman. She is gorgeous,' said Ryan with a touch of admiration in his voice. 'How long are we going to babysit Alex for?'

'Until I am sure that he is safe and in no danger,' retorted Chris. 'Why the hurry? Are you missing a TV programme, or going on a hot date, or something?' he said with a note of sarcasm in his voice.

Ryan just smiled sheepishly. But in his mind he said, yes Mr Horsman it's, or something, and that something could be dangerous to my health and I need to get away if I can.

Seated just twenty metres from Chris and Ryan in a semi-obscured booth sat the man codenamed Cyclops. He was talking on his phone to Alkis Eleftheradou alias The Fixer.

'They have Andonis Papaspiro here in the hotel. The whole of the top floor has been sealed off and is guarded by officers from the EKAM unit which is headed up by Yannis Spanos,' said Cyclops.

'We don't have enough men to storm the place here in Edessa yet. The two brothers that did the job on the statue in Salonika will be here in half an hour though,' said Alkis the Fixer.

'We can wait. I've spoken with Zeus and he wants it done soon so it can't delay too long. It needs to be a precision hit because I am in the ground floor restaurant,' warned Cyclops.

'What restaurant stays open all through the night?' questioned Alkis.

Cyclops laughed. 'Good question. 'It's a restaurant by day and a supper club at night. A sort of night club for those who like their music smooth and quiet. How are you going to do it?'

'Rocket launcher. But it's going to make a hell of a mess. It will probably destroy some of the floor below too.'

Cyclops took a sip of his whisky and blew out his cheeks while he thought about what the fixer had just said. The restaurant was six floors below the target floor so barring a major error, the ground floor should not be damaged at all. The fixer had not failed him yet so he had to trust him.

'Okay, go ahead as fast as you can.'

'Right, it'll take me time to get the rocket launcher ready, wait for the other two, and get over there. Probably can be there in forty minutes.' The fixer checked the time. 'It'll get light in one hour at around five-thirty. I want to have it done and be back here before light.'

'Agreed,' said Cyclops. 'Good luck.'

Cyclops went back to his supper little knowing that only a few hundred metres from where he was sitting was the Prime Minister, in a bungalow in the grounds of the hotel. If he had known that the instructions for the fixer would have been quite different.

In the bungalow Alex and Gitta had just finished showering and were sitting in their towelling robes on its small balcony.

'Okay,' said Alex as he sipped a glass of white wine. 'Tell me all you know about our friend Eckersley. How did you manage to infiltrate his organisation anyway?'

'Oh that was easy,' Gitta said. She too was in a towelling robe, but it was far too big for her and the front kept opening up and slipping below her nipples. After several times of trying to keep it from falling she abandoned the idea and took it off, sitting there naked placing her Beretta between her thighs. Seeing the look on Alex's face she said, 'What? Nobody is around at this time of the morning so the only person that can see me is you, and I'm sure you don't mind darling.'

Alex laughed and pretended he was embarrassed by the sight of her naked body. He said, 'seriously now, how did you get into Eckersley's organization?'

'He advertised the position in The London Times on one of his trips to the UK. The CIA requested that I apply for the job. It was only after I had got the job that Chris told me that the CIA with MI6's blessing, had cornered Eckersley's personal assistant and offered her enough money to persuade her to resign, forcing Eckersley to advertise for a replacement.'

'Are you privileged to have access to all his records and plans?' asked Alex.

'No about two thirds. The other third I have to sneak around, try to overhear conversations, or discreetly place recording devices. The latter is tricky because every now and then he orders his guards to do a sweep, so I have to collect them, then re-position them after the sweep has finished.'

'I know that we have a debrief with Chris late morning tomorrow...well I mean today,' said Chris looking at his watch. 'But do you believe that Eckersley poses a danger to Greece?'

'Most definitely, he is an extremely dangerous and clever man who is ruthless in achieving his ambitious strategies.'

Gitta suddenly got up from her chair announcing that it was such a beautiful and balmy warm night they should walk in the grounds before going back to bed again. They both got dressed in similar outfits, faded jeans and a t-shirt for Alex and faded jeans and a white short sleeved blouse for Gitta. Both wore thong style sandals, and both had Berettas tucked into their belts in the small of their respective backs.

'Where did you get the Beretta from darling?' asked Gitta.

'Chris gave it to me. I must admit I feel safer having my own gun. Come on let's go,' said Alex taking Gitta's hand.

It was five o'clock when they set out for a walk round the grounds of the hotel. Grounds which were immaculately landscaped with narrow paths snaking between huge rhododendron bushes, trees, small clumps of rose beds and the occasional water feature. The way was lit by fairy lights of assorted colours, which ran beside all the pathways, strung like twinkling stars through the bushes and trees. It was made for lovers on hot summer nights. Some other bungalows in the grounds had their porch lights on and some were completely dark. But there was nobody about as Alex and Gitta holding hands strolled down the winding pathways.

As they reached the edge of the hotel's grounds near to the main road that connected the hotel to Edessa, they heard the sound of an engine. It did not sound like a car engine but sounded like a van's engine.

'Behind this bush Alex,' half whispered Gitta as she nudged him behind a massive rhododendron bush. Alex heard the urgency in her voice and moved fast pulling his beretta from his belt as he stepped off the path until he was hidden from the road.

'You're very suspicious aren't you sweetheart?' said Alex.

'The engine sounds like a van darling. If it was a car in all probability it was someone returning late to the hotel. A van however makes me suspicious because it's too early for any sort of delivery so what is a van doing on this road at five-fifteen in the early morning?' said Gitta as she stepped behind the bush next to Alex so she too was hidden from the road.

Suddenly the sound of the engine disappeared and all they could hear was the sound of rubber on a macadam road as the van coasted down the gently inclined road.

Gitta said, 'Notice something strange?'

'Yes no engine noise,' said Alex.

'Not just that Alex, no headlights, well no lights actually.'

'You're right I didn't twig, that confirms your suspicions.'

Gitta parted some fronds in the bush so she could see what was going on without being seen herself. She kept up a commentary to Alex as she watched what was going on. The white van had slowed to a halt just before the long drive up to the hotel entrance, one hundred metres from the bush where Gitta and Alex were. There wasn't a fence bordering the front of the property so the men in the van could clearly see the hotel some two hundred metres away.

Three men got out of the front doors of the van leaving the doors open and quickly moved to the double doors at the rear. Gitta watched as one of the men leaned into the van and handed a pistol to each of the other two men before taking out of the rear doors what looked like a shoulder rocket launcher without the rocket.

'Sorry Alex but we have to stop them. Are you going to be okay with a fire fight?'

Alex who knew what was going down from Gitta's description, nodded, and said, 'Don't worry about me we're together in this.'

'Good,' whispered Gitta. 'We don't have much solid cover from this bush but we have the element of surprise. You take the man with the rocket launcher and I'll concentrate on the other two. On the count of three okay.' She blew Alex a kiss then counted down. 'Three, two, one.'

They both stepped out from cover, Alex to the left and Gitta to the right, the silence of the night punctured with the sounds of gunfire and ricocheting bullets. Alex heard a loud clang as one his bullets struck the rocket launcher just as the fixer was trying to arm it with a rocket. The launcher fell from his grasp and clattered onto the road. Another of the men dropped his gun then clutching his arm let out a yelp, as a bullet either struck him directly or simply grazed him.

The fixer had already decided that prudence was the better part of valour and was scampering around to the driver's side keeping the van between himself and the shooters in the grounds of the hotel. The other two men followed his example, both scurrying towards the passenger door as fast as they could. Now Gitta and Alex were out in the open still firing at the men.

'The tyres Alex, shoot the tyres,' shouted Gitta.

The wounded man of the two had now reached the open door and was climbing into the van as fast as he could. The other man turned and let off a couple of shots covering his mate as he climbed in. Gitta yelped and hit the ground. Alex started running to where Gitta lay. The fixer gunned his engine, the back wheels spun spewing loose hardtop behind the van which was now accelerated away in the opposite direction to the way it had come, with the second man clinging onto the running board for dear life.

'Gitta darling, are you alright,' Alex cried, his heart sinking as he dropped down on his knees beside her. He could see blood on the path but didn't know from which part of her body it had emanated. He vaguely heard the sound of running feet and heavy breathing behind him.

'Alex, move away,' ordered Chris as he knelt beside Gitta. 'Torch Ryan,' he said. Ryan shone the torch on Gitta. It was obvious to all of them that the blood spreading out in a black pool on the ground was coming from her head.

Chapter 15
17th August 2013 – Edessa Region – 05:30

Two kilometres north of the Aigai Hotel on the road from Edessa to the North Macedonian border some thirty-five kilometres distance, the white van driven by Alkis, took a right turn onto the road that crossed the mountains before descending back into Edessa itself. Alkis did not reduce his speed at all, so soon the van was careering along, swaying from side to side as he desperately attempted to avoid the numerous potholes peppering the road. A road that was deteriorating the further the van travelled away from the hotel.

'Τᾳμοτω!' Fuck! Alkis swore under his breath. 'Damn and blast! This road is getting worse the further we ascend up the mountain.'

'We have to turn around and go back the way we came,' said the man that had been shot in his shoulder. 'You have to take me to a hospital and the nearest one is in Edessa. This road goes nowhere.'

'We can't go back the way we came. How are we going to get passed the hotel? They'll have a roadblock up in no time at all. No, you'll have to wait for your hospital. Anyway, you're an illegal immigrant from North Macedonia. As soon as you check in at the hospital with a gunshot wound they will call the authorities,' said Alkis, his voice getting shriller and shriller as he remonstrated with animated hands, which to the other two men's extreme worry, were hardly touching the steering wheel.

'The bullet hasn't passed through my shoulder, it's still in there,' moaned the injured man. 'I will have to take my chances.'

'Look,' said Alkis. 'This road goes back to Edessa through the mountains. It won't be too bad and it'll only take an hour longer than using the road we came on from Edessa.'

'I'll be dead by then,' moaned the wounded man.

Alkis slowed the van and stopped at the side of the road. 'Let me look at your wound,' he said, turning to his injured colleague. He examined the wound which was bleeding quite profusely despite the best efforts of the injured man to keep pressure on the injury.

'You're right,' agreed Alkis when he had finished examining the wound. 'It needs looking at sooner rather than later. But I have a solution.'

The buzzing of his burner phone interrupted what Alkis was about to say. He opened the connection. It was Cyclops.

'What the hell went on out there in the hotel's grounds. Was that you Alkis?'

Yes sir, we were ambushed as soon as we had drawn up outside.'

'Who by, do you know?'

'Too dark to see faces clearly but one of them was definitely a woman.'

'A woman did you say?' said Cyclops in astonishment.

'Yes and she knew how to shoot. A professional I'd say. Although she was hit just before we managed to get away. How badly we don't know.'

'I'll find out from this end who the woman was. Any casualties at your end?'

'Just the one sir.'

'Badly?'

'Needs hospitalization.'

'You know that can't happen, don't you?'

'Yes sir, I know.'

'Get rid of the problem, you know what to do?'

'I do sir, don't worry.'

'Good, I'll be in touch. Get back to your hotel in Edessa and wait for my call,' said Cyclops. 'They'll send up a drone to track you down soon, so don't use your lights. By the way, your men did well in Salonika. Twenty-five dead is a decent count. Kalfas's polling numbers will fall a few more points at least.' Cyclops broke the connection.

Alkis put the phone onto the shelf beneath the steering column, turned to the injured man and said. 'Cyclops thought you did a decent job in Salonika and asked me to thank you for your fine work. He's sorry that you have been injured but he was quite definite that a hospital is out of the question for you.

'What does he expect me to do?' moaned the injured man. 'If I can't stop the bleeding I'll bleed out. I have an idea! Why don't we turn around and take the road to the border with North Macedonia. There is a hospice with a good doctor just over the border. We can be there in twenty minutes.'

'I have a better idea,' said Alkis. Then quite nonchalantly, he picked his pistol up from the same shelf that his phone was in, turned in his seat and shot the injured man once through his heart.

'Dump the body on the roadside, will you,' said Alkis to his remaining partner. 'We need to get going sharpish. And don't stare at me like that, you have just killed at least twenty-five innocent people in Salonika. Anyway, rules are rules, you know that.'

Suddenly Alkis noticed headlights coming towards them down the mountain road.

'No wait!' he shouted. 'I have an idea. Alkis started the engine of the van then manoeuvred it until it straddled the road so as to prevent any vehicle to pass.

'Get out and pretend you are checking the right hand front tyre,' ordered Alkis.

No sooner had the other man got into position by the front tyre, around the bend in front of them came a car bathing them in the glare of its powerful beams. The car slowed then the driver realising that he could not pass the van hit the brake and the car came to a stop twenty metres from the van.

As soon as it had stopped Alkis was out of the van, Glock in hand. Before the driver of the car could react Alkis had reached the driver's door, opened it, and pulled the driver out onto the road. The driver screamed and at that moment Alkis realised it was a woman. His partner had reached the front passenger door and was struggling to wrestle the passenger, who had realised he was fighting for his life, out of the car.

After several minutes, the man and the woman, trussed up like turkeys, were sitting on the floor in the back of the van.

'Now what?' said Alkis's partner.

'We take their car. If they do deploy a drone it'll be looking for a white van, not a car. Especially a luxury car like their Lexus. I'm going to enjoy driving that.'

'But the drone will spot the van is stationary and will realise we have switched vehicles.'

Alkis grinned, tapping his index finger to his head. He said, 'They won't spot the van on the road because we are going to push it off the road into the ravine below. Even if they do spot it they will think that we have suffered some sort of accident and gone off the road. By the time they figure it all out we shall be safely in Edessa in our hotel. Come on let's get the van off the road.'

Alkis put the van into neutral, released the hand brake and as his partner pushed, he leant into the van with one hand turning the steering wheel until the van was pointing at right angles to the road towards the drop to the ravine. Alkis got behind the van to help with getting the van over a semi-grass verge and through the wire fencing, that instead of crash barriers, was a feature of many mountainous roads in northern Greece, which did not carry much traffic.

The two hostages inside the van realised what was happening and began screaming and shouting in fear. Even as the van disappeared over the edge and started its fall to the ravine floor, their screams could be heard in the still early morning air, until they too faded into silence. Alkis watched the progress of the van as bounced down a steep incline, miraculously staying on its wheels before it soared off the mountainside and dropped out of sight. The sound of it crashing onto the ravine floor was just about audible to the two men watching.

'Let's go,' said Alkis. Then he said in a matter of fact voice. 'They'd have died well before the van had gone off the edge of the mountain, bouncing around inside the van would have broken every bone in their bodies. Shame because the woman was pretty.'

They were soon on their way. Alkis enjoying driving the luxury saloon, which after the van's noisy engine, gave them a nice quiet ride, as the car glided around the mountain bends. He was thinking that they had been lucky that there had been an opportunity to change vehicles. He wasn't bothered that it had cost another two lives. Once you have killed two or three people you become accustomed to the feeling of dread at the prospect of not going to heaven and don't take much notice of it.

He was a Greek Orthodox of course and had been brought up like most Greek children with religion an important part of daily life. But, he had managed to compartmentalise his killings, as an occurrence which had nothing to do with him. It was as if they happened to someone else, perhaps his alter ego. It amused him to think that he was proud that he had become the best at what he did. He was the perfect assassin.

Twenty-five minutes later feeling smug that they had outwitted the authorities, they were descending the twisting road down the mountainside into the outskirts of Edessa and heading to their hotel. Not long after reaching Edessa they had parked without further incidence in the car park of the hotel.

However, they wouldn't have felt so smug if they had known that in addition to deploying a drone to search for them on the mountain, she had also ordered the diversion of one of Greece's spy satellites to overfly the northern regions of Macedonia. During one of its passes it had recorded images of them pushing the van off the road. However, by the time the information from the satellites passage was processed, a couple of days would pass.

Chapter 16
17th August 2013 – Aigai Hotel – 06:20

Back at the Aigai Hotel in the bungalow where Alex and Gitta had made love, only a couple of hours ago, Gitta was sitting up in a chair being attended to by a doctor, who was staying at the hotel. Alex and Chris had carried Gitta from the scene of the firefight to the bungalow, while Ryan had hightailed it to the hotel reception to ask them if they had a doctor as a guest. As luck would have it they had.

Although there had been a lot of blood the bullet had only grazed Gitta just behind the temple. The doctor cleaned and dressed the wound, gave her a couple of pills to dull the pain and advised her to rest-up for a couple of hours. Alex decided to stay with Gitta to make sure she did as the doctor ordered. He had already called Kaliope at the Four Seasons and authorised her to deploy a reconnaissance drone to track the van, then come to the hotel, bungalow No.7.

He decided to leave Aliki, his Minister of Culture at the Four Seasons because she had the unveiling of the King Philip of Macedonia statue in Alexander the Great Square in the centre of Edessa that morning and probably needed to work on her speech. Ironic that the statue of one Greek hero was destroyed a few hours ago and the statue of another Greek hero, Alexander's father, was being unveiled here in Edessa.

'I'm going to go back to the main building to find Leonidas and Yannis Spanos,' announced Chris. 'We need to have a meeting before we get any more surprises.'

'I agree,' said Alex. 'And we need to do it before Gitta has to leave for her day job at Eckersley's villa.'

'Right,' said Chris. 'I'll be as quick as I can. It's six o'clock now, let's say we convene at six-twenty.'

'Agreed,' confirmed Alex.

Chris headed for the hotel lobby. As he drew near the entrance he saw that Ryan was talking to a man who looked vaguely familiar. Chris stopped and ducked behind a tree. He was curious to know who the other man was. He was a big man, at least six foot four inches tall, but also well built like a boxer. Where had he seen this man before? He took out his mobile phone and took a photograph, then sent the photo to Alex's phone.

Just as he came out from behind the tree, a taxi drew up at the hotel entrance. The man who was talking to Ryan immediately picked up his briefcase and headed out of the hotel and got into the taxi. Why the hurry Chris wondered as he entered the hotel lobby. He went up to the reception desk, picked up the house phone and spoke to Yannis Spanos, telling him about the meeting at the bungalow and to bring Andonis Papaspiro along as well.

Chris found Leonidas talking to Ryan at a table just inside the bar, which was now closed, and instead a buffet breakfast had been set up for the hotel guests.

'Morning Leonidas,' greeted Chris. 'Sorry to interrupt you but Alex wants to see you in bungalow No. 7 in five minutes. Alex has ordered breakfast for all of us there.'

'Alright,' said Leonidas stifling a yawn. 'Sorry, but I am knackered. I Didn't have any sleep last night.'

Chris, on seeing the yawn wondered if the man had taken a room with the woman he was with last night or had stayed in the supper lounge all night. He said, 'We won't keep you long, afterwards you can go back to the Four Seasons and sleep all you want.'

Ryan started to get up but Chris stopped him saying, 'No need for you to come Ryan. I'll fill you in later, but I want you to stay in the lobby and watch for any suspicious persons, either leaving or coming in. By the way who were you talking to in the lobby earlier?'

Ryan just about managed to stop his face going red. He felt like a child who had been caught with his fingers in the sweet jar. He decided to bluff it out, fairly sure that Leonidas had not seen the man he had been talking to. If he had he would definitely have known who it was.

'I don't know,' lied Ryan. 'Just another hotel guest who asked me for advice on the best places to go in New York. He had obviously heard my accent and figured me for a New Yorker.'

'Oh, I was only asking because I thought I recognised him. Perhaps I was wrong. I'll see you later. Come on Leonidas, follow me,' Chris said, turning around and striding out of the bar area.

Five minutes later, Gitta, Kaliope, Leonidas, Yannis, Chris, Andonis and Alex were lounging in whatever chairs they could find in bungalow No. 7. Each person inside the bungalow was balancing a plate and a mug of coffee or tea on their laps. The only table of any size in the bungalow was covered in typical continental breakfast foodstuffs, juices plus tea and coffee urns.

Yannis had also brought along his no. 2 Dimitris Moustakas to guard the bungalow and he was now sitting outside the front door of the bungalow supposedly protecting it. The kidnappers of Dimitris's wife had already contacted him earlier in the morning reminding him that time was running out, and if he wanted to see his wife again he only had a few hours before the deadline. To emphasis their point the kidnappers transmitted a photograph of Dimitris's wife to his phone, which when he saw it caused him to retch uncontrollably.

'Right ladies and gents,' said Alex. 'Firstly I would like to offer our condolences to Andonis for the terrible tragedy that befell his family yesterday. I can't imagine the hurt you are feeling Andonis but we are grateful that you have agreed to help us bring whoever perpetrated that to justice. Now before I forget. Kaliope would you please order another reconnaissance drone to patrol the area around

Alexander the Great Square in Edessa where Aliki is performing an unveiling today.'

'On it,' said Kaliope, taking out her mobile phone.

'Andonis, why don't you tell us what you discovered,' said Alex.

'So, the other night I was checking the share register, something I do as an audit every couple of months if I can, when I noticed that there had been purchases of Hellenic Aluminium shares which looked suspicious. There were three purchases all for a 4.8% of the share capital. Under Greek law, and international law as it happens, if a person or an entity purchases 5% or more of a public company's shares they must publish their intentions. So several, well three in fact, purchases of 4.8% made me very suspicious that something wasn't right,' said Adonis taking a sip of coffee.

Adonis continued, 'So I called Yannis Blounas, the securities officer at our operations site in Edessa. He did some checking and discovered that the securities register had been hacked, and the purchases, although done on different days, had been posted with a fraudulently time stamp, which makes it difficult for us to pick up. My guess is that the purchaser intended to accumulate enough of Hellenic Aluminium shares to become a major shareholder, who would, sooner than later, announce a hostile takeover.'

'Wouldn't they run the risk of prosecution?' asked Kaliope.

'In theory, yes,' said Andonis. 'But in practice the remaining shareholders would want to see their shares increase in value, which is what the stock market would make happen, because whoever was attempting to buy Hellenic Aluminium would have to apply a large premium to the number of shares that needed to be bought, to be able to own over 50% of the company, and thus persuade the shareholders to sell. So the shareholders would create such a stink that the individual or entity seeking to take Hellenic Aluminium over would probably just pay a heavy fine.'

'That's the reason poor Blounas was killed,' said Chris. 'The poor guy knew too much. I don't suppose he told you who was behind the share purchases, did he?'

'No, he didn't, but he did find out the brokers who participated in the share purchases. I'm pretty certain though it was the work of one hacker working in their company. He should be easy to find if the police and the Financial Services Authority raid the broker's premises this morning and audit their IT systems.'

'I'll get onto that right away,' announced Kaliope as she brushed away at her fringe with her hand.

'It has to be Eckersley, either as an individual or through another company vehicle that he is using, who is buying the shares. He has the money, the power, and the knowhow,' reasoned Leonidas. 'I wouldn't be surprised if he were behind the bombings too.'

They all nodded in agreement.

'I think we all have come to that conclusion too, Leonidas. Let's hope that Gitta can get the evidence we need to arrest or deport him,' said Chris. 'Why don't you tell us what you told Alex and me earlier.'

Gitta still looked strained and still had a thumping headache, but she managed to summon up a smile saying, 'It's no secret Eckersley is looking to buy up bauxite mines wherever he can on the planet. Only last month he bought up over half of Turkey's mines. Greece's mines have become more desirable since the discovery of new deposits of bauxite in this region. From what I have managed to glean so far he is open to obtain the mines through legal and illegal means.

He has hired a small mercenary army from John Dexter's Black Hawke company and I believe that he will use them for a land grab of whatever he can get of Macedonia. He fanatically believes that North Macedonia was the birthplace of Alexander the Great and that once upon a time the land that North Macedonia owned extended all the way to Salonika.'

'My god!' interjected Kaliope. 'We have a serious situation on our hands. We should get some eyes on the border Alex.'

I agree. Why don't you deploy a drone in the border area. Use one of our Reaper drones fully armed just in case we have to move fast.'

Once again Kaliope got busy on her phone.

'One other point we need to discuss is the possibility of a potential leak,' announced Chris. 'Both Gitta and Alex are certain that the rocket launcher's target would have been the top floor of the hotel and that Andonis here was the target. Only a few people knew that he was holed up there. It was a lucky break that Alex and Gitta were out walking when the van arrived.'

'And they probably think that they have a snitch in their midst too, and that they were ambushed,' commented Alex.

'Very perceptive Alex,' praised Chris. 'You'll make a good agent yet.' Chris teased. 'Seriously, I have an idea where our leak is unfortunately.'

Chris relayed the conversation that he had with Ryan the previous evening when Ryan seemed too impatient to leave the hotel and this had triggered a nasty itch in Chris's mind. The type of itch that invariably proved that Chris's suspicions were correct. They all sat in shocked silence trying to absorb what they had just heard.

'Yannis, I'm going to take the guard you have outside a cup of coffee and a croissant,' said Chris. 'I take it you don't mind. I feel sorry for the poor bugger. He must be starving without having breakfast. By the way Alex, did you get the photograph I sent you earlier? I recognise the face but can't place it.'

'It's the President of the Golden Dawn party, Dimitri Karagianis,' explained Alex. 'As you know they are an extreme right wing party. They are constantly causing trouble but they are popular with the elderly and some undesirable elements of the unemployed younger generation.'

What the hell was Ryan doing talking to him, mused Chris to himself. Could he be behind the bombings or is Eckersley using the Golden Dawn party as a conduit to destabilise Alex's Government.

'I'm going to stretch my legs. I have a plan of action in my head but it would be interesting to see what you produce while I'm out,' announced Chris as he grinned from ear to ear. He knew they would take it as a challenge and it would be interesting to see if they came up with some of his ideas too. 'Bye the way I'll take some breakfast to that poor man outside, he must be starving without his breakfast this morning.'

Chris went over to the table laden with breakfast foodstuffs, poured a mug of coffee, took a tray, put the mug on it and filled the rest of the tray with croissants, some pieces of cake and some fruit. He unlatched the French doors that led off of the bedroom and moved onto the veranda. Moustakas was not there. He was probably round by the front thought Chris.

He had started to descend the steps that led onto a path that encircled the bungalow when he heard muffled conversation coming from the other side of the building. Instinct warned Chris not to make a sound as he placed the tray on the steps then moved to the corner of the building from where the conversation was coming. As he moved nearer the conversation became clearer and he realised that it was the guard talking on his mobile. The words he was hearing made his blood run cold.

Near the corner Chris stopped, faced the wall then carefully edged his way along it until he could peer around the corner. He saw Moustakas on his mobile, his back to the wall, facing towards the main hotel complex. Chris drew back, pulling out his Glock as he did so. He peered around the corner again. Moustakas was now facing away from Chris's position, some fifteen metres from him, still talking animatedly on the phone.

Chris debated whether to go back for backup but then decided against it as he had the element of surprise. He stepped out into the open facing Moustakas, legs akimbo, gun held in two hands straight out in front of him, pointing at Moustakas's face. It was the only shot he had because Moustakas was wearing a bullet proof vest and was wearing the typical anti-terrorist issued helmet.

'Dimitris, drop your phone and turn towards me very slowly,' shouted Chris. Dimitris Moustakas froze, then started to turn towards Chris.

'Here, take it but don't shoot,' yelled Dimitris, as at the same time he tossed the phone in Chris's direction. Chris was slightly distracted by the flying phone and took his eyes off Dimitris for a split second. When he refocused back on his target Dimitris had dropped to one knee and had his service revolver in his hand, a hand that was swinging up towards him.

It was all a blur after that. Chris fired twice as he flung himself sideways. He felt a searing pain in his side but despite that as he hit the ground he managed to get a third shot off which struck Dimitris in the throat, passing through the jugular vein and out the other side. Blood fountained out of Dimitris neck as he pitched forward onto the ground a pool of blood quickly spreading around his head.

Chris heaved a huge sigh of relief and attempted to get up but the pain in his side was too intense and he sank back down again. They'll be out in a jiffy he thought. I might as well stay down.

Chapter 17

17th August 2013 – Eckersley's Villa – 11:00

Arthur Eckersley sat behind his trademark desk, a grey marble top on a mahogany base. It was big; four metres in length by two metres deep. As with most men who have many enemies, Eckersley always sat with his back to the wall. In front of him, the open plan, eight-hundred square metre, one story villa stretched out towards the large kitchen at the other end of the building.

It was a large villa, far too large for one man, but Eckersley loved opulence, decadently large spaces, and light. The villa had all of that and more. It had history, for the villa had been built using the walls and stones of the two bakeries and one stable, built in the late nineteenth century, that had stood there before the villa. It boasted six bedrooms, five bathrooms, a huge lounge with a centre piece open log fire and dining area big enough to comfortably have twenty people at one sitting. The furniture throughout was modern with clean lines except for one area which was furnished with materials and ornaments of distinctly Turkish origin.

Outside, a fifteen metre wide patio stretched completely around the villa, with a swimming pool, barbecue, and bar area gracing one side and on the other side gardens filled with fruit trees and vegetable plots. The villa was accessed through the main double gates at the front of the gardens or the rear double gates at the rear. By the main entrance were spaces for five cars. In one corner of the grounds was a small four bedroom property which housed his staff and sophisticated communications equipment. Eckersley was using part of that equipment to have an untraceable conversation with Cyclops.

'What happened to our man on the EKAM team?' asked Eckersley.

'He was shot by that CIA agent who is in the Prime Minister's party,' replied Cyclops. 'He must have made a mistake and it cost him his life.'

'And Alkis?'

'Safely back with his colleague in his hotel in Edessa.'

'I'm going to relocate them back to the staff quarters here. I've already got the two men who were eavesdropping on the telephone bugs in Hellenic Aluminium offices, here in the staff quarters with their equipment. My god it's damn hot in here,' complained Eckersley as he wiped his sweating brow with a clean white handkerchief. He rose from his desk and moved nearer the air conditioning unit to cool down. The villa was built of stone which while aesthetically beautiful, was unfortunately like an oven as it retained heat. When the temperature outside was forty Celsius, as it was today, even the air conditioning and wearing a pair of shorts and a sleeveless vest couldn't keep him cool.

'Good idea,' agreed Cyclops. 'Alkis is the best assassin we have so we need to keep him safe. 'What do you want to do about Andonis Papaspiro? He has obviously told them all he knows because the Hellenic Aluminium operations offices were hit by the police and FSA early this morning.'

'We do nothing. I am already a majority shareholder with the 13 ½ % of shares in the name of my holding company. Our aim now is to purchase at least another 37% of shares so that we own the company outright. We do this by offering high premiums to existing shareholders to entice them to sell their shareholdings.'

'And if they are reluctant to sell?' asked Cyclops.

'We threaten them and their families.'

'What shall we do with Dimitris Moustakas's wife. She is in pretty bad shape from the torture she has suffered?' Cyclops asked.

'Keep her for your men to play with or kill her. It's up to you,' said Eckersley. 'Now what about our campaign to destabilise Kalfas's Government. What are you planning?' asked Eckersley.

'Our next targets are as we had discussed last week. Target no.1 is a bomb under the Alexander the Great statue in central Athens. Target no.2 is the White Tower in Salonika and Target no.3 is a high profile Government minister.'

'Which minister?' asked Eckersley.

'Don't know yet. There are several contenders, it really depends on finding a suitable time, and place, then we will strike.' confirmed Cyclops.

'Good,' said Eckersley. 'Hopefully by tomorrow we will have John Dexter's mercenaries on standby just across the border. You might need extra support to hit all three targets on the same day.'

'Thanks,' said Cyclops. 'I'll keep you updated.' He shut his burner phone down, opened the back of the phone, took out the SIM card, then broke it in half before slipping both halves into his pocket. He made a mental note to himself to throw away each half in a different place at least half a kilometre distant, to ensure they avoided being compromised.

Eckersley put his burner phone down quite confident that the equipment installed in the staff quarters would prevent anyone eavesdropping on his conversation or tracing the call. He had seen Gitta enter the villa from the front door and go into her office while he was on the phone. He needed to speak to her. He pressed an intercom button on his desk.

'Yes,' said Gitta.

'Come to my office a moment,' said Eckersley.

Gitta stood up from behind her desk, then checked herself in the long mirror which had been already hanging there on the day she had moved into her office. It was most likely a bedroom before being converted to an office, she thought, and it makes me look good.

To detract Eckersley from asking too many questions about the plaster that could be seen under her hair, she had changed into a pair of truly short white shorts that hardly covered her cute backside and a boob-top in the same colour, that barely covered her breasts. She wore nothing on her feet as she had discovered many years ago that men found her sexy when she walked around in bare feet.

'Good morning my dear,' greeted Eckersley as Gitta walked into his office. He had watched her as she walked down the length of the villa from her office to his. He could feel himself getting hard and he chided himself under his breath for it. Until the news from the UK he often allowed himself a fantasy that one day he would have her, but the news rather dampened his ambitions for her body.

'You look lovely today,' continued Eckersley. 'Sit down will you.' He pointed to the seating area. Then, noticing her plaster for the first time, asked, 'Whatever have you done to your head?'

'Nothing, really,' replied Gitta. 'My heel broke causing me to fall and hit my head. It's fine, just a little sore.' It being sore was the truth at least, thought Gitta.

'Well be careful, you never know what dangers lurk around the next corner.'

Was that a veiled threat, wondered Gitta. Or just a general statement?

Eckersley continued. 'I've just heard some unwelcome news from the UK which has upset me a little. Do you remember my personal assistant who gave you a one-day induction program just before she left after her resignation and you joined the organisation?'

'Yes I do,' said Gitta, wondering what was coming. She recalled that her name was Amanda. Last she had heard she had been given a new identity, a lot of money and relocated far away from Malton, North Yorkshire where she had lived.

'The police found her body, well, parts of her body, a couple of days ago lying in a ditch.'

'Oh my god,' exclaimed Gitta. 'Do you know what happened? Even as she asked the question she dreaded what the answer would be.

'Well only what we have managed to pry from friends in the North Yorkshire Constabulary. It seems she fell in with a bad lot, got into drugs and stole a lot of money. She was badly tortured I'm afraid, as an example, the police assume. They believe she suffered horrendous pain from what was left of her body. It seems she had limbs removed while she was still alive.'

Gitta felt sick to her core. How on earth had Eckersley found out where the authorities had relocated her to. He either has infiltrated MI6 or the CIA with his own people, or, he has someone high up, probably in MI6, on his payroll. In her eyes Eckersley was a dead man; she would be the one to end his life.

'You look shocked my dear,' said Eckersley.

'I am and although I didn't know her except for that one induction day. I am sad for her, I wouldn't wish that kind of suffering and death on my worst enemy,' said Gitta.

Eckersley looked directly into Gitta's eyes and Gitta gave an involuntary shudder, for his eyes reminded her of a shark's eyes, two black holes showing no emotion whatsoever. His next words made her blood run cold.

'You see what unpleasant things happen when someone crosses a powerful organisation my dear? As I said earlier, you never know what dangers lurk around the next corner, do you?'

Gitta was just about to say something when Eckersley's land line rang. He strode to his desk and picked up the receiver. She was surprised that he hadn't dismissed her before he began to talk. But she was grateful he hadn't, as she had been unable to place a bug on that phone. She listened intently to Eckersley's side of the conversation.

'I'd rather you called on my mobile.'

'It doesn't matter now.'

'Interesting, you think it's a head wound.'

'Yes tomorrow, both events at the same time.'

'You will deal with the Minister, good.'

'Alkis will come with me today.'

'The official bid will be announced this afternoon.'

'Goodbye.'

Eckersley put the phone down and said to Gitta. 'Sorry I had to take that. If you don't have anything for me, then I think we are done for now. I'm going into North Macedonia this afternoon for a meeting but I'll be back before you leave for the day.'

'Well, enjoy your trip and I'll see you later,' said Gitta getting up from the couch. 'I'll finish the report you asked me to do and have it on your desk by the time you get back.'

Gitta left Eckersley's office and returned to her own. Sitting at her desk she was deep in thought weighing up the options that were open for her. She would have loved to know who was on the other end of the line. Two events tomorrow. What sort of events and where were they taking place? Who was the Minister and what was the deal? The official bid was probably the announcement of the take-over but the most worrying things she had heard, at least for her safety, was the news about Amanda and the mention of a head wound. She was certain that Eckersley knew she was a plant, but did he suspect she worked for a Government agency? If it was both, her life was in great danger.

While Gitta had been deciding her next move, Eckersley had called his bodyguard into his office.

'If Gitta tries to leave before I get back kill her, but make it look like an accident. Is her car in the parking area inside the gates?'

'No sir, she usually parks it outside the main gate.'

'Okay, well just make sure she doesn't slip by you and out of the gate. I won't be pleased if that happened and you'll be sorry. Is that understood?' Eckersley looked menacingly at his bodyguard.

'Yes sir, I understand.'

An hour later Eckersley heard the toot of a car horn outside the main gates. He hurried out to where the bodyguard had already opened the door to the side of the main gate that was used as a pedestrian exit from the villa. Alkis was waiting in the car and as soon as Eckersley had got into the vehicle, he gunned the engine and sped away towards the border.

Gitta heard them go and decided to make her move. This morning instead of parking her car outside the main gates she had parked it outside the back gates. Well done me, she thought, my intuition was spot on. She had realised that her days of being Eckersley's personal assistant were numbered. Initially, because the head wound would make him suspicious, which it did. But the revelation about what Amanda had suffered, obviously at the hands of Eckersley's men, and using it to warn Gitta that crossing his organisation, was a dangerous thing to do, was another reason for her to leave. Eckersley was too close to finding out that she worked for a Government agency.

She left her office and headed for the kitchen area. Beyond the kitchen was a large pantry and wine cellar. At the back of the wine cellar was a door that opened out onto a path that led to the back door which in fact was a tradesman's entrance. She pulled her Glock from her holster just in case she met any of Eckersley's staff, particularly the bodyguard. Fortunately, she reached the back gate without incident, opened the pedestrian door in the gate and stepped out into the road.

Her car was parked just one hundred metres away, just beyond the outer perimeter wall of the villa. Still feeling apprehensive because it had seemed much too easy, she quickly text Alex, telling

him about Amanda, where Eckersley was going, and that she was on
her way to the Four Seasons Hotel. She continued to hold the Glock
while making her way to her car, all the while, scanning the olive
trees which were densely planted in neat rows, on the opposite side
of the road. Reaching her car she breathed a sigh of relief, unlocked
the door, and gratefully slumped into the driver's seat.

She didn't so much hear anything as felt a presence behind her.
Her hand grabbed for her pistol but before she could reach it she felt
the muzzle of a gun, being pressed hard into the back of her neck.

'It's far too early to clock off work Ma'am,' said a voice behind
her. 'Now get out of the car slowly keeping your hands where I can
see them, and face away from the car.'

Gitta did as she was told.

'Let me introduce myself,' said the voice. 'You can turn around
now. My name is Alkis, others have nicknamed me the 'fixer,' and you
have been trumped.'

With a sinking heart Gitta turned around to face whom she
knew was also known as the 'smiling assassin.' He should have been
with Eckersley on the way to the border. They had set a trap and she
had walked straight into it. Alkis motioned with his gun for her to
start walking towards the back entrance of the villa she had recently
used. As she walked she wondered what she would face over the
next few hours. Whatever it was, she knew that it would not be in
the least bit enjoyable and she needed to steel herself for what was
coming.

Chapter 18

17th August 2013 – Edessa The Four Seasons Hotel – 15:40

In Suite 710 at the Four Seasons, Alex sat back from the table rubbing his eyes. He was tired, both physically and mentally, it had been a long day. And he was worried because Gitta had not shown up yet, especially as she had text him around midday, that she was leaving Eckersley's villa. He was also waiting to hear from Kaliope, about the outcome of the EKAM operation which was starting within the hour.

He had met with Kaliope, Leonidas, Chris, Ryan, and Yannis earlier that afternoon at two-thirty. Aliki had successfully completed the unveiling of the King Philip of Macedonia statue without any trouble and by all accounts her speech was well received. She was now on her way to North Macedonia in a coach, with a United Nations cultural team who were looking into the claims that Alexander the Great was born and lived in the region now known as North Macedonia. This region they claimed was originally Macedonia, incorporating an area which extended all the way from Skopje to Salonika on the Aegean Sea.

Before the meeting he had ordered Kaliope to deploy a drone to follow Eckersley to the border. When they commenced their meeting at two-thirty, Kaliope had a technician set up a monitor which had the pictures from the drone relayed to it. They watched as Eckersley crossed the border and drove a further five kilometres before entering what looked like a farm. He had parked in front of the farmhouse, then walked up to the front door, unlocked it, and entered the building.

'He has a key to a black ops site,' murmured Chris. 'Does the drone detect heat signatures Kaliope?'

'Yes, hold on while I relay the instructions.'

They watched transfixed as the monitor's screen darkened except for bright areas of fire-like body shapes. They counted twenty-six bodies. 'So Eckersley was meeting a band of twenty-five men.' Chris said.

'Must be the mercenary force that Gitta had mentioned,' said Alex. 'We need to keep a drone watching that black ops site, twenty-four-seven.'

Chris suggested they discuss the deployment of drones. He was concerned they were outgunned as well as outnumbered. Eventually, everyone agreed that three reconnaissance drones would be deployed, one at the black site, one at Eckersley's villa and one watching the Aigai Hotel, where they were using the top floor as a safe house for Andonis Papaspiro. They would hold off deploying the more powerful Reaper drones but would keep them on standby in case they were needed later. Alex thought that keeping them on standby rather than on patrol would lessen the risk of a trigger happy accident. Each Reaper drone was armed with two Hellfire air-to-ground missiles and a Paveway laser-guided bomb. They packed quite a punch.

Kaliope had updated them on the latest forensics from the bombings in Athens and Salonika. She confirmed that all the detonators and the C4 materials had been manufactured in North Macedonia. There was no trace of the men that had perpetrated the bombing in Salonika. Despite the drones and the citywide police activity. They had disappeared off the face of the earth it seemed. Although not quite.

'We had a breakthrough from a spy satellite pass after the gun battle at the Aigai Hotel. The satellite photographed two men pushing a white van off the mountain road leading to Edessa. There was another car parked nearby and we assume they used that to drive back to Edessa. I sent out a recovery unit and forensic personnel to the ravine which the van had fallen into.

There were two people, a man, and a woman, trussed up like turkeys in the back of the van. Both of them in extremely bad shape. Broken bones, deep gashes and suffering major blood loss. Miraculously both were alive, just. We managed to get the woman to tell us what happened. As we had surmised the two men had staged an accident in the hope we would think they had crashed down the ravine, then they had hijacked the couple's car.'

'Were they taken to the hospital in Edessa?' asked Leonidas.

'Unfortunately, neither of them made it,' said Kaliope. 'However, there was another man in the back of the van with them. He had been executed by one of the men who had pushed the van off the road. We were able to match the bullet with a bullet we found embedded in one of the trees where the Prime Minister and Gitta had their gunfight. He had another bad gunshot wound in his shoulder and the bullet was still in there. Forensics matched the bullet to the Prime Minister's gun.'

Kaliope paused to give them time to digest this latest information.

'It gets better,' she continued. 'Forensics found trace materials of C4 on the man's hands. The only logical conclusion we could come to was that he was one of the men who perpetrated the bombing in Salonika.'

She paused again to take a sip of her coffee. Yannis Spanos jumped in,

'That means that the second man is still here in Edessa. We got lucky because after identifying the couple from the white van, we found their registration number in the vehicle licencing database and luckily managed to trace the car by searching footage of Edessa's few traffic cams.'

'This is fantastic, where are they?' Alex could barely contain his excitement.

Kaliope grinned. 'Right here in this hotel.'

'In this hotel!' exclaimed Chris. 'Unbelievable. Are they in their room right now?'

'We don't know because we have only received this information a few minutes before we convened this meeting. I have ordered half of my squad to return from the Aigai Hotel,' said Yannis. 'We plan to raid their room at five-thirty this afternoon.'

'We have the police watching all the hotel entrances with orders to arrest them if they attempt to leave the hotel.

'Wonderful,' enthused Alex. 'Now we are getting somewhere. I'm grateful to all of you.' Alex beamed as he looked around the table at everyone. He even managed to keep the smile up when looking at Ryan, a feat at which he was immensely proud. 'However, I'm worried about Gitta. It's been several hours since she sent the text message that she was leaving Eckersley's villa. I'm concerned that she has been taken hostage or worse still killed.'

'There wouldn't have been a reason to kill her,' explained Chris. 'If she has been taken hostage she will be much more valuable to Eckersley alive, rather than dead. What we are overlooking is the possibility she met with an accident on the road back to the hotel.'

'I think we would have heard by now if that had been the case,' said Yannis in a matter of fact tone.

He regretted what he said the moment he had said it. The Prime Minister was obviously distraught and so excluding the accident option and leaving the hostage option wouldn't have helped his mental state.

'I agree,' said Kaliope, tipping her head to one side and giving Yannis a wide smile, then hoping against hope that she hadn't been so obvious. She thought he was the sexiest man she had ever met.

The conundrum she had was how could she let him know without seeming too forward.

'I think we should wait until morning and if we haven't heard from her, or from her captors, if she has been taken hostage, then we will plan our next moves,' said Chris. 'Yannis why don't you tell us about this afternoon's raid.'

'Right,' said Yannis looking at his notes from the iPad he had just picked up from the table in front of him. 'The hotel has four means of access. The main lobby entrance, the fire evacuation doors at the back of the hotel, the tradesman's entrance which accesses the kitchens, and lastly the underground car park. We have pulled five of my team from Salonika and five from the Hotel Aigai.'

'How many men are still guarding Andonis?' asked Alex.

'Five at the moment, that should be enough. So, we will have two men on each entrance and the remaining two, plus myself, Chris, Ryan, and Kaliope will breach the hotel room at five-thirty.'

'Kaliope! Isn't that a dangerous move, what do you feel about it Kaliope?' asked Alex.

'Don't worry, I asked if I could join them. Yannis will kit me out in the EKAM combat gear and I'm also a trained firearms expert. It's not as if I'll go in first once the room is breached, I'll be hanging back,' replied Kaliope, studying the expression on Alex's face. He didn't seem alarmed at what he had heard, in fact now he looked quite relaxed about it.

Alex turned to Yannis saying, 'I'm okay with that but keeping her safe is on you Yannis.'

'Don't worry Prime Minister, no harm will come to her.' Yannis turned to Kaliope and said, 'I have some spare sets of combat gear in the EKAM transport vehicle. I'll bring one up to your room later if that's okay with you?'

Hoping that no one could see the flush she felt rising through her tan Kaliope said, 'Why don't you come up at four o'clock, I'll get coffee in.'

Yannis nodded in agreement.

'Leonidas, I think you ought to go and see Spiros Emmanuel the CEO of Hellenic Aluminium to appraise him of the situation regarding Eckersley,' said Alex.

'Good idea, I'll do that,' agreed Leonidas.

With that the meeting broke up at three-thirty, with those involved in the raid on the hotel room agreeing to meet at the second floor fire exit door at five-twenty five. From there they would walk up the stairs to the third floor where the target's room was. Leonidas who was thankful he wouldn't be around when the raid took place called Melita on her mobile, arranging to meet her at her house after his meeting with Spiros Emmanuel.

At the time that Leonidas was talking to Melita, a burner phone in room 322 of the Four Seasons hotel rang with an annoying shrill tone. One of the guests answered it.

'Hello.'

'Cyclops here, can I speak to Alkis.'

'He is not here.'

'Where has he gone?'

'To Eckersley's villa. I don't think he'll be back tonight.'

'There's going to be a raid on your room by EKAM at five-thirty. You'll have to leave somehow. EKAM officers are on every exit.'

'Okay, five-thirty you say. I'll be ready with a major surprise, don't you worry.'

'Excellent.' said Cyclops before disconnecting the call.

In suite 512 of the Four Seasons, Kaliope was feeling nervous, like a teenager on a first date. But it's not a date she kept telling herself. Nevertheless, she had showered with a very fragrant soap, done her hair, put on makeup and selected her favourite Paco

Rabanne perfume. She pondered what one wears under an EKAM uniform. She reasoned that it must be a heavy material and therefore she should wear something lightweight especially as it would still be in the upper twenties Celsius at that time of the afternoon. So she put on a white t-shirt without a bra, and a pair of what she called Greek blue shorts, the blue of the Greek flag.

She looked at herself in a full length mirror and liked what she saw. Her legs which she thought was her best feature were long, tanned and perfectly formed. She had ordered Greek coffee for two with a shot of brandy in each. She reclined on the sofa and looked at her watch. It read three fifty-five. Just five minutes to go she thought. She was certain that Yannis would be exactly on time, after all he was military.

There was a faint knock at the door which she barely heard. Kaliope jumped up, took a quick glance in the mirror, then headed for the door. In her excitement she forgot to look through the peephole, feeling sure it was Yannis on the other side of the door. She flung it open a wide welcoming smile on her face.

What she saw wiped the smile away in an instant. She attempted to close the door again but there seemed to be a terrible weight on the door. Then a blur of movement and she felt a searing pain on her temple. The room started spinning in front of her while her legs didn't seem to be able to support her body. She fell to the floor her eyes barely focussing on the black boot in front of her face, then everything went black.

Chapter 19

17th August 2013 – Edessa The Four Seasons Hotel – 16:00

Yannis Spanos rapped on the door of Suite 512 with his gloved knuckles. He heard nothing from inside the room. He thought that perhaps Kaliope had fallen asleep. He knocked again, a little louder this time. Still nothing. Yannis put his ear to the door. Not a sound. Then he had an idea. He called the hotel reception with his mobile and asked to be put through to the room. If Kaliope were asleep the sound of the telephone ringing out would surely wake her up. He didn't have to put his ear to the door as he could quite clearly hear the phone from his position outside Kaliope's door.

The phone stopped as Yannis closed the connection and put his own phone away. As he did so he was looking directly at the spyhole in the door and he thought he detected a slight change in the light. It was so subtle that Yannis wouldn't have noticed it if he weren't looking directly at the spyhole. As it was he now doubted he'd seen anything but even so he allowed his mind to go into investigative mode.

He went back to his room to retrieve a listening device which was standard issue to EKAM officers. While in his room he called Chris Horsman and told him that he suspected someone was in Kaliope's suite. Chris agreed that they needed to investigate further but was at loss as to think who might be in the room.

'Let me check around the rest of the team to see if anyone has seen Kaliope at all,' suggested Chris.

'Good idea,' said Yannis. 'I'll check with my team too. Let's meet at 16:30 hours outside Suite 512.'

They synchronised watches before going off to talk to their respective team members. A few minutes later Yannis was on the third floor corridor talking to the two undercover EKAM officers who were watching room 322.

'Has anyone left the room at all?' asked Yannis.

'No sir. We have been here since four o'clock and no-one has left the room. There is a food tray outside their door though.'

'Just the one?' queried Yannis.

'Yes sir.'

'Right, thank you men, as you were.'

Yannis pondered what he had heard. He thought it probably confirmed that only one man was in the room. Was it the driver of the white van or was it the second bomber from Salonika? Whichever one it was they would get him within the hour.

Yannis's mobile phone rang. It was Chris.

'What's up Chris?'

'I can't trace Ryan,' said Chris. 'No-one has seen him in the last hour and that worries me.'

'You don't think,' Yannis stopped in mid-sentence.

'He's in Suite 512!' Chris finished the sentence.

'There is only one way to find out,' suggested Yannis.

'I realise that,' said Chris. 'We have a slight problem though. Alex wants to join us. He says that Kaliope is one of his key cabinet members and wants to help out.'

'I know he is in the CIA but he is the Prime Minister of Greece. He can't get involved in any more shoot-outs which is what it might come down to. Anyway he is an amateur compared to us.' If Chris could have seen Yannis he would have seen his hands energetically moving in time with his words in typical Mediterranean style.

'I know but I can't dissuade him, he's an extremely stubborn man. We'll meet you on the fifth floor at four-thirty as we said.' Chris wasn't going to argue, he knew Alex would never change his mind.

'Okay,' said Yannis resignedly.

While he waited, Yannis moved down the fifth floor corridor towards Suite 512. Taking great pains not to make any noise whatsoever, he managed to reach the door of the suite. He took his listening device from his pocket, a device which looked similar to a water glass, but much more sensitive to sound.

He heard several voices but although he could pick up the occasional word he could not follow what they were talking about. He surmised that was because the voices were not coming from the lounge area of the suite but from the bedroom area. The conversation was between two males voices which caused Yannis to wonder if Kaliope was indeed in the room. Then he heard what could only be described as a whimper, a sound which tugged at his heartstrings and at the same time made him furious. He had to apply maximum self-restraint to stop himself storming into the suite on his own. He prayed that Chris and Alex would arrive soon.

Up on the seventh floor Alex started to make his way down to Suite 512. He was deep in thought going over the events of the last few days. Ten minutes ago he had received a conference phone call from his policy advisors in Athens who were concerned that his popularity ratings were falling and the gap between his party and the Golden Dawn party was narrowing quite dramatically. With only a few months to the General Election things were not looking good.

He was told that the public were afraid after the bombings in Athens and Salonika and the assassination of Andonis's family in Edessa. Questions were being asked in parliament and all opposition parties were demanding that he and the Home Office Minister come to the parliament to give answers as to what was going on. Alex told them to tell the Leader of the House to say something to quieten the clamour down. He should say that Alex and his team were dealing with the problem, had identified the perpetrators of these atrocities, and were hoping to bring them to justice in a few days.

Alex thought that the president of the Golden Dawn party Dimitris Karagianis was cunningly clever, using the public's anxiety to further his cause. He had mobilised his party members and some of his MP's to move into areas where predominately elderly people lived, escorting them on their shopping trips, banking appointments and even café and restaurant visits. Alex was feeling badly battered. Twice he had had to go on national television to try to calm the public's mood after the bombings in Athens and Salonika. The death toll now stood at forty-nine and there were twenty-eight people still in hospital suffering from life changing injuries.

No more deaths please, Alex prayed. That was exactly why he was on his way down to Kaliope's suite and precisely why he would save Gitta if he possibly could. It was going to be his personal vendetta. Alex pushed those thoughts to one side as he descended the final steps and entered the fifth floor corridor. He spotted both Chris and Yannis near the door of Kaliope's suite with another man whom he had never seen before.

'Who is this?' Alex said quietly, as he approached the men.

'Our way in,' said Chris. 'This is Theo, one of the hotel's receptionists.'

Alex stared at Theo thinking that he looked embarrassingly uncomfortable, terrified even. 'What is in that envelope?' whispered Alex pointing at a large brown envelope that Theo was holding.

'Nothing,' said Chris. 'But we are using it to get whoever is inside, and Yannis believes it's two people, to open the door to Theo. If they don't come to the door Theo has a master pass card and he will open the door himself'

'Supposedly, there is a coded communique from the cabinet office in Athens for Kaliope in the envelope.' explained Yannis.

'You're a brave man Theo. I hope we are paying you well?' said Alex.

'Yes Prime Minister, very well.'

'Right, silencers on now,' ordered Chris as he screwed his own one onto his Glock. The others followed suit. Alex was feeling excited as his silencer went on, suffering from the intense adrenalin rush he always felt before some action. At the same time though he felt a little guilty believing that a Prime Minister shouldn't in all honesty, be playing cowboys and Indians with real bullets.

Chris checked that both Alex and Yannis were ready before motioning to Theo to go ahead and knock at the door. Alex positioned himself next to Chris, flat against the wall, Yannis was on the hinged side of the door so he would be the first to see into the room when the door opened.

Theo, making sure he was positioned in front of the spyhole rapped hard on the door. He waited thirty seconds before giving the door another hard rap. Another twenty seconds passed and then a voice said. 'What do you want?'

'I have an important document for Ms Vlachos the Home Office Minister. It's stamped urgent in big red letters,' said Theo holding up the envelope to the spyhole.

'Wait!' said the voice. Everyone waited hardly daring to breathe. Then they heard the lock turning from the inside and a gap starting to appear as the door was slowly opened. 'Give me the envelope,' said the voice, his hand reaching through the gap for it.

As the envelope was passing from Theo to the man on the other side of the door Yannis acted. Thrusting his leg out with great force his boot smashed into the handle of the door, forcing it inwards causing the man behind the door to stumble back. The door was free, and Yannis burst through driving his body into the man, forcing him onto the floor.

Chris with Alex following right behind him, ran through the small vestibule, passed the two men fighting on the floor and into the lounge area. Alex heard a squeal coming from the open door to the bedroom on his right. Sprinting towards the door with Chris hard on his heels, Alex suddenly found himself running towards a man who had appeared in the door. He stopped in his tracks. It was Ryan.

'What the hell are you doing here?' shouted Alex, in his excitement not noticing that Ryan was holding a gun and bringing it to bear on him.

'Get down!' screamed Chris, at the same time letting off two shots at Ryan. Alex dropped to the floor; as he did so he felt the air pressure of the two bullets as they passed remarkably close to him. Two bright red blotches appeared on the left hand side of Ryan's shirt about where the heart was. He swayed and in his eyes was a momentary look of disbelief before he crashed face downwards onto the floor.

Alex got up from the floor, retrieved his Glock which had fallen out of his hand when he had hit the floor, then followed Chris into the bedroom. The sight that greeted them would have melted even the most hardened heart. Kaliope had been tied to the bed, on her back, in a star shape. Both legs and arms extended taut. They could see her sinews under her skin stretched to their limit, or so it seemed. She was blindfolded and had a muzzle over her jaw and mouth which would prevent her talking but allowed some sounds to pass her lips. Her left hand was covered in a makeshift blooded bandage, the blood still dripping slowly down her arm. She was moaning softly.

Chris and Alex heard a noise behind them. It was Yannis, a bit blooded but seemingly physically all right, holding a blooded knife in his right hand.

'No, no, no!' exclaimed Yannis as he rushed to her bedside. He immediately cut her bonds with his knife, cradled her in his arms and in his anguish rocked her like a baby.

Chapter 20

17th August 2013 – Eckersley's Villa – 17:30

The Reaper drone which had followed Eckersley into North Macedonia and then back to his villa was now circling at three thousand metres above the villa. Its video was being relayed in real time back to Tatoi Air Force Base where the pilots who controlled the Reaper drone and all the other surveillance drones were situated. The video was processed at the base before being uploaded to a highly classified and tightly secure Government cloud, where it could be accessed by those senior Government ministers or senior armed forces personnel who had special clearance to view the data.

Eckersley, who had been briefed by Alkis earlier went directly to the house in the villa's grounds where the staff were quartered. In the basement workshop he found Alkis sitting in a chair positioned six feet in front of Gitta, who was hanging by her tied wrists from an iron bar. The bar was fixed to the ceiling via a pulley system which allowed her to be moved either higher or lower. The only thing supporting her were her toes and this was making her sway uncontrollably as she tried to maintain balance.

Eckersley could see that she was exhausted, how long she had been hanging there he did not know. Her eyes had sunk into their sockets, her hair was matted over her head and there were what seemed like scratches on her arms and legs. Her outer garments, which looked as though Alkis had ripped them off, were in a pile at her feet. Eckersley, walked around behind her and saw the raw welts from the whip which Alkis was still holding in his hand.

'Has she talked?' said Eckersley as he walked around in front of Gitta.

128

'Nothing yet,' said Alkis. 'Keep your distance she could hurt you being that....' Before Alkis had finished his sentence Gitta had pulled up her legs, then thrust with what strength she had left, hitting Eckersley in the chest with her tied feet. Eckersley let out a cry of pain and fell backwards onto the stone floor.

'Fuck you!' shouted Gitta through teeth clenched with the pain from the movement she had just made.

Eckersley gingerly got to his feet still fighting for breath. He looked around the basement for some kind of weapon to hurt Gitta in retaliation for the pain she had inflicted on him. Alkis tossed him the whip.

'No,' said Eckersley. 'Get one of the men to go to the tool room and bring me the nail gun.'

Alkis grinned, this is going to be fun he thought, as he exited the basement.

Gitta raised her weary head, her green eyes reflecting hatred for the man standing before her.

'I'm going to kill you,' she said matter-of-factly her voice showing no emotion.

Eckersley laughed. 'You are not in a position to kill me or anyone else for that matter. If you tell me who you work for and how much does that weak man of a Prime Minister and his CIA crony know about my plans, I promise you it shall be a quick death for you. However, if you don't talk you will wish you were dead long before we have finished with you.'

Eckersley sat down in the chair Alkis had vacated and looked Gitta over.

'You are a beautiful woman my dear, you have a desirable body and an exquisite taste in underwear. Wouldn't you like to keep it that way and take the easy way out because the hard way will leave you ugly and disfigured and in excruciating pain?'

Gitta continued to stare malevolently at him and so strong was the hate she radiated that Eckersley shivered involuntarily. It wasn't hate for what he might do to her but hate for what he had done to the girl she had replaced in his organisation, and the deaths he had caused in Athens and Salonika. She was certain he was behind them all. What she had to do now was to harness all her CIA training and remember the ways in which pain can be ignored and even suppressed. She had to relax both in her mind and her body, become without emotion but at the same time every now and again make her torturers angry because an enraged torturer makes mistakes. She prayed that she would last until the cavalry arrived in the form of Alex and Chris.

'Perhaps we can come to a deal,' offered Eckersley breaking into Gitta's thoughts. 'A quid-pro-quo arrangement where I tell you part of my plans then you answer some of my questions. What do you say?'

Gitta thought about it for a moment. How much information is too much, how much information would satisfy Eckersley. It was a difficult call. Perhaps it would be better to say nothing and ignore his stupid deal. She could lie of course, skew the information without giving too much of the truth away. It would be interesting to learn what he was planning over and above what she knew.

'Agreed,' said Gitta. 'You start.'

At that moment Alkis walked in with a nasty looking nail gun in his hand. He plugged the lead into an electrical socket and handed the gun to Eckersley.

'Okay I'll start,' said Eckersley. He was pondering which part of Gitta's body to fire the first nail into. He owed her one for drop kicking him, but he didn't want to maim her at this stage. The torso would be too dangerous because of the profusion of major blood vessels. The pelvis has too many nerve endings and could cause paralysis. Arms and legs are good, buttocks are better and so are hands and feet.

'First things first though my dear,' said Eckersley offering her a cold smile. 'Alkis would you please lower the lovely Gitta here so that her feet are flat to the floor. Then shoot her with the nail gun in the left buttock from about twenty feet.'

Gitta initially tensed but then calling on her CIA training she relaxed and thought about how she was going to kill Eckersley. Alkis had lowered her down so her feet were flat to the floor. She heard him walk behind her, then stop. Alkis got down on one knee, aimed the nail-gun at her left buttock and fired.

'Thonk!' Gitta had hardly registered the sound of the nail-gun firing, when the two inch nail, travelling at sixty metres a second, buried three-quarters of its length into Gitta's left buttock. She flinched and involuntarily uttered a cry as the nail buried itself. At first there was no pain but after a few seconds the pain began to radiate outwards from the point at which the nail had penetrated, and blood begun to ooze out around the nail.

'Shall I pull it out,' asked Alkis,' grinning from sheer pleasure at the thought of inflicting more pain on Gitta.

Before Eckersley could answer his mobile phone rang.

'Yes?' he said.

It's Cyclops. Things haven't gone too well at the hotel. Both Ryan and Rousos have been killed.'

'How?' asked Eckersley.

'Instead of leaving the hotel before the raid by EKAM, they took it upon themselves to kidnap the Home Office Minister in her own suite. When she didn't answer the door to two of her colleagues, they became suspicious. Realising that something was wrong, they burst into her hotel suite and killed both Rousos and Ryan.'

'Is the Minister alive?'

'Yes.'

'Does that mean we have to cancel tonight's operation?'

'No, it's going ahead as planned,' confirmed Cyclops.

'Right, get some more people up from Salonika. Make sure they are good.' Said Eckersley.

'Don't worry, this doesn't change anything,' said Cyclops and disconnected the phone.

Eckersley was not pleased at hearing this news. All his assets except for Alkis and his secret trump card in Edessa were now dead. He might have to mobilise Dexter's men sooner than he wanted. The news that he was now the major shareholder in Hellenic Aluminium was made public earlier in the day, so tomorrow he would be talking to other major shareholders making them offers he hoped they could not refuse. He turned to Alkis.

'We need to talk. Not here but over at the villa. Besides I'm hungry and so must you be. Hoist her up so that she is barely on her toes and pull out that nail, we wouldn't want the wound to turn septic just yet. Join me at the main house when you are done.'

Eckersley left the basement and headed for the villa. Alkis did as he had been ordered. He raised Gitta up until she was barely taking her weight on her toes. Her arms were stretched to the limit, the sinews taut and clearly visible through her skin. Alkis went around behind her to extract the nail from her buttock but Gitta was ready for him. Waiting until he was about to extract the nail, summoning all her strength she used her arms to swing herself forward and then drove her buttocks back towards Alkis. The nail struck him on his cheek and opened a three inch gash which immediately spurted blood. Alkis screamed in pain and so did Gitta as the force of the blow drove the nail further into her buttock.

'Fucking bitch!' yelled Alkis. 'I'm going to kill you, wait and see.' He picked up the nail-gun from the floor where he had left it, turned towards Gitta and without taking aim fired twice. One nail missed her completely but the other passed through her side just below her breasts and clattered to the floor. She yelped at the pain which brought tears to her eyes.

Alkis calmed himself down knowing that Eckersley would be extremely angry if Gitta died at his hand. Anyway, he needed to see to his gashed cheek. He left the basement; it would be dark soon.

Gitta was left hanging by her wrists, her toes barely touching the floor. She was tired, hungry, and thirsty. She was in excruciating pain from the wound in her side and her buttock. It was going to be a long uncomfortable night and she needed all her resolve.

Chapter 21

17th August 2013 – Edessa The Four Seasons Hotel – 20:00

In Suite 512 of the Four Seasons Hotel, Kaliope sat on her sofa, a glass of white wine in her hand and her ever present mobile in the other. After being rescued from her ordeal at the hands of Rousos and Ryan, a doctor had been called to deal with her various injuries, the worst one of which was the extracted fingernail on her left pinkie.

Earlier, at 5 o'clock the news had broken that Bauxite Mining, one of Eckersley's companies in his Xplore Industries group had accumulated enough shares for a majority shareholding in Hellenic Aluminium, and that they intended to make a take-over bid. This was not a surprise to them, but it was to the stock markets and the other shareholders. The shares had responded by closing at a price ten percent higher than its opening price. Alex had sent Leonidas his Business and Industry Minister to meet with the CEO of Hellenic Aluminium to assure him that the Greek Government would do everything in its power to prevent a hostile takeover.

Kaliope's mobile phone rang. She looked at the display and saw it was Thomas Davanellos the Commander of EKAM the counter terrorist squad and Yannis's boss.

'Thomas,' said Kaliope. 'How are you?'

'Hello Kaliope, I think a lot better than you must be feeling right now.'

'No, I'm fine now thank you. The only major damage is my missing pinkie fingernail,' Kaliope tittered in her embarrassment. 'What news from Athens?'

'We have picked up some chatter on the internet which leads us to believe that tomorrow there will be an attack on important monuments in Athens and Salonika.'

'Any idea which monuments?' asked Kaliope.

'We're not certain, but one of our informants has revealed that the Golden Dawn are actively recruiting from organised crime men who are C4 explosive experts.'

'The president of Golden Dawn was here in Edessa yesterday. Thomas do you have any indication that Eckersley and the Golden Dawn are working together?'

'Nothing concrete but there have been too many coincidences in the last few days. The bombings are intended to destabilise the Government and give the Golden Dawn a chance to get enough seats to form a coalition Government with another party at the general election. It's also a distraction from Eckersley's goal of taking over the bauxite mines of Hellenic Aluminium.'

'Not only that,' said Kaliope. 'We are sure that North Macedonia is mixed up in this too. Our drones discovered a small mercenary army just over the border of our Macedonia. If only we could have arrested at least one of the bombers instead of killing them, we might have some more answers,' Kaliope sighed.

'Perhaps we should concentrate on guarding monuments of heroes whom North Macedonia is claiming as their own,' said Thomas.

'Good idea,' agreed Kaliope. 'I suppose the most obvious in Athens is the Alexander the Great statue.'

'Yes, it is and in Salonika as they have already hit Alexander's statue, the White Tower would be the next logical target. They have built a replica in Skopje, so they obviously believe that it is one of their own cultural treasures.'

'I'm afraid I dare not spare any of Yannis Spanos's men who are here in Edessa, however he has left half of his unit back in Salonika. You could use them to keep an eye on the White Tower,' said Kaliope.

'Right, I had those men in mind. Could you authorise a couple of reconnaissance drones, one for Athens and the other for Salonika?' requested Thomas.

'I'll get onto it right away don't worry.' Kaliope assured him.

'Thank you,' said Thomas. 'I wish you a speedy recovery from your ordeal.'

'I'll be fine don't worry. Keep me updated please.'

'Will do,' said Thomas then cut the connection.

Kaliope liked Thomas and respected him too. She liked the way he took the initiative and made decisive decisions. He was a good man as the Commander of EKAM.

She poured herself another glass of wine, her thoughts turning to the mercenary army close to the Greek border. Would Eckersley use them to invade Macedonia? It's possible she thought. North Macedonia has had its eyes on northern Greece from the border all the way down south to Salonika, because they believe that Alexander the Great and his father King Philip II of Macedonia were born in the country now known as North Macedonia. But that could be just an excuse to take Macedonia, an area of land that is the most popular tourist destination, that is not an island, and is fourth overall in Greece, outperforming all other regions of mainland Greece. She, herself loved vacationing in an area that offers four UNESCO sites and many other cultural wonders blending into a backdrop of magnificent tree covered mountains and colourful agricultural plains.

Perhaps this is what North Macedonia wants, she thought. The economic potential of an area that boasts over half of Greece's industrial output in the form of bauxite and copper mining would be invaluable to them. Of course they couldn't justify invading and taking Macedonia by force, just for its assets. But, if they had proof of their claims regarding Alexander the Great and King Philip II, who knows what an international court might decide, especially in this woke-ridden age, piracy could very well be forgiven. Greece's own overtures to the UN to not recognise the name North Macedonia looks at the moment like a losing battle. Likewise, Greece's plea to the EU to not invite North Macedonia into the EU club, looks as though it too will fall on stony ground. Kaliope sighed, how many times had Greece been on the losing end of international decisions and conflicts. However, surely history was with them this time.

She recalled her Greek history in which she was taught that the Macedonians in ancient times circa 4000 BC were a tribe that came from the south called Makednoi. They named the territory they settled down in, Macedonia, a tranche of land that today, comprises the whole of central Macedonia. Kaliope laughed inwardly. What had caused her humour was the thought that what she was thinking probably was exactly what Aliki Traka the Minister of Culture would be talking about on her visit to Skopje tomorrow.

She would be telling them that the Macedonians during the time of King Philip II and his son Alexander, some five hundred years before Christ, were in control of a territory stretching from the Ionian Sea in the east to the Turkish border in the west and had built their ancient capital Pella, which is now a modern town and the capital of the region of Pella in central Macedonia. Under King Philip II, Macedonia had become a powerful Hellenistic State. Then after the assassination of King Philip II, his son Alexander became King of Macedonia and began his historic and successful campaigns to the north, as far as present day Skopje, and to the east as far as Afghanistan.

Kaliope surmised that there is no way that North Macedonia could legally claim that King Philip II and Alexander were their cultural sons. Okay, so over the years after Alexander's death, Macedonia was invaded many times, and its name changed by the empires of the Romans, the Slavs, the Bulgars and the Magyars. Then in more modern times the Byzantium, the Ottomans and in the early twentieth century, the Bulgarians. But the territory had always reverted back to the name Macedonia once the invaders had been repelled. Anyway, North Macedonians were Slavs from the north and history has written that the Macedonians came from the south. There could be no connection between the two.

Satisfied with her reasoning, she leaned back against the back of the sofa, closed her eyes, and tried to relax. She was feeling excited at the thought of Yannis coming to see her. He had shown in the way he held her after her rescue that he had strong feelings for her. Reliving those moments in her mind she felt the urge to touch herself but she resisted and instead rearranged her clothes to make herself more desirable. She undid the highest button on her blouse, showing more of her cleavage, which was not as obvious at it would have been if she were wearing a bra, but it would do. The blouse was white showing a nice contrast with her tanned body. The skirt she was wearing had a slit down one side. She had chosen it purposely with the sole intention of sitting there with her legs crossed, revealing one exquisite thigh. He probably wouldn't immediately notice she was not wearing panties, but she didn't want him to have to fumble around with them, although he was probably adept at removing ladies' knickers with his teeth too. Another urge to touch herself flooded her loins as those thoughts shrouded her mind. Kaliope sat back again, closed her eyes, and concentrated on breathing nice and composed.

Two minutes later Yannis knocked at her suite door. He saw that she had not shut it properly and nudged it open. Entering the small vestibule he stopped, transfixed by her beauty.

'Hey,' said Kaliope, giving Yannis her best whiter than white smile.

Yannis smiled back, kicked the door gently shut, and walked towards her. 'Hey, you,' he almost whispered. Kaliope couldn't stop her heart starting to race. He was wearing a black t-shirt which showed off his well-muscled torso and a pair of denim shorts which came down to his knees but as Kaliope observed, as he poured two glasses of wine, showed of his well-formed buttocks.

'Για μας, κούκλα μου' said Yannis as he clinked her glass.

Kaliope reciprocated. 'Cheers, handsome,' she said, feeling the blood rushing to her face because he had called her his little doll.

Yannis sat down beside her and kissed her on her cheek. He took her hand and held it lightly resting on her thigh. Kaliope gazing into Yannis's piercing blue eyes found her desire for him becoming uncontrollable. It seemed her senses had become so heightened that even though his arms were not moving she could sense his muscles rippling under his toned skin. She deliberately uncrossed her legs as she guided the hand that held hers till it was touching the bare flesh of her thigh. At his touch, her body trembled as if an electric current had passed through it.

Yannis feeling this, slid his hand further up her thigh leaned forward and kissed her full on her mouth. Her lips parted and their tongues touched then started a sensuous dance. Kaliope moaned as Yannis's fingers touched her now wet vagina. She put her hand on his lap and through the material of his shorts she felt his hardening manhood. She was breathing fast now as the waves of desire for Yannis coursed through her body. She wanted her flesh against his flesh now. She stood up facing him, undid her skirt and let it drop to the floor, then she undid the remaining buttons on her blouse, discarding it. She stood facing him for a few seconds while he drank in her beauty and finely sculptured body.

She could see the desire in his eyes too. She leant down and deftly undid the belt on his shorts before pulling them together with his underpants down to his ankles. His manhood stood up, strong and tall in a salute. Kaliope climbed onto Yannis's lap in a crouch astride his thighs, positioning herself above his penis she took hold of it and guided into her waiting flower. She gasped as his entire shaft slid deep into her pussy. They locked mouths and Yannis held her buttocks helping to support her as she began to rhythmically slide up and down his shaft her strong thighs keeping her in the crouch.

Slowly at first, they savoured every second, but their desire was stronger than their patience and Kaliope began to move faster. They disengaged their lips and gazed into each other's eyes as Kaliope brought them both to the edge of their orgasms. Then, with a soft scream Kaliope felt the waves of ecstasy enveloping her whole body. Shuddering uncontrollably she felt Yannis's juices gushing into her as he too moaned with his own orgasm. Her thighs were pulsing now and could not hold her in a crouch, so she collapsed onto her knees keeping Yannis inside her still. They embraced and let their sweat mingle as it ran down their naked bodies, both feeling completely fulfilled and both radiating the love they felt for each other.

Later as they lay in each other's arms in Kaliope's bed, drifting in and out of sleep, oblivious to them both, events elsewhere which had no correlation to love or sex, were playing out, bringing Macedonia and North Macedonia closer to a flashpoint.

Chapter 22

17th August 2013 – North Macedonia Border – 21:00

The white Pullman coach with the words United Nations emblazoned on its sides, and with its smoked glass windows reflecting the setting sun's rays like dancing streaks of light, made the final turn from its journey down the mountain. Two kilometres of a treelined flat straight road lay ahead before the border with North Macedonia. Beyond the border more mountains with narrow twisting roads lay ahead. The coach which had left Edessa some ninety minutes earlier was heading for the North Macedonian capital of Skopje with twenty-six UN representatives on board. One of these was Aliki Traka the Culture Minister of Greece.

Alex Kalfas had begged her not to go, but Aliki had insisted she must, saying that her experiences during the second world war in Nazi occupied Greece, were far worse than she would face in North Macedonia. Alex had considered sending a surveillance drone to follow the coach but had been talked out of it by Kaliope who reasoned that it would probably cause a diplomatic incident if the drone were spotted in North Macedonian airspace. Besides the Reaper drone that was on station watching the road between Eckersley's villa and the border was eyes enough. Alex reluctantly gave her permission to go.

The border crossing turned out to be a non-event as there were no border guards to be seen, just a small wooden hut, which served as a border post. After initially slowing down to cross the border, the coach then sped up when the driver realised that there were no guards at the post. The Reaper Drone cruising at twenty-nine thousand feet above them, saw and recorded all this. At its height it was able to see in detail, sometimes twenty feet above the terrain, if

141

the pilots so chose the whole area from Eckersley's villa to the border and beyond. The pilots themselves were under orders from Kaliope to be vigilant and report immediately on seeing any danger to Greece or its assets in the area.

As the coach crossed the border John Dexter the CEO of Black Hawke was talking to the men in his private army. He had taken a chance coming over from Turkey to North Macedonia because as the American Government had contracted him to police the border between Turkey and Greece to ensure that Turkey did not violate any international or NATO treaties, any contracts which concerned a NATO ally had to be ringfenced. So he was permitted to contract out other mercenaries under the Black Hawke umbrella but not get involved personally. His intention was to speak to Captain Knowles the commander of the group about the United Nations delegation heading their way. Once that conversation was over he would head back to his headquarters in Thrace near the Turkish border with Greece.

This mercenary group had taken over a farmhouse located just three kilometres beyond the border in North Macedonia, the same farmhouse that the reconnaissance drone, which had followed Eckersley earlier that day, had used its heat seeking technology to discover that there were twenty-five men in the building. One of the men was looking out for the coach, and he was up on the flat roof with a pair of powerful binoculars. He had his binoculars trained on the border post when the Pullman coach crossed into North Macedonia. He spoke into his field microphone attached to his helmet.

'Transport crossing into North Macedonia,' he announced.

'What type,' asked Knowles who had moved onto the radio console as soon as he had heard the announcement.

'A Pullman coach belonging to the United Nations by the look of it.'

Excellent thought Knowles. Now is the chance to ruffle some feathers. He called Eckersley at his villa and told him about the coach. Eckersley immediately saw an opportunity to put some pressure on Alex Kalfas's Government and told Knowles to apprehend the coach and take it and its passengers to the farmhouse.

It was now twilight and light around the farmhouse had taken on a mauve hue typical of twilights in this part of Europe. The coach's headlights shone brightly now as it approached the road's nearest point to the farmhouse. One hundred metres from the entrance to the driveway the coach driver was almost blinded by a pair of headlights belonging to a black SUV four-wheel drive vehicle, as it sped up the road towards the coach. He slammed on his brakes and brought the coach to a stop. The SUV also stopped, straddling the road so blocking any chance of the coach driver suddenly wanting to be a hero and trying to drive away.

Four armed men in army fatigues climbed down from the SUV and stood in front of the coach, one of them gesticulating to the driver to open the front door. It took the driver several seconds to understand that they wanted the door open, but eventually it dawned on him, and he complied to the request. One of the men climbed into the coach and stood facing the passengers.

'We don't want to hurt you but if you don't do as we tell you, we will,' shouted the man. Turning to the driver he ordered, 'Follow the SUV!'

As soon as the SUV had turned around in the road and the remaining three men got in, the driver complied and followed the SUV down the drive towards the farmhouse, there he parked the coach in front of its main entrance.

The Reaper drone silently watching far above recorded and transmitted the video of the entire incident. The drone pilots who had seen the events in real time and immediately realised its importance, had transmitted the video evidence to the mobile phones of Alex, Kaliope, Chris, and Yannis.

In suite 512, the mobile phones of Kaliope and Yannis pinged simultaneously, rousing them both from their slumber.

'Oh my god!' exclaimed Kaliope. 'Have you seen this Yannis?'

'Just looking at it,' said Yannis. 'Alex will be asking for a meeting any second now. What they have done, kidnapping a coach load of civilians, is an extremely serious matter.'

Kaliope was flicking at her hair which now didn't look too great. It was tossed and tangled from their lovemaking, although Yannis thought it made her look sexy. She didn't feel sexy though. If anything, she was slightly fearful that Greece could be on the brink of a border skirmish. She voiced her fears to Yannis.

'It might come to that,' he said. 'Our problem is that we have lost the advantage of the Reaper now because we can't use it for fear of collateral damage to the United Nations delegation.'

'We'd better get dressed. It wouldn't do to go into a meeting with the PM in our state of undress,' said Kaliope giggling.

Yannis slipped off the bed and stood up. Kaliope opened her eyes wide feigning astonishment at the sight of his naked but well-honed body.

'You have gorgeous buttocks,' she complimented as Yannis did a pirouette. 'And you're modest too!' Yannis laughed as he disappeared into the bathroom for a shower.

While Yannis was in the shower Kaliope rang Alex and they arranged to meet within the hour in Alex's suite.

Meanwhile, quite oblivious to what was going on at the border, Leonidas Papadakis was sitting in the living room of Spiros Emmanuel, the CEO of Hellenic Aluminium, with a glass of Spiros's home-made red barrel wine. Opposite him sat Spiros and to his right much to his delight sat Melita. He had not expected her to be a dinner guest tonight, neither had Spiros because she hadn't been invited, but had turned up out of the blue and Spiros didn't have the heart to refuse to let her stay.

During dinner Leonidas had appraised Spiros of the reason Andonis had been targeted and the current situation regarding the shares that Bauxite Mining, a company owned by Xplore Industries group, had been purchasing, and that the Greek Government was committed to not letting Hellenic Aluminium fall into foreign hands. Spiros was shocked when he heard about Gitta and the mercenary army waiting near the North Macedonia border. Leonidas had had to reassure him that the Government would do everything possible to protect him and his staff and that even as they spoke a drone was being specifically made ready to be on station over his house within a few hours.

Leonidas looked at the grandfather clock in the opposite corner of the room. The time was approaching ten o'clock, it was time for him to check-in. Alex had insisted that he check-in via text, every hour on the hour, even though his phone had the standard issue panic button installed. If he was in danger and it was activated, it transmitted an intermittent tone to the phones of all the other members of the Edessa team.

'Excuse me, nature calls,' he said as he made his way from the living room towards one of the bathrooms which were accessed from the large hallway.

He waited an obligatory two minutes in the bathroom after sending the text, then he flushed the toilet, ran the taps for a few seconds, then left the bathroom.

As he approached the living room, he thought he heard a thud. He couldn't be sure, but a voice in his head reminded him to be careful, so he put his hand in the pocket where his mobile phone was and put his thumb over the panic button. Leonidas opened the door and entered the room.

What he saw caused the blood to drain from his face, without thinking his thumb depressed the panic button on his phone sending an intermittent signal to Alex, Kaliope, Chris and Yannis.

He imagined that there would alarm bells at the hotel, and he wasn't far wrong.

Chapter 23

17th August 2013 – Edessa Four Seasons Hotel – 22:00

In Suite 710 on the seventh floor of the hotel, Alex, Kaliope, Chris and Yannis sat round a table discussing the kidnapping of the United Nations delegation.

'I suppose we have the advantage that they don't know we know about the kidnapping yet,' said Alex.

'Not really Alex. Now that they have hostages, we lose our option of using the Reaper drone for fear of too much collateral damage,' said Chris.

'Too right,' agreed Kaliope. 'We don't want to cause a diplomatic incident involving the United Nations delegation.'

'Wait a minute, we can't just leave them to their fate. You know that they will be used as leverage to get Eckersley everything he wants,' said Yannis.

'Why don't we just arrest Eckersley and charge him with the bombings?' asked Alex.

'No hard evidence.'

'Come on Kaliope, the bastard has kidnapped Gitta,' said Alex, exasperation clearly evident in his voice.

'Even that we are not sure of, we suspect that's what has happened, but we have no evidence yet,' said Chris. 'But that doesn't mean that we are going to do nothing about the kidnapped delegation. There are ways in which we can force them to give up their hostages without using force.'

'What do you suggest Chris?' said Alex.

'We should let them know we know about the hostages. Not directly but indirectly by issuing a news communique. That way we get the world on our side.'

'I agree,' said Kaliope.

Yannis murmured, 'me too.'

'What's the matter Yannis,' asked Kaliope, realising he was preoccupied with other thoughts.

'I can't hang around doing nothing, you know that. So I was thinking we should have a plan, a military plan as a last resort. We may never use it but as a contingency we should devise one,' said Yannis.

They all looked at Yannis, then at Alex. 'Go for it,' he said. 'Kaliope would you draft the communique please. We should get that out so it hits the newswires before morning.'

'On it!' said Kaliope using her favoured response when asked to do something by Alex.

'Kaliope can you give us the latest on preventative measures in case the rumoured disruption in Athens or Salonika actually happens?' said Alex. But before Kaliope could respond, their phones started beeping, dot, dot, dot, dash, dash, dash, dot, dot, dot.

'It's Leonidas,' yelled Yannis. 'He's in trouble!'

'Where is he?' asked Chris.

'He's meeting with the CEO of Hellenic Aluminium for dinner,' said Alex.

Yannis immediately took over. This was his territory and he sprung into animated action.

'Chris, Kaliope, and Alex on me! I'll get some of my men to meet us near Spiros Emmanuel's home,' barked Yannis.

Ten minutes later a black SUV tore out of the car park and headed west. Yannis was driving and giving orders to his number two who was still in the Aigai Hotel to send four men to meet them at the house. Spiros Emmanuel's home was five kilometres outside of Edessa, so Yannis reasoned that a ten-thirty-five rendezvous was doable for both parties.

At the house itself, Leonidas was just recovering from the shock of seeing Melita standing astride the groaning body of Spiros, whose head looked as though it had been pistol whipped it was so blooded. The small pistol she was holding was pointing at Leonidas and although his initial thought was could she use it? By the look on her face and the confident way she stood astride Spiros, hinted that she was competent enough. However, whatever the answer was, he was not going to test any theory out.

'Come in Leonidas,' said Melita, beckoning him in with the gun. 'Sit down over there,' Indicating with the gun that he should sit on the sofa opposite her.

'What the hell is going on Melita?' said Leonidas, his voice breaking as he said it.

'My homeland is taking back its rightful lands, that's what's going on Leonidas,' she said in a low fierce voice. 'Soon Salonika and the whole of Greek Macedonia will be back in the arms of their lawful owners.'

'But you are Greek,' whined Leonidas, his face laced with puzzlement as he sat rubbing his forehead which was glistening with his sweat.

'No, Leonidas,' she said, with a voice full of pride. 'I was born in FYROM, the former Yugoslavian Republic of Macedonia, in a village close to the Greek border. My father was Greek, my mother Serbian, perhaps that is why you took me for a Greek.'

While she was talking, Melita had stepped over Spiros and had sat down in an armchair near to the open French doors which led out to the patio. From there she could see down to the gate at the end of the brightly lit drive and although she was confident that no one would be coming, she felt psychologically safer being able to see the drive.

'What are you going to do with us?' said Leonidas, moistening his dry lips with the tip of his tongue.

'We,' said Melita emphasising the word we. 'Are going to kill you both.' A mocking smile playing on her lips.

Leonidas's heart sank at her words. He found it hard to believe that she had changed so dramatically from the woman he had fallen in love with and whom he thought had fallen in love with him. She had been so caring, and so loving these past few months. Mata Hari couldn't have acted out her charade any better.

'So, it was all a pretence,' said Leonidas, a sudden look of anger passing across his face.

'Not all of it. I was, no, I am very fond of you,' she corrected herself. 'But I'm afraid my country comes before any personal wants or needs.'

Spiros had stopped groaning now and had pulled himself into a sitting position against the leg of a small table. His head had lolled forward against his chest and the blood continued to drip from his wound onto clothes which by now were wringing wet with his blood. Leonidas wondered if Spiros were dying but he knew that he could not give him the help he needed with Melita calling the shots. He could try, however.

'Spiros needs medical attention,' said Leonidas with a note of firmness in his voice as if he knew what he was talking about.

Melita's eyebrows lifted in surprise. 'Are you qualified to treat him?' she said, her mouth faintly mocking him. 'Or are you expecting me to help him after I have put him in this state.'

Melita's mobile phone chirped indicating a text had arrive. With one hand still pointing the pistol at Leonidas she managed to retrieve the phone from her bag and read the text. A smile curled the edge of her mouth as she said, 'Alkis will be here in ten minutes to take you both to Eckersley's villa where you will join one of your colleagues who has been a houseguest for a couple of days now.' She gave a throaty little laugh. 'I understand that Eckersley will make you very welcome.'

Leonidas's heart sank when he heard those words. He knew now that if help didn't arrive before Alkis did, he would never see the light of day again. It had been twenty minutes since he had hit the panic button so where were they?

Outside the villa all was still and quiet except for the low noise of the breathing of seven men crouching low behind the wall around the property. They could see that going up the drive would be madness because it was lit up. However, one thing to their advantage was the style of the villa. It was modern with large areas of windows, so Yannis was able to see into the lounge area beyond the patio. He saw Melita quite clearly. She seemed nervous because she kept glancing up the drive and waving her pistol around.

Yannis whispered into his comms microphone to the others, describing what he saw.

'But what I can't see,' he said, his voice almost a hiss. 'Is if there is anyone else in the room. I'm going to climb over the wall and work my way round to where I can see deeper into the room.' Without waiting for an answer Yannis scaled the wall and jumped down onto the soft earth of a well-watered flower bed. He quickly moved deeper into the garden; his night vision googles lighting his way as if it was still daylight. After crossing the garden behind the house he moved down the side of the property back to the front garden, only this time he was on the opposite side of the drive. There were plenty of bushes for cover right up to the patio, so he was able to see the whole lounge quite clearly.

'Melita is holding Leonidas at gun point and it looks as though Spiros is dead, if he's not he soon will be as he has lost a lot of blood,' reported Yannis into his mic, with a voice devoid of emotion.

'Don't kill her,' whispered Chris. 'We need her to give us as much information as possible.'

'I have an idea,' said Yannis. 'We need her to turn around so that I can shoot her gun arm and make her drop the weapon. So, Chris and Alex, come up the drive talking animatedly and loudly. That will attract her attention and being an amateur, she will turn towards the sound and give me the small window I need to shoot her gun hand. You other three men stay watchful around the perimeter of the house in case we have any unwelcome visitors.'

'Let's do it,' said Chris. Then turning to Alex, he turned off his mic and whispered. 'Listen Alex, I think Yannis is too confident that this will be easy. Melita has managed to neutralize Spiros and capture Leonidas. She isn't as naïve as Yannis believes. Draw your gun and keep it out of sight and don't hesitate to shoot if you have too.'

Alex pulled his Glock out of his shoulder holster with his right hand and let his arm hang down his right side where neither Yannis nor Melita could see it. As he stepped onto the drive with Chris to his right, he felt a chill crawl down his spine, and he felt as if every single muscle in his body was taut as a bow string.

In the villa Melita had felt rather than seen, a change in Leonidas. He no longer seemed afraid and now instead of slumping forward in defeat as he had been doing, his torso was now straight, he looked alert. She noticed his feet were in a new position and looked as if he was ready to spring away from the sofa he was sitting on. His eyes too had stopped focussing on her but were looking into the garden beyond the patio.

Her body tensed and her mind cried a warning. She swivelled around and seeing Yannis climbing up the patio steps fired two shots before Yannis could react. Yannis dived to the ground and rolled behind a glass patio table. Too late he realised what was going to happen. Melita fired another two shots into the glass, and it exploded from the force of the bullets sending shards of glass everywhere. Fortunately, Yannis was wearing the standard anti-terrorist helmet so his face and especially his eyes were protected. His bullet proof jacket protected his upper torso, but a particularly large shard of glass lodged in his thigh.

At the moment that Yannis had dived behind the table, both Alex and Chris had brought their guns to bear on Melita. She too had realised that two men were coming up the drive and had turned towards them. A fusillade of shots cut through the night air between Melita and the two men on the drive. Alex managed to get two shots off before he hit the ground with such force, that to his dismay, his gun was dislodged from his hand. Chris meanwhile was in a crouch position his gun still barking as he emptied his gun's magazine towards Melita. She collapsed in a heap onto the living room floor her gun spinning away towards the sofa that Leonidas was now standing in front of.

He rushed to her side; she was still alive but only just. Leonidas could see that she was losing a lot of blood from two gunshot wounds in the centre of her chest. A bullet had also smashed her knee and Leonidas felt a little queasy seeing the kneecap at a crazy angle to the knee. Her gun hand had also taken a bullet and Leonidas could see a neat hole through her palm.

'Don't bother to call an ambulance,' uttered Melita in a barely audible voice. 'I know I'm dying; it'll never get here in time.' She felt a sudden chill sweep through her body, then her body felt as if it was floating. Leonidas could see that she was fading away.

'Is there anyone I should contact?' he asked, as he gazed down into her eyes. Melita raised her eyes to his; she nodded; her throat too dry for speech. Then something between a laugh and a sob escaped from her mouth as her eyes glazed over, then in an instant the light in her eyes went out as if someone had turned a switch. Leonidas knew she was dead.

Outside the villa Alkis who was driving Eckersley's Mercedes, spotted one of Yannis's men skulking in the darkness, as he drove passed the villa. He wasn't keen on stopping and getting into a firefight; besides, he didn't know how many EKAM forces were in and around the villa. Fuck, he thought, if Melita has been taken and although he knew that she could hold out for some time, eventually she would break, and tell them everything she knew. That would be damaging to the cause. They had to make Gitta talk; the important thing was to keep Cyclops's identity a secret; he had to know if they knew who Cyclops was and now only Gitta could tell them.

Once out of earshot of the villa, Alkis gunned the Mercedes's engine and headed for Eckersley's villa and his rendezvous with Gitta.

Chapter 24

17th August 2013 – Eckersley's Villa – 22:45

It was almost pitch black in the basement but there was enough ambient light to allow Gitta to see shadows. Earlier Alkis had entered the basement and had been taunting her, telling her what he was going to do to her, and how he was going to hurt her. He had let her down none too gently, but in the almost dark basement he did not see that she had managed to gather an extra two metres of rope. Now she was no longer dangling with just her toes supporting her, she was lying down with the extra rope hidden from view beneath her. It was just as well that he had let her down because she had been in agony and at the time had actually felt grateful that he had, even though he had a pair of darts in one hand and a hedge cutter in the other.

He had put down his tools of torture and told her to turnover and lie on her stomach. She did this while cleverly manoeuvring the rope so it remained hidden from him. He had then retrieved two fifty-kilo weights from under the long workbench that stretched the length of one wall, and two pieces of rope. He proceeded to tie her right leg to one weight, and then taking her left leg he had forced her legs open. Just as he was about to tie this leg to the other weight his phone had rung. It was Eckersley.

'You need to go to Spiros Emmanuel's villa right away, Melita needs our help,' said Eckersley.

'Why what's up?' asked Alkis, a hint of frustration in his voice as he realised, he wouldn't be able enjoy hurting Gitta just yet.

'She has both Emmanuel and Papadakis virtually prisoners in Emmanuel's villa. Go and help her bring them to the villa. Put them in the basement with Gitta.'

'On my way,' said Alkis. The news that another two prisoners were joining Gitta cheered him up. He was looking forward to having some fun later.

Once Alkis had gone, Gitta got to work. She had to grit her teeth against the pain racking her body but the thought of being free gave her the motivation she needed. Alkis had left the hedge cutter where he dropped it earlier just over one and a half metres from her. She crawled using her elbows and knees towards the hedge cutter hoping she could reach it before the weight attached to her ankle stopped her forward momentum. It did for a moment, but she was able to pull it with her attached leg and move it the few extra centimetres she needed.

Reaching the hedge cutter, she rubbed the bonds around her wrists up and down against its cutting teeth until the rope frayed and broke. Her hands were numb, and she had to massage them to get the circulation going again. The pain was excruciating but she knew that it would be short lived and she would need her hands working as they should if she was going to escape from the villa. Once she had all feeling back, she was then able to undo the rope tying the weight to her leg.

She stood up, then immediately sat down in one of the chairs as waves of nausea washed over her. Gitta looked around for a clock, there was none. She estimated that fifteen minutes had passed since Alkis had left. She needed to move, there was no way of knowing when Alkis would return. She needed to boost her energy levels, then she spied a small fridge on the end of the workbench. Hopefully, it had snacks and refreshments for the men when they worked down here. She grimaced as she made her way towards the fridge, something caught her eye, something that appeared black in the gloom. It looked like a bag, a woman's bag. It was her bag; they must have thrown it under the workbench when they brought her into the workshop. Gitta punched the air with delight and then frowned when a stabbing pain emanated from her injured side.

She was happy because she always carried amphetamines in her bag and they would give her the stimulus she needed to escape from the villa. She opened her bag and breathed a sigh of relief. Not only were the amphetamines in the bag but so were two bananas, and amazingly her COP Magnum Derringer, that had two barrels, one round in each. But that was more than enough for protection at close quarters. Gitta scoffed the bananas, then opened the fridge, spied the bottle of cold water, and used the water to wash down a couple of amphetamines as well as quench her thirst.

Gitta was ready, well almost, she suddenly realised that all she was wearing was skimpy underwear. Still, she thought, it wasn't cold and besides some bikinis showed more skin than her underwear. The small meal and pills she had just consumed were now taking effect and she felt much stronger now. Treading very carefully in her still bare and blooded feet, gun in her right hand, she opened the door to the basement workshop and peered out. The corridor leading to the stairs was deserted so Gitta was able to ascend the stairs without fear of being seen. As she approached the top of the stairs voices could be heard coming from an open doorway just off to the left. She figured that it wouldn't be Eckersley's big bodyguard, he would be in the villa with Eckersley. They were probably guards, and they were almost certainly armed so it might be prudent to avoid a confrontation. Gitta reached the top of the stairs and looked around. She could see bunkbeds in the room from where the voices came from. Must be a bedroom, she thought. There were another two doors further along the corridor which were of no interest to Gitta as she needed the front door. She looked to the right, scanning the room, her gun following her gaze across the room. It was a kitchen which thankfully was empty and the front door she desired was on the other side.

One minute later Gitta was out in the night air, a light warm breeze tugging at her dishevelled hair. On the other side of a small orchard of fruit trees the swimming pool was ablaze with illuminations. Gitta peered through the trees to see if anyone was sitting by the pool. Nobody was about, probably all in bed at this time she thought, allowing herself a wry smile through her pain. How she wished she could be tucked up in her own bed or even nicer in Alex's bed back at the Four Seasons Hotel.

Gitta spent the next ten minutes navigating her way in the darkness through the villa's grounds towards the front gate. The back gate would have been nearer but she was afraid that at this time of night it would be locked up and she was in no fit state to scale it tonight. The front gate was well lit as were the parking bays just inside the grounds. Gitta kept in the shadows as she searched for the sign of any guard on duty. She spotted a spiral of smoke coming from behind the only car that was in the parking bays. The guard must be smoking out of sight behind the car. Gitta crept forward, her Deringer in her right hand, finger caressing the trigger. She'd have to get close, in order to muffle the sound of a shot, if she needed to shoot him, the barrel of the gun had to be against the guards clothing. There was no other way, she was too weak for hand to hand combat. She crept on.

The guard never heard her coming, the first thing he knew was the feel of a gun muzzle against his back.

'Don't make a sound or this bullet will shatter your spine,' Gitta hissed, pressing the gun harder into the guards clothing. The guard stiffened, then froze. Gitta could see that he wasn't holding a weapon.

'Spread your legs and put your arms straight up,' she ordered. The guard did as he was told, then with her left hand Gitta frisked him the best she could. He didn't seem to have a weapon.

'Lie down on your front and put your hands behind your back,' whispered Gitta with as much authority as she could. The guard did as he was told. Gitta sat astride him, retrieved a plastic tie from her bag and slipped it around his wrists and pulled it tight. Good old Chris, she thought, it was a tip he had taught her. Always carry plastic ties in your bag he had said, they will come in handy if you need to subdue someone. She looked around for something to gag the guard, anything would do, an old rag perhaps. She spotted just that on a small workbench which had several cans of motor oil and other vehicle maintenance accessories on it, including some duct tape. Much better than an oily rag she thought.

After gagging the guard with the tape, she exited the villa grounds and started walking towards Edessa. It wasn't far, roughly eight kilometres she remembered. She just needed to watch out for oncoming headlights in case it was Alkis returning from his errand. She was glad that there was no moon tonight, she would be less visible to straying eyes. Of course, if she saw headlights, she would leave the road and go into the olive trees and stay hidden until the vehicle has passed.

Even though there was no moon, from high above, she had been watched for the last ten minutes by the drone which Kaliope had deployed earlier that morning to watch Eckersley's villa. Unknown to Gitta, it had been transmitting pictures in real time of her progress to the drone pilots, and they had forward them to Kaliope's smart phone. She had alerted Alex, Yannis and Chris, who were still at Spiros Emmanuel's villa, cleaning up, and they had immediately taken Yannis's black utility vehicle and were at this moment speeding towards Eckersley's villa.

Alkis, who was also heading towards the villa was not speeding. He was a couple of kilometres from the villa when he noticed the headlights of a speeding vehicle about half a kilometre behind him and catching him fast. In the closing UV Yannis recognised

Eckersley's Mercedes and realised that it wasn't Eckersley who was driving. He took an executive decision and before Chris and Alex had realised what was happening, the UV instead of passing the Mercedes, rammed into the back of it, causing it to jump forward and Alkis to lose control.

The Mercedes twisting like a snake as Alkis tried to bring it under control, left the road, miraculously avoiding the first few olive trees before hitting a fairly sturdy one head on. There was the sound of tearing metal and breaking glass, then the slow hissing of a hot engine cooling down. Yannis managed to bring the UV to a stop a hundred metres from where he had rammed the Mercedes, and as soon as he had stopped, they all piled out of the UV and ran towards the crash site. Yannis was the fittest so he was first on the scene. He headed for the driver's door which was open but hanging on one hinge. He peered into the car; it was empty, Alkis was nowhere to be seen.

'Unless we get a search party out here there is no way just the three of us can find him,' declared Yannis.

'Agreed,' said Chris. 'Even the drone could not find him through the trees.'

'Wait a minute, I thought drones had heatseeking software,' said Alex.

'You know....' Yannis stopped in mid-sentence and put his finger to his lips. Then he drew his gun and motioned to the others to move behind the car. He had seen a movement behind Alex further into the trees. Moving gingerly trying to be as quiet as possible Yannis moved towards the shadowy figure, holding his gun with both hands, his left hand clasping his right wrist steadying his gun hand.

'Yannis, is that you,' cried a female voice. Yannis recognising it was Gitta shouting, holstered his gun and ran towards her. On reaching her he gathered her in his arms and kissed her long and hard on her lips.

'I was so afraid I'd lost you,' he managed to say in between kisses. 'I missed you so much.'

All thoughts of trying to catch Alkis went out of their heads now that they had found Gitta and they returned to the UV intent on getting Gitta back to the Four Seasons Hotel as fast as possible.

Fifteen minutes later, a fuming Alkis walked through the front gates of the villa, immediately heading for the basement of the staff's house.

'The bitch is going to pay for tonight,' muttered Alkis. Little realising that Gitta had flown the coup.

Chapter 25

18th August 2013 – North Macedonian Farmhouse – 07:00

Aliki Traka struggled to wake up. It was cold in the farmhouse, there were draughts everywhere. Broken windows, holes in the roof and walls, many places where chilly air might enter. It might be hot during the day but at night, out of the blazing sun, the temperature dropped quite significantly in the early morning. She hadn't slept at all well during the night, not because she was afraid but because she had been recalling the last time she had been taken hostage by a foreign power. It was in January 1943, during the German occupation of Greece.

Aliki, who was now eighty-four years of age and by far the oldest cabinet minister ever to sit in a Greek Government, was the youngest of three siblings. She was born in 1925, her elder sister, Voula, in 1923, and her elder brother, Nikos, in 1918. The suburb of Athens where Aliki grew up was one of the most fashionable and expensive areas of the capital. Her father was a self-made man, working mainly in shipping, and was able to afford a large house to bring his family up in. Life was wonderful for Aliki and her siblings, waited upon by the two maids, schooled by tutors and attending the best school in Athens.

Then in 1939, the second world war broke out, but for a year Greece was not involved, however Aliki could sense that her parents were fearful of what might be coming in the future. Her brother was conscripted into the army aged twenty-two and posted immediately to northern Greece in the Macedonian province, near the Albanian border. On October 28th, 1940, the Italians invaded through Albania. The Greek army fought hard and managed to push the Italians back into Albania. Aliki's brother fought in the mountains in the deep snow, where, because of his and others inferior quality footwear he got frostbite and lost two toes. The Greek army's courageous feat in pushing the Italians back, annoyed the German hierarchy and Hitler was forced to re-route his army from Yugoslavia towards Greece. So, on April 6th, 1941, the German army entered Greece and by the end of May, an overrun and exhausted Greek army surrendered.

Aliki vividly recalled the fearful look on her father's face when the Athens radio station ERT announced that they were shutting down because the Germans were entering Athens from the north. Four hours later she discovered why her father looked fearful. It was siesta time, the hours between two o'clock and four o'clock in the afternoon when Greeks slept off their lunches.

There was a sudden loud banging on the front door of the house. Her father took his time answering the door even though he knew that delay would annoy the Nazis whom he was sure were the ones knocking his door down. Aliki, Voula, Nicki and their mother ran to the landing wooden guardrail, which overlooked the front hall of the house, just before the front door was opened.

'Michaelis, please be careful,' shouted Hero his wife. 'Do whatever they say.'

As Michaelis opened the door Aliki could feel her heart pounding in her chest. She watched as her father just stood there looking at the three Nazi officers standing in the porch.

One of them stepped forward, gave a Nazi salute 'Heil Hitler,' he shouted, giving my father a full on glare. Aliki's father didn't move but just kept staring at the three Nazis.

'My name is Major Deiter Meyer,' said the saluting officer in broken Greek. 'May we come in please?' Then without waiting for a reply he brushed past Aliki's father followed by the other two officers. 'Thank you, these gentlemen are my fellow officers Captain

Fischer and Captain Muller,' he said pointing in turn at the two other men.

The three men took their time in looking around the front hall, noting the number of rooms, the stairs, and the three faces staring down at them from the landing rail.

'Come down please,' said the major in broken Greek. 'We will not hurt you.' Then turning to Aliki's father he asked, 'Is this all your family?'

'My son is at the university studying to be a lawyer.'

'Was he a soldier in the Greek army?' questioned the major.

Aliki's father hesitated for a second, then proudly stood straight and replied, 'Yes of course, he is an officer in the Greek army and a patriot.'

The major stared at Aliki's father who did not flinch or avoid the major's eyes. The major started a slow clap then indicated to his two captains to do the same. 'Bravo,' said the major. 'You are a proud and brave man.'

By now he had an audience of Voula, Aliki and Hero, who all had descended from the upstairs floor.

'This is a lovely house,' said the major. 'And it is ideal for our needs as we need an HQ in the northern suburbs of Athens, so I'm afraid we are going to confiscate the house and you will have to find alternative accommodation. You can only take your personal possessions, nothing else. You have forty-eight hours to comply,' he said a sanctimonious smile on his face.

Aliki's father spent the next two days searching for a home as near to the sea as possible and as far from the centre of Athens as possible without leaving Athens itself. He also had to look for a school for Aliki and Voula. Voula was in her last year and Aliki had two more years to go. They had been attending Arsakion School in Athens, one of the best private schools. Unfortunately, the Germans took the school over to use it for the overall command centre of Greece and the Greek islands.

Forty-eight hours later the family was settling into a rental property in a suburb called Paleon Phaleron. The house was much smaller than their house in Psychiko but at least it was only a few hundred yards from the shore. A suitable school had been found but as the Greek summer term finished in early June both Voula and Aliki only had a few days to go before the summer break.

The next day the whole family had to register at the local police station giving detailed information including family roots. Each police officer was shadowed by a German officer who processed the information and sent it to the German Command Centre in Athens. The Germans, who Aliki's father was relieved to see were not Nazi's, were billeted in a local hotel which had a small dance floor in its outside restaurant area, and they invariably asked local girls to join them in the restaurant. There was nothing sinister about their invitations it was just a time of relaxation with tasty food and Greek bouzouki music.

Because Aliki and her sister Voula were both exceptionally beautiful they were approached several times to attend the dances at the hotel. Aliki's father encouraged them to attend, telling them to keep their ears and eyes open and report back to the resistance anything they heard of importance. One of the officers whose name was Major Jurgen Schneider, a typical good-looking blonde, blue eyed Arian, had taken a liking to Aliki and had encouraged her to accept food offerings such as eggs and bread. Under the occupation food for the Greeks was scarce and what was available was very expensive. Aliki's father was selling valuables and carpets for a few eggs or a loaf of bread at a time. So, the meagre food that was on offer was gratefully accepted by Aliki and her family.

Once Jurgen had fully trusted her he used her as a food runner, and she used her bicycle to transport food to other army bases or the German Command Centre. Aliki felt embarrassed because she knew that he was in love with her and she could not reciprocate the emotion, but also because she began to steal food from the parcels and drop the food off at the nearest resistance safe house on her route. She knew she was playing a dangerous game and love her or not she was sure that Jurgen because of his fear of the Nazis, would turn her over to the them if he ever caught her taking food. Her parents too knew what she was doing and were growing increasingly fearful that as she took more and more food someone would notice and she would be caught.

Her luck held however until the middle of the January 1943; then it ran out. It was a very cold evening after the snow of the previous day and she had picked up two bags of food from Jurgen, which as usual she put in the two paniers on her bike. On her way to the German Command Centre she stopped and looked to see what food she was carrying. It consisted of the usual eggs, some fruit, some bread, and quite unusually, five fresh fish, Barbouni. Aliki stared at the fish, she had not had fish for eighteen months, for although they were living near the sea, the local fisherman had been forbidden by the Nazis to sell their catches to anyone but the occupying forces.

Aliki could not resist it; she took two fish, some bread and put them in her shopping bag. At the Command Centre as was the usual procedure a Nazis lieutenant emptied the paniers.

'Anything to return?' asked Aliki.

'Wait, while I check.'

The lieutenant disappeared inside the building then appeared again just as another two soldiers holding a young woman between them exited the building and roughly threw the woman onto the ground. Aliki could see that the woman had been badly beaten and she shuddered inwardly.

'What happened to her?' asked Aliki.

'Nothing, you may go,' said the lieutenant. Then as an afterthought he said. 'She is a food runner like you. That's what happens if you try to cheat on the Third Reich.'

Aliki's instinct was to help the woman if she could but she knew that they would forcibly stop her from helping her. She mounted her cycle and headed towards Syngrou Avenue and home. She had not gone more than a couple of kilometres before a grey military car screeched to a halt in front of her bike. Two Nazi officers jumped out of the back and before she had realised what was happening she found herself in the back seat of the vehicle squashed between the two officers. One of them had her shopping bag on his lap and neither of them said a word to her.

She thought of the young woman she had seen a few minutes before and her heart seemed to plummet into the pit of her stomach. There was no heating in the car and a cold tremor ran through her body but she wasn't sure if it was the cold or the thought of what they might do to her. The two officers and driver wore greatcoats and were obviously oblivious to the cold. The car drew up at the Command Centre and the two officers escorted her into the building, taking her to the office of Major Deiter Meyer.

He recognized her at once even though it had been almost two years since he had thrown her family out of their house.

'Well, well, well, what do we have here?' Meyer said, as he eyed her up and down. 'You're the young lady of the family whose house we commandeered for our HQ in northern Athens aren't you?'

'Yes,' mumbled Aliki. She disliked this man intensely. He had a hooked nose which made him look like a bird of prey especially the way he stared at her through his paper-thin framed glasses.

'Speak up woman,' commanded Meyer irritatingly.

'Yes,' said Aliki more loudly this time.

Meyer turned to the two officers who had brought Aliki to him. 'What has she done?' he asked.

'The food parcel she brought here was supposed to contain five fish but it only had three. When we searched her shopping basket we found two fish in it,' explained one of the officers.

Meyer smiled at Aliki but the smile wasn't matching his eyes which were ice cold. 'You Greeks are not at all grateful to us for letting you live in relative freedom. How do you show your appreciation? I'll tell you how, by stealing from us, or blowing up a bridge here and there, or just plain obstruction of our duties. Which billet has she come from?' he asked one of the officers.

'Paleon Phaleron, major.'

'Put this woman in a cell and in the morning call the army base in Paleon Phaleron and tell whoever is in charge of food parcel distribution that I want to see them.'

Aliki was taken away and locked in room that was sparsely furnished with just a bed and a table and chair. She realised she had been lucky that the Command Centre had been a school and not a police station. The room was luxurious compared to a jail cell. Perhaps not that lucky she thought, after realising there was no heating, the bed had one thin blanket for warmth, and there was a draught roaring through the split wooden frame of its solitary window. She slept fitfully through the night; her feet and hands numb with cold. No amount of rubbing would keep the blood circulating in her extremities. She was frightened and anxious at the same time that her parents would be frantic with worry, not knowing where she was or what had happened to her.

Finally, at seven o'clock in the morning, her door was unlocked and a soldier brought in a bowl of cold water, a dirty flannel, and a tissue thin light blue towel, for her to wash with. An hour later Major Meyer walked into the room with Jurgen Schneider.

'Good morning Aliki,' said Jurgen. 'It seems there has been a misunderstanding,' he continued apologetically. 'The major's officers' have been a little overzealous with their accusations. I explained to them that in return for your excellent work ethic running the food parcels around Athens I occasionally reward you with a fish or two, maybe some eggs or a loaf of bread.'

'You are far too generous,' commented Meyer with a quizzical look on his face. It was obvious he did not believe a word of what Jurgen had said. He couldn't do anything about it though as he and Jurgen were the same rank. Turning to Aliki he said, 'You can go with Major Schneider.' He had no intention of apologising to her or to him.

'Heil Hitler!' Meyer said with enthusiasm, clicking his heels and extending his right arm in the Nazi salute.

'Very good,' said Jurgen. Then taking Aliki by the arm he ushered her out of the room.

Later, in his car on the way back to Paleon Phaleron he gently admonished Aliki saying. 'We were lucky this time but maybe next time we won't be. You are fortunate that I hate the Nazis probably as much as you do. Major Meyer is no fool and he could have, if inclined, made it more difficult for me. From now on if you and your family need more food don't take it, ask me for more. Promise me you'll do that?'

I promise,' said Aliki, pressing herself further into the seat feeling the warmth of the car heater lulling her to sleep.

Aliki's reverie was suddenly interrupted by one of mercenaries shouting for the UN delegation hostages, to line up and collect their breakfast; a Greek coffee and a small plate of olives.

Chapter 26
18th August 2013 – Salonika – 10:30

The battered eight year-old dark blue VW Golf parked on Avenue Sophias, one hundred metres from the White Tower in Salonika became an object of interest at precisely ten-thirty hours on the 18th August 2013. The drone that had been deployed on the Home Secretary's orders, to comb the area around the White Tower for any suspicious activity. They had earlier flagged the car, together with another fifteen vehicles, because they had been stationary for over an hour, quite legally, on a major thoroughfare. Undercover EKAM officers had been sent to investigate all sixteen vehicles, while the drone used its infrared technology to scan the cars for heat signatures of humans and metallic objects.

In one of the cars the undercover officers found a couple having sex on the back seat of their car, another two cars had their owners curled up on the back seat fast asleep, three cars were stolen, and the rest, except for the battered VW, were empty waiting for their owners to return. Inside the VW were two men, one in the driver's seat and the other in the back. Both men who were ex-mercenaries, had been hired by the Salonika representatives of the Golden Dawn to blow up the White Tower, one of Salonika's and Macedonia's iconic landmarks.

The back seat of the VW had a metre square piece cut out of it and protruding through that gap was the business end of two RPG's. The drone using its infrared technology had picked up the signature of the RPG's at ten-thirty precisely. At ten-thirty-two the swarthiest of the two men reached into the hole in the seat and took hold of one of the RPGs, with his grubby hands and broken fingernails that had long since forgotten what a manicure was and passed it to the driver in the front seat. An RPG is almost two metres long so manoeuvring it within a car was not easy. He then pulled the other RPG out and lay it across his lap. It just about fit between the two rear doors.

'How the fuck are we going to aim and fire these things from inside the car?' swore the man in the back.

'I'm going to get us so near that you won't need to aim. It's a big target you know,' said the driver in his distinctive accent from the Mani region of Greece.

'We'd better rock 'n' roll then, there are wankers out there who keep on talking to their watches,' said grubby hands.

The VW moved into Avenue Sophias at precisely ten thirty-five the exact same time as Kaliope gave the go ahead for an assault on the VW. She prefaced the go ahead order with the word 'Celsius' which meant 'no prisoners.' On hearing that word, the rear doors of a van marked Salonika Plumbing, opened and an EKAM plain clothes operative holding an RPG appeared in the doorway.

The rocket was on its way towards the rear of the VW before the driver could react. The last thing he did was an involuntary pull of the trigger on his own RPG whose rocket hit the passenger door at the same instance as the rocket from the EKAM RPG hit the fuel tank. The resulting explosion vapourised the VW's driver and grubby hands, leaving the car itself as a twisted pile of metal.

When Eckersley heard what had happened in Salonika, he became terribly angry. He called Dimitri Karagianis the president of the Golden Dawn party.

'Dimitri! What the hell is happening? Things have not been going well lately. Talk to me!' he shouted down the phone as he marched up and down his office.

'Calm down Arthur, said Dimitri. 'The technology that the Yanks have given to Greece is being made excellent use of. They use their drones to good effect and their intelligence network is unfortunately too good. But, you haven't had it all your way up there either have you? Failing to kill the Business Minister, letting the woman agent slip through your fingers and failing to get rid of the Home Secretary.'

'At least I have a big card left to me, in that I'm holding hostages over the border and have a mercenary army that could be in Edessa and take over the Aluminium mines within hours,' boasted Eckersley.'

'The people were starting to lose faith in the Kalfas Government after the bombing in Athens and the destruction of the Alexander the Great statue in Salonika. The Golden Dawn party was benefiting from the mistrust for a while but the foiling of the White Tower attack could have started a reverse in sentiment. We need something big to hurt the Government,' said Karagianis as he paused for thought.

After several seconds he continued, 'What you are suggesting wouldn't work or lead to the public sentiment hardening against the Kalfas Government. The drone technology the Government possesses would destroy your mercenary army before it could advance two kilometres into Greek territory. We need something which would convince the public that the Government is not in control.'

'Such as?' queried Eckersley in exasperation at the negative vibes coming from Karagianis.

'Use the hostages as an umbrella,' suggested Karagianis. 'They wouldn't dare use the drones on your army if you did that.'

Eckersley liked that idea but he wasn't going to give Karagianis the satisfaction of thinking he was excited by it. 'Would that be enough to move the public's sentiment against the Kalfas Government?'

'Perhaps, but I think we need something more, something that the public would absolutely get off their feet and protest in the streets about.'

'Who do you know in the media world?' asked Eckersley.

Karagianis thought for a moment. 'There are several editors who would do me a favour for the right price. Why? What are you thinking?'

'What if the press ran with a story accusing the Government of being on the verge of recognising the name North Macedonia and willing to pull their veto of them joining the EU?'

'Brilliant!' exclaimed Karagianis a broad smile lighting up his face. 'I'll make sure that the story is on the front page of at least two papers tomorrow morning.'

'Make sure we have at least one broad sheet and not all tabloids. It has to look like a genuine story that sticks in the public's perception,' said Eckersley.

'Don't worry I know what's needed,' said Karagianis, feeling a little peeved that Eckersley didn't trust him to do it properly. Eckersley sensed that, and afraid that he would lose the only ally he had in Greece said, 'Look Dimitri I appreciate everything that you are doing to further my and your ambitions. I look forward to reading tomorrow's papers. Enjoy the rest of your day.'

As soon as the connection was cut Karagianis keyed in an international number.

'Yes,' said a male voice with a distinct American drawl.

'How soon can you get to Athens?'

'I could catch a Lufthansa flight out of Berlin and be there around sunset.'

'You are in Europe already?'

'I'm always prepared for sudden changes of plan, it's all part of the service,' said the man with pride in his voice. '

'You're booked into The Grande Brittania hotel on Syntagma Square in the name of Carter, James Carter. Your requested tools will be in your room.'

'I think I have a passport in that name,' said the man with a chuckle. 'I'll let you know when I've checked in.'

'Have a safe flight,' said Karagianis and cut the connection.

The man in Berlin unlocked the safe in his hotel room and picked out five passports. He sorted through them till he found the one with the name James Carter. He then called down to reception.

'Reception, how can I help you Mr Donovan?' said a gushing female voice.

'I'm checking out, please get me a cab to the airport.'

Yes sir, Mr Donovan, right away.'

Chapter 27
18th August 2013 – Athens – 19:30

Earlier that day Alex, Leonidas, Chris, Gitta and Yannis had flown from Edessa to Athens. They were now in the cabinet room of the Megaro Maximo, the Prime Minister's office, and residence, waiting for Kaliope, who earlier that day had flown to Salonika to thank the local police, and EKAM officers, for a successful operation against the men planning to destroy Salonika's White Tower. Also in the room were the Finance Minister, Achilles Nikolaou, and Argi Tsibouka, the Foreign Minister.

Alex and Chris had discussed whether Gitta should join the meeting but decided against it as it might have caused to many raised eyebrows in the room. They couldn't introduce her as a CIA agent in case her cover was compromised, nor could they introduce her as Alex's lover as that would not send the right optics at all.

Alex surveyed the people around the table, whiling away the time until Kaliope turned-up. He could see why she was smitten by Yannis, just his presence oozed confidence, strong facial features, framed in a shock of black hair. Piercing blue eyes that could be both cold and hard when needed, also flirtatiously soft, a characteristic which made him so attractive to women. And, thought Alex with a pang of jealously, what women would call a fit body. But then Alex never had been one for serious gym work, anyway he had come to like his slight paunch, especially after Gitta had told him that she thought it sexy.

The door burst open cutting short Alex's musings, as Kaliope almost ran into the cabinet room, flushed from her exertions of running up the stairs.

'So sorry Prime Minister,' she said excitedly, her face a bloom of colour. 'We've managed to arrest three men just before they initiated an attack on the Alexander the Great statue here in Athens.'

'Well done Kaliope,' enthused Alex. 'I don't think the public could take another national icon being destroyed.'

'Thank you, but we can't be complacent, there might be another target that we don't know about,' said Kaliope.

'I agree with Kaliope,' said Yannis, offering Kaliope a broad smile which evidenced his feelings for her.

'The chatter on the internet is quite intense in Greece, implying that something is afoot but as yet we haven't managed to make any sense of it,' added Kaliope.

'Keep up the good work,' praised Alex. 'Now I should explain why we have a stranger to some of you at our meeting today. Of course I'm referring to Chris Horsman. He is CIA station chief here in Greece, working for the American Government and under the agreement which our Government made with the Americans in 2010 he is helping to ensure our international and domestic security is not compromised. Without him we would never have found out that Eckersley poses a great danger to our country. I hope you all are happy with the arrangement and his presence here?'

Alex looked around the table as each person signalled either with a thumbs-up or a nod that they had no problem.

'Good, now let's move on. Argi what are the vibes from our allies regarding the hostage situation?' asked Alex, directing his gaze towards her.

Argi characteristically gathered her thoughts as she usually did before replying to questions. 'I spoke with the UN Secretary General earlier today about the hostage situation and he was very keen that we left it to the UN to find a solution. Apparently they are negotiating with North Macedonia for the hostages release which is a little bizarre as the mercenaries holding the hostages are claiming to be a group called MNM, Macedonia for North Macedonia.'

'That's ridiculous,' exclaimed Alex. 'How on earth could they believe the MNM is a North Macedonian group?'

'They don't, but there is no one else they can negotiate with,' said Argi. 'Besides they are afraid that we might take unilateral action ourselves if there were no negotiations taking place.'

'I might decide to do just that,' admitted Alex.

'Hold on a minute Prime Minister, we can't endanger the hostages. Besides, we have no concrete evidence that it is Eckersley behind this,' pointed out Chris.

'What about Gitta's kidnapping?' asked Achilles. 'Surely that's enough evidence?'

'Are you worried that we are consuming too much of the public's money on this case?' asked Alex. 'How much have we spent so far?'

Achilles stopped shuffling his papers around and then proceeded to hand out one sheet to each person around the table.

'Thank you, you've certainly come prepared,' approved Alex as he started reading the numbers on the page. 'Why don't you run us through these Achilles?'

'Sure thing. Well as you can see the money we had set aside to cover security contingencies has been all but spent. The drones are very expensive to use and have utilized the bulk of the budget,' explained Achilles.

'Well you'll have to ringfence some more funds Achilles because drones are the only defence we have against terrorists,' said Alex. 'And in answer to your question about proof, we only have Gitta's word against Eckersley's word; so far we only have circumstantial evidence which won't stand up in court.'

'Why don't you,' said Alex addressing Chris, 'take Yannis, Kaliope, Leonidas and Argi into the meeting room next door and brainstorm a next steps' strategy. Meanwhile, I'll go over the budget with Achilles ready for his spending round in two weeks.'

After they had left Alex got up to get a cup of coffee from the espresso machine. He stood at the picture window which faced the National Park and the rear of the parliament building. He could see in the distance the top floors of the five star hotels which were a feature of the north side of Syntagma Square. A square which, although he could not see it because it was obscured by the trees of the national gardens, he imagined at this time of the evening, it would be teeming with tourists and Greek families, out for an evening meal.

I should see how Gitta is, he thought to himself. He had been worried about her ever since she had escaped from Eckersley's villa. She had not recovered that composed, confident persona that he loved about her and since her escape she had not allowed him to touch her. It was as if she was ashamed of her scars. He looked at his watch, it was half-past nine. He should head up to his personal quarters and see how she was. He took one last look over the trees towards Syntagma Square.

At the moment that Alex was looking out towards Syntagma Square, the man now called Donovan was looking through the high powered telescope sight of the Accuracy International rifle, which lay disassembled on his bed. To Donovan it appeared as if Alex was staring directly at him. But of course that was just an illusion. 'Tomorrow my friend,' said Donovan in a low voice. 'Tomorrow my rifle and I will introduce ourselves.' Smiling to himself Donovan swung the sight around until he was looking into a room at the Astra Hotel on the opposite side of the square, a couple of floors below the level he was on. Nothing exciting there; he panned to the room next door. A young couple were unpacking, no doubt excited at the prospect of a vacation in the unique sunlight of Greece and a chance to swim in the warm Mediterranean waters. Hmm, I like her underwear thought Donovan as the woman produced several colourful thongs from her case. She had a good body but perhaps a little too skinny for Donovan's taste. He watched just the same as she continued unpacking, finally producing the biggest rabbit he had ever seen.

Just at that moment there was a knock at Donovan's door. Reluctantly he put down the scope and with a few long strides reached the door and peered through the eyehole in the centre of the door. A woman stood outside. A rather striking one at that, long dark shoulder length hair mirroring a friendly face with soft brown eyes, a pert nose, and full lips, which were smiling, showing an array of even teeth. Donovan had never seen her before. As ever always on the alert he picked up his Glock from the hat stand beside the door. 'Who is it?' he asked.

'My name is Conchita,' said the woman. 'Mr Karagiannis sent me to welcome you to Greece and to make sure you have everything you need.'

Donovan opened the door and indicated, with a flourish of his left arm, that she should enter. He watched her as she walked passed him, a slight lazy swaying of her hips. She was wearing a white T-shirt, a pair of black shorts, which showed off her lightly tanned legs, and open sandals. Her shoulder bag swayed in time to her hips. She turned around to face Donovan, slipping the bag from her shoulder and reaching for the fastening. In two long strides Donovan had clamped his hand around hers, stopping her from opening the bag.

'Drop the bag,' he commanded.

Not showing any fear Conchita took one step back and calmly said, 'I have a letter from Karagiannis to give you, not a bomb or a gun, although I do have a gun here.' Before Donovan could move a muscle she had reached behind her back and produced a small derringer from her waistband in the small of her back.

Donovan allowed a slow grin to develop on his face as he said, 'You're fast, one of the fastest I've seen.' Before Conchita could respond his left hand had shot forward grabbing the gun and at the same time sliding one of his fingers between the trigger and the back of the trigger guard so that she could not fire the gun. Simultaneously straightened his right hand which was still holding his Glock, pointing the muzzle at her forehead. 'Checkmate,' he said chuckling.

After her initial surprise Conchita allowed herself a smile and conceded that Donovan was much faster than she was. She took stock of the man as her recently released gun hand replaced the Derringer into the holster in the small of her back. He looked very fit she conceded, just over two metres in height, clean shaven, with piercing blue eyes which she could see were appraising her too. She liked his hair, no hair loss but a mane of dark grey, which he wore a little long. His age she reckoned was late forties but he wore his white chinos and black t-shirt well for his age.

She retrieved the letter from Karagianis and handed it to Donovan. His name was Irish but he certainly did not look Irish, too swarthy. More middle eastern, perhaps Israeli. She wasn't far wrong as the name on Donovan's birth-certificate was Moshe. He was Israeli and had served in the Mossad until five years ago when he decided to drop out of sight, contracting himself out as an assassin. He was now the most sought after wet man in the world, with a kill rate of ninety-five percent.

Donovan read the letter; his eyebrows raising when he got to the bit confirming that the mark was the PM. Then with a shrug of the shoulders he placed the letter in an ashtray, picked up the table lighter next to it and set light to the letter. Both of them watched it burn until the paper was just blackened ashes.

'Where did you learn to shoot?' asked Donovan. 'And be so cool under pressure?' he added.

'I was a member of EKAM the anti-terrorist arm of the police here,' replied Conchita. She looked over to the bed eying the components of what was obviously a rifle. 'I know something about rifles too. That is an Accuracy International with a .338 bore, bolt action and moderated. How far are you going to shoot with that thing?'

'Very good,' said Donovan smiling and putting on the charm. 'If you had said that it had a silencer I would not have believed that you know guns. But the use of the professionals' word, *moderator* instead of silencer tells me that you do know your guns. Why the word silencer is ever used beats me. A gun emitting a low phut sound is not silenced.'

'I told you so,' said Conchita. 'So you can put the gun away now please.' She pointed at his Glock still in his right hand.

'How do I know that you are not undercover for EKAM? You said you worked with them?'

'I had the letter from Karagianis which he asked me to give to you and which you have just burned in that ashtray,' Conchita said pointing at the guilty receptacle.

'There are any number of ways you could have got hold of that letter and besides the letter made no mention of you.'

'Call him then! He will vouch for me.'

'I aim to,' conceded Donovan. 'Listen, I'm sorry that I'm being such a pain but I have many enemies because of what I do. Governments, police, and security services all want a piece of me. I'm impressed with your knowledge of firearms, your reaction speed and coolness under duress. But, I can't trust you until I have confirmation that you are Karagianis's envoy.'

'I'll call him and you can talk to him,' said Conchita.

'Yes but tell him to come here. I want to see him in person.'

Conchita did as she was told and Karagianis agreed to come to the Grand Brittania Hotel where they would meet in the bar in one hour. Fit, good looking, no stet that, more like sexy looking, thought Conchita, and charming too. How can I impress him even more? Yes, that's it, she thought.

'I'll put that together in no time,' she boasted pointing at the disassembled rifle on the bed. And you didn't answer my question about how far.'

Donovan chuckled at her persistence. 'When I am satisfied that I can turn my back on you without fearing a bullet or a knife between my shoulder blades,' he said. 'Let's go down to the bar I'm dying for a drink,' he said, putting the Glock into his waistband before slipping on a jacket.

Chapter 28

18th August 2013 – Athens – 21:30

Alex knocked softly on the door of his and Gitta's bedroom in the Prime Minister's suite in the Megaro Maximo. He did not want to wake her if she was sleeping. There was no answer, so he opened the door quietly, and seeing Gitta safely tucked up in bed, he breathed a sigh of relief that she was safe. Walking over to her bedside he marvelled at how shallow her breathing was when she slept. Sometimes he really had to concentrate to spot her chest rising and falling with her breathing. Tonight he felt himself welling up with love and happiness as he gazed down at her.

His mobile phone began chirping and he quickly hit the green call button so that the sound would not wake Gitta.

'Yes?' he said quietly into the phone.

'Alex, it's your friend Stavros.'

'Hello Stavros, for what do I owe this pleasure?' Stavros was the editor of the daily broadsheet Hellenic News, the newspaper that the Greek Government invariably used as a conduit for its leaked sound bites.

'Alex, we have been friends since our university days haven't we?'

Alex frowned wondering what was coming. 'Yes my friend,' he said.

'Then why have you leaked the Macedonia story to the tabloids?'

'What are you talking about Stavros? My Government hasn't leaked anything,' declared Alex. 'I am loyal to those who have been loyal to me and you are a dear friend too. Which tabloids are we talking about?'

'The two right wing newspapers The Freedom Times and Democracy,' said Stavros. 'They are reporting that you have come to an agreement with North Macedonia to uphold their claim for

Pella in central Macedonia where Edessa and the Bauxite Mines are situated.'

'And the birthplace of Alexander the Great. What utter bullshit!' exclaimed Alex visibly shaking with rage. Luckily for Gitta, Alex had stepped out of the bedroom so Gitta would not hear him. 'You have to believe me Stavros I would never sell Greece out like that.' Alex put a hand to his forehead as he felt the beads of sweat dripping onto the front of his shirt. Anger does make your blood boil he mused.

'I know Alex,' said Stavros, but where did the story come from and if as you say it's a complete fabrication, a lot of arm twisting must have gone on to enable those headlines to be printed.'

Alex stood in the hallway, his mind racing, trying not only to take in what Stavros had told him but also figure out the implications to him, to his Government and to the people, when the story is published in the morning.

'Alex! Alex!' said Stavros in a raised voice.

'I'm thinking, sorry Stavros. I suppose there is no way we can stop them from printing?' asked Alex.

'It's too late in the day for an injunction, there is no way your lawyers could get the papers ready and to a judge before the presses start to roll. I would start thinking about your response and through what media channels you will give it. A written statement of denial in my newspaper would not be enough.'

'You're right,' agreed Alex. 'But it has to be refuted quickly, at least by tomorrow evening at the latest, don't you think?'

'Yes I do. You'll need evidence too.'

'We have plenty, don't worry. Leave it to me and thanks Stavros for the heads-up. I'll talk to you tomorrow.'

After cutting the connection Alex returned to the bedroom. Seeing that Gitta was still sleeping, he hastily wrote a note explaining that he was in the meeting room with the others. He then hurried to the meeting room keen to let the team know what was being published in the papers next morning. As he entered the room he could immediately sense that Kaliope had taken charge, as she stood at the end of the table cajoling Achilles to produce some temporary budget figures.

'Sorry Achilles,' apologised Alex. 'I had to take that call and you did right to join the others in here. Okay, listen up everyone we have another problem to find a solution to.' When he had their undivided attention he relayed the conversation he had just had with Stavros. They sat there transfixed, the expressions on their faces quickly changing from mild interest to outright astonishment. Then there was uproar as everyone started talking over each other.

'The share price of Hellenic Aluminium will plummet,' said Leonidas.

'Can't we slap a D-notice on the newspapers in question?' asked Kaliope.

'Pella, of course. That's why the Alexander The Great statues were targeted,' mused Yannis.

'Has to be Karagianis and the Golden Dawn,' mused Chris.

'My god, the international community will think we have gone mad,' said Argi.

Can't we stop them?' said Achilles.

Alex held up his hands towards them.

'Stop!' he shouted. 'One at a time please. Let's all get back to the cabinet room and discuss this. There is no recording device in this room so we can't discuss official business and policy issues in here.'

When they were all seated in the cabinet room and the audio and video recorders woken from sleep mode by the sound of their voices, Alex opened the discussion.

'We have to mitigate any damage to the Government that could come out from their poisonous lies. And, before you ask, we can't stop publication because the presses have been running for a good few hours now and to stop distribution would be impossible. Until we can refute their story with solid evidence we will be taking a lot of flak, not only domestically but also internationally.' Alex stopped talking and looked around the table. He could see that he had their undivided attention. Alex continued.

'I know we are all exhausted, it's been a long day, but we need to have formulated a strategy by midnight, because just after that, the newspapers will begin appearing on the news grills of the night kiosks in the major cities and towns. But before we discuss the newspaper article issue tell me what you guys have come up with regarding getting the UN delegation back safely.'

They looked around at each other, no one willing to jump in and take the lead, until Chris took the bull by the horns and said, 'Kaliope you take the floor.'

'Thank you Chris,' said Kaliope. 'So, what we have concluded is that it would be difficult to draw the men out from the farm building and therefore using drones would endanger too many innocent lives. However, we could use drone technology to support a night raid on the farmhouse, using infra-red to locate the positions of the mercenaries inside.'

'How would you differentiate between the good guys and the bad guys?' asked Alex.

'We would use heat signatures to detect where the guns were. No one in the delegation is carrying, so matching a guns heat signature to an infra-red image would be simple.'

'Yannis would lead the raid,' said Chris. 'And he would take ten of his best men with him plus myself, so we would be twelve in all, half the size of their force, but we would have the element of surprise.'

'Do you need the adrenaline rush Chris?' laughed Alex.

They all laughed at Alex's remark.

Chris continued, 'It will be impossible to conduct the raid by crossing the border on foot, we have to go in by air and parachute in at night, about five kilometres behind the farmhouse. But we would need North Macedonia's radar installations knocked out for a few minutes while our plane was in their airspace.'

'Who and how?' questioned Alex.

'We thought you could talk with the American Secretary of State, Dominic Ferrara and I could smooth the way by talking to my boss at the CIA,' said Chris. 'What we want is a plane to deliver a small Electromagnetic Pulse burst to temporally knock out North Macedonia's power grid for a few minutes.'

'And that would knock out their radar too?' asked Alex.

'Yes, and any backup systems too,' said Chris.

'The UN and EU are as usual working at a snail's pace on this and won't be too happy that we pulled the rug from under their feet. We need a heavy hitter supporting us and because of Gladio we think he will approve of our plan,' said Argi.

'Good idea,' agreed Alex. 'As soon as we're finished here I'll get onto it. Now, what are we going to do about the newspaper article which is due on the kiosk newsstands in just over an hour's time?'

While they focused on the problem at hand, five hundred kilometres to the north in the region of Pella, another disaster was brewing, which by morning would headline most of the dailies, except for the two right wing tabloids.

Chapter 29

18th August 2013 – Pella Region – 23:00

Five kilometres north of the village of Roses, just one kilometre inside the tree line of the Grammaticus forest, three men were hard at work preparing incendiary devices. The weather and wind direction was perfectly aligned for what they were about to do. The extremely hot weather, which Greece had enjoyed for the last three weeks, had parched the earth, and made the pine needles on the trees, which made up the majority of the flora in the Pella, a giant tinder box.

It only needed a stray flame, a discarded match, a piece of glass or an abandoned smouldering cigarette butt, to start a dangerous fire. But, the existence of the Meltemi hot winds direct from the Sahara, blowing strongly towards the north, in the mix, had the potential for a perfect storm. This south wind would blow the flames northwards devouring and destroying everything in its path.

Alkis, the fixer, was instructing his men on where and how to deploy the incendiary devices. He had worked out that placing the devices one hundred metres apart in a three kilometre long line, and setting them off simultaneously, would create an instantaneous wall of flame travelling north at five kilometres an hour. Far too fast for the fire services to react in time to be able to control the fire.

A few hours earlier Eckersley had called Alkis into his office and told him about his idea to start a forest fire which he hoped would embarrass and damage the Kalfas Government.

'Have you calculated the possible loss of life and property?' asked Alkis.

'The property value that has the potential to be destroyed runs into the millions,' said Eckersley. 'There are twelve villages which could be destroyed and of course there is a possibility that the conflagration could reach Edessa.'

'And life?' questioned Alkis.

'What, have you suddenly got a conscious?' laughed Eckersley.

'Fuck no, I just wanted to know if you have estimated loss of life at all.'

'No, because no doubt villages will be evacuated, so loss of life is an unknown,' reasoned Eckersley. 'Take a couple of men and thirty or so incendiary devices to an area just north of Rose village. You decide on spacing etc. as you are supposed to be the explosives expert around here.

So Alkis took two men whom he trusted and they were now setting the final few devices. All the devices were blue toothed to Alkis's smart phone so that he could set them off with one button press. Alkis could see between the trees the glow of torches about a kilometre away, whose owners seemed to be getting nearer his position. He thought it a bit too early for his men to have finished, so playing safe he stood behind a tree and watched the approaching flashlights.

He soon realised that it wasn't just two people but what seemed like a family, two men, a woman, and a child. He realised that they had been hunting, as both men were carrying hunting rifles. Alkis could see that they were dangerously close to one of the incendiary devices. This was not good, he thought, if they discovered the device and they realised what it was, he couldn't let them report it to the authorities. He watched in trepidation. As he had feared the child, a young girl about ten years of age, stumble on something and shouted to her parents.

'Daddy, look what I've found,' the child shouted.

'What's that dear?' questioned the mother.

'Looks like a bomb,' screeched the girl.

The father and his male companion laughed at the girl, then they walked over to where the girl was, to appease her curiosity.

'My god!' exclaimed the father. 'It certainly looks like a small bomb. What do you think Vangelis? Weren't you something to do with bombs in the army?'

The man called Vangelis nodded, then bent down and shone his torch on the device. 'It's an incendiary device,' he said matter-of-factly.

'Hadn't we better report this?' asked the father.

'This device has a steady green light. Run!' shouted Vangelis as he realised the device could go off at any moment. 'This might blow any minute now. Let's get out of here!'

The mother grabbed her daughter's hand and started to run towards the edge of the forest. Then she stopped dead in her tracks as two shots rang out from behind a tree in front of her. She screamed and looked back at her husband and Vangelis. Both were lying on the ground writhing in agony, each one with a kneecap that seemed to have exploded, peppering the area around them with blood and bones. The mother instinctively ran towards her husband as the little girl shrieked with fear. She never reached him as Alkis's third shot passed through her neck ripping out her carotid artery. She dropped like a stone, her hands desperately trying to stem the blood flow. Before she died the last thing she saw was her daughter being slammed backwards by Alkis's fourth shot. The daughter didn't move. The mother made a feeble attempt to try and get up on her feet to get to her daughter but she had lost too much blood and the effort was her final act as her heart stopped. There was no blood to pump.

Alkis was in a hurry now, he didn't know if the shots had been heard but he wasn't taking any chances. He dragged the four bodies one by one further into the woods and lay them where once the fire started they would be consumed by it. He hoped the others were now below the line of incendiary devices out of harm's way. Alkis punched the code into his phone and it transmitted a Bluetooth signal to the device nearest to him. That in turn transmitted the signal onwards to the two devices either side of it one hundred metres away. Withing a few seconds all the devices had received the signal and they simultaneously exploded.

Alkis watched with a grin on his face as a wall of fire three kilometres wide started its inexorable march towards the north devouring everything in its path.

By the time the fire authorities had been alerted to the fire it had really taken hold and had advanced two kilometres further into the forest and had managed to become four kilometres wide.

It was to become one of the worst instances of arson in Greece's history.

Chapter 30

19th August 2013 – Mega Maximo Athens – 06:00

Alex hadn't had a good night's sleep worrying about the bad press that his Government would face in the morning. Several times he had woken Gitta with his tossing and turning. She had managed to sooth him back to sleep each time but only for him to wake up once again. Finally, she decided that it felt right to allow Alex to touch her once again since the traumatic events at the hands of Alkis in Eckersley's villa. So they had made love, tentative at first but then gradually with more passion. When their passion had been satisfied and Gitta lay in the arms of Alex, she spoke for the first time in depth about her ordeal.

Alex had been shocked at her description of what she had gone through at the hands of the monster Alkis and to a lesser extent Eckersley. He vowed that Alkis would not stand trial but instead would die as horrible a death as possible. He told Gitta what he had sworn expecting she would welcome his future for Alkis; however, she said nothing. Alex fell into welcome asleep before he had any sort of response from Gitta. While he slept Gitta lay awake making plans on how she would save Alex the trouble by making sure that Alkis would stand trial, but with life changing injuries inflicted by Gitta herself in just retribution for all the pain he had caused her and the many people who had died at his hand. Just before 05.00 hours she woke Alex, made him a light breakfast, then sent him downstairs to his suite of offices, telling him that despite the seemingly insurmountable problems she was certain he and his team would overcome them.

Alex now stood in his office looking intently at the morning newspapers which were spread over his office desk in front of him, at the same time as he was reading the papers' headlines; he also had the morning news on TV. It wasn't going to be a good day.

The two right-wing papers, The Freedom Times and Democracy had not minced their words and their front page story was a damning indictment of the Greek Government betraying its promises to the people of Greece, around its stance on the ceding of Macedonia to North Macedonia. Their headlines were remarkably similar Alex noted. The Freedom Times headline read *Kalfas Betrays Our Homeland,* and Democracy's was *Kalfas Betrays The People.* Someone doesn't like me, thought Alex with a wry smile.

All the other dailies led on the hostage crisis in North Macedonia and the failure of the Greek Government and the UN to broker a deal that would release the hostages. Alex hoped that Yannis and Chris had managed to work out the logistics for a night raid and Argi, following Alex's call to the President of the United States, where he had persuaded him to allow the use of a small electromagnetic pulse bomb, had made the necessary arrangements.

He picked up *The News* and was relieved to see that his friend had, as promised published the Government's response to this allegation. Alex felt that it was a strong response which should deflect some of the dissension heading the Government's way. But, the soundbites coming from the experts being paraded across his TV screen were not what he wanted to hear. A couple of snap polls conducted by two major TV companies showed that his personal rating had dropped to under forty percent and the Government was now five percentage points behind the New Democracy party and only one percentage point in front of the Golden Dawn party.

Then, to his horror the TV station went live to Macedonia, showing the world the out of control forest fire heading northwards, driven by the Meltemi winds, and destroying everything in its path. My god! The news of the fire hadn't made the papers but now the TV news wouldn't let this go until they have something or someone to blame. In a way Alex figured, it might divert the public from the alleged Macedonia scandal. He heard the sound of animated voices coming from the cabinet room. Alex figured that it was going to be a lively session. He pressed the intercom for his secretary Maria's desk.

'Maria, would you bring these papers into the cabinet room and I don't want to be disturbed until we are finished please.'

'Yes sir,' replied Maria.

Alex walked into the cabinet room to be greeted by a cacophony of voices throwing questions at him. Kaliope was on the phone in front of a large map of Northern Greece, Yannis and Chris were in deep conversation, and Leonidas, Achilles and Argi were watching the live feeds from Macedonia. As if a switch had been closed, as soon as Alex entered the room, all conversation ceased and they took their places around the cabinet table.

'Kaliope, please fill us in on the damage wrought by the fire in Macedonia,' said Alex.

Kaliope pointed in the general direction of Macedonia on the map. 'Unfortunately, the fire is still out of control despite the best efforts of the fire services. There are over two hundred fire fighters on the ground plus five planes and two helicopters.'

'Where are the planes and helicopters getting their water from?' interrupted Alex.

'The lake.'

'What lake?'

'Lake Vegoritida to the west of Grammaticus Forest where the fire started. It is currently marching steadily north fanned by the Meltemi wind, unfortunately it is heading towards the Edessa area,' said Kaliope, pointing to the precise area on the map.

'How long before Edessa is in danger?' asked Argi.

'Current projections are ten hours. I have put all army units within fifty kilometres on standby in case we need to evacuate. Three villages have already been evacuated by fire fighters.'

'Do we know what started the fire?' asked Yannis.

'The first response, fire fighters found four bodies a kilometre in from the edge of the forest. Three of the bodies were grouped together here, a family by the look of it, husband, wife, and a female child. The initial forensics examination shows that they each died from a bullet wound, and they were dead before the fire engulfed them,' explained Kaliope.

'They must have seen more than they should have,' murmured Chris.

'Yes,' said Kaliope. 'The bullet wounds were apparently all kills which makes me think that the shooter was a professional.'

'And the fourth body,' asked Alex, 'was it shot too?'

'No, forensics believe that the man was burnt alive. He might have been one of the arsonists, as his body was found very near the remains of an incendiary device here, one of twenty that have been found so far.'

'This smacks of an Alkis operation, particularly the precise nature of the killings,' said Chris.

'I concur,' said Yannis. 'I'd like to wring that bastard's neck!'

'The share price of Hellenic Aluminium has been gapped down ten percent before the markets open,' announced Leonidas. 'Are any of the mines in the line of fire Kaliope?'

'None is in immediate danger but if the wind direction changes slightly towards the west the Vruta mine might be compromised.'

'So apart from embarrassing the Government another purpose of the fire is maybe to force the share price of Hellenic Aluminium down, enabling Eckersley to buy the company more economically,' said Alex. 'Keep me abreast of the market movements today please Leonidas, and Kaliope I would like half hour updates.'

'Right sir,' said Kaliope.

'Now Argi, your turn, is the operation planned for tonight going ahead?' asked Alex.

Argi, immaculately dressed as usual and looking fresh despite the hour, rose from her chair and walked over to the large map, pointing to the specific areas as she described the operation.

'The Americans have leased one of their troop carrier gliders to us. This will enable Yannis and his team to cross the border quietly and because of the Meltemi wind, the tow plane can release them out of earshot of the farmhouse where the hostages are being held. At precisely one o'clock tomorrow morning the electromagnetic pulse bomb will be deployed just before the scheduled release of the glider. There will be army vehicles waiting for the hostages on the Greek side of the border, out of sight until the hostages are freed.' Argi stopped while she took a mouthful of coffee. 'Yannis will command a force of twenty men including Chris, a number which Yannis assures me is more than capable of doing the job.'

'Excellent Argi,' enthused Alex. 'Some good news today at least. When are you heading up north Yannis?'

'Within the hour we shall take a flight to the Salonika air force base where we will meet up with the rest of the team. Until the operation gets underway we shall spend the day running through the logistics and constructing a back-up plan in case something goes wrong. There will be a drone in the air photographing the whole thing.'

'I'm sure nothing will go wrong Yannis. Well, good luck and I hope you, Chris and the rest of your men make a safe return. Head out whenever you want to.' Alex stood up and saluted Yannis who returned his salute, then nodded to Chris and they both left the room.

'Right next on the agenda is coffee,' declared Alex as he went over to the coffee machine by the window. They all relaxed and joined Alex by the window relieved that for a moment that the tension had left the room. As Alex poured his coffee he looked out over the National Park towards Syntagma Square where he could just make out the outlines of the hotels through the morning haze. It was going to be another scorcher today.

Even as Alex looked over the National Park, the man called Donovan was sitting in front of the open French windows leading out onto his balcony, with his rifle now sitting on a tripod in front of him. He was sighting the telescopic lens on the very window which Alex was looking out of.

Donovan and Conchita had met with Karagianis, the leader of the Golden Dawn party, the previous evening in the hotel restaurant. Donovan had relaxed the moment that Karagianis had vouched for Conchita, so he had not objected when after Karagianis had left and they were having Sambuca, she had suggested a night cap in his room.

Three hours later Donovan was lying exhausted on the floor after having been taken on a sexual adventure and heights of pleasure which he could never have imagined. The journey took him from tantric sex, through gentle love making to high energy fucking and oral sex where Conchita's suppleness was erotica itself. While Conchita was in the bathroom he went over to his bed and seeing that she had placed another shot of Sambuca on the bedside table, downed the drink in one go and sat back against the headboard. Conchita came out of the bathroom naked and standing at the foot of the bed showed off more of her suppleness. Donovan started to get hard again watching her amazing erotic show, but he was also tired, his eyes began to close against his will. Before long, the sleeping agent which Conchita had spiked his drink with, won the battle and Donovan fell fast asleep.

Conchita sprang into action, gathered her clothes which were strewn all over the room, she dressed quickly, then looked around for the ammunition which Donovan would use in the morning. At first she could not find it but then she checked the rifle itself and saw to her relief that he had already loaded the gun. She expelled the two bullets, then from the false bottom of her bag took out a tool which looked like a small clamp. She placed one of the bullets in it and turned the small handle. The clamp's surface was slightly uneven so it made some minute indentations on the surface of the cartridge, which could not be seen with the naked eye. For an accurate shot over one kilometre the surface of the bullet should be perfectly slip-streamed, now it wasn't. She did the same with the second cartridge, then reloaded both into the rifle.

Replacing the rifle where she had found it, she checked the room making sure everything was as it should be. She took his empty glass and washed it before pouring a small drop of Sambuca on the bottom, placing it on his bedside table again. You never know, she thought, he might be suspicious in the morning and get the glass tested. Conchita was feeling quite wicked and turned-on by the sight of Donovan's naked body spread-eagled on the bed. She contemplated giving him a blowjob while he slept or better still making him hard and then sitting on his penis. She relented to her lust and threw her clothes off and got to work on his manhood. Five minutes later, sweat pouring off her body she noticed Donovan's eyes flutter. She thrust even harder; she felt his hands around her waist as he helped her motion. Fully awake now, he also thrust in rhythm with Conchita, so for the fifth time that night he exploded into her as she screamed out her orgasm.

Donovan, now sitting sighting his rifle recalled those moments, but not once did the possibility of a sleeping potion cross his mind. Conchita had left, now he was a professional killer attending to his business, all thoughts of Conchita and the night banished from his mind. He lined up the rifle sight on Alex's head, the cross hairs in the middle of his forehead. Donovan took an intake of breath, then slowly squeezed the trigger.

A loud *phut* sound sounded as the .50 BMG cartridge left the barrel at a speed of over eight hundred metres per second, spinning from the spiralling grooves inside the barrel which help make the bullet go in a straight line over a long distance. One and a half seconds later, through his telescopic sight Donovan saw Alex thrown backwards onto the floor.

Giving a small grunt of satisfaction Donovan began to dismantle the rifle and get ready to check out of the hotel. What he didn't know was that the bullet did not travel as true as he would have wanted. Due to the tampering Conchita had done the previous night, it had deviated a few inches to the left before it had struck Alex in the head.

Chapter 31

19th August 2013 – Mega Maximo
Athens – 08:00

Alex was thrown backwards, not so much from the force of the bullet but an almost instinctive reaction to avoid what was coming his way. He lay on the floor clutching the left side of his head; he could feel the blood oozing through his fingers. I'm not dead he thought, but I could be dying he reasoned. I'm losing a lot of blood. Then he remembered what his doctor had once told him a while back, when he had cut his finger and had needed stiches. A little blood goes a long way, the doctor had said to a complaining Alex, who was saying that by the time the doctor had completed the necessary administration procedures, he would have bled to death.

Both Chris and Yannis had acted in unison even before Alex had hit the floor.

'Down everyone,' they yelled as they threw themselves to the ground pistols drawn.

'Sniper?' said Chris looking at Yannis.

'Must be, but I don't know where the sniper is. We'd better stay low for a few minutes,' said Yannis.

'Kaliope, could you take a look at Alex and see what the damage is, but make sure you keep low?'

Kaliope crawled over to Alex. She had taken all her emergency medical courses months before and as she moved herself towards Alex, using her elbows and lower arms to pull herself along, she was hoping she could remember what she needed to do. When she reached him she saw that he had been incredibly lucky. The bullet had grazed the side of his head just above the temple. Yes, it was bleeding a lot but the wound was definitely not life threatening. There was a first aid kit in the cupboard on the opposite side of the room away from the window. Argi, who was no fool was already opening the cupboard doors. She had correctly reasoned that the side of the room where the cupboard stood wasn't in the line of sight of any shot from a sniper. She threw the first-aid kit across to Kaliope.

Argi was pushing numbers on a mobile phone when Chris realised what she was doing.

'No Argi! Not an ambulance. Call Alex's private physician, he can be trusted not to say anything. It doesn't look like an injury that needs hospitalisation,' said Chris.

'I agree with Chris,' said Kaliope who was attending to Alex. 'It's superficial, rather a lot of blood that's all.'

'If the shooting gets out the stock market will go through the floor,' warned Leonidas wiping his brow as he sat on the floor in the furthest corner of the room from the window, his face still ashen from the shock of it all. 'And if Hellenic Aluminium follows suit then it makes it all the cheaper for Eckersley to purchase the shares he needs to take control of the company.'

'Agreed,' said Kaliope. 'This must be kept hush-hush.'

'What I don't understand,' said Chris. 'Is how a professional sniper could miss the target by so much?'

Before anyone could answer Yannis's mobile rang.

'Good work,' pronounced Yannis into the phone. 'Be careful, don't blow your cover.'

Yannis's last remark caught everyone's ears and Chris as suspicious as ever was the first to react.

'Who shouldn't blow their cover?' asked Chris. 'Is there something you haven't been telling us?' Chris said in an agitated voice as he turned to Yannis. He hated anyone keeping information from him. 'We're a team and we should all have the same information.'

Yannis visibly blanched at Chris's outburst. He looked around the room and saw that they were all looking at him expectantly. I'll have to tell them now he thought. Yannis walked across the room passing in front of the window the sniper had fired the bullet through.

'Yannis you're crazy!' yelled Kaliope. 'get down!'

'Okay calm down everyone, the sniper has gone from the room he fired from,' said Yannis as he sat down in one of the empty chairs around the conference table. He invited the others, all except Kaliope who was still attending to Alex, to sit down too. When they were settled he continued.

'Some time ago, well before this latest crisis, and before Alex became PM, I didn't like the direction of travel that the political extreme right arena was heading, particularly Golden Dawn. So I decided to assign an undercover operative with the job of infiltrating the Golden Dawn organisation. The operative was a female who adopted the name Conchita. She has managed to climb to the top of their organisation during the last two years and in the last couple of weeks became very close to Karagianis. Yesterday evening she was sent by Karagianis on an errand to the Grand Brittania Hotel. She was to contact a man called Carter, real name Donovan, who had been hired to assassinate Alex. He was checked in to one of the suites on the top floor. The only one which had line of sight into this room.'

'Were you aware that this man Donovan or Carter was in Athens specifically to kill Alex?' asked Kaliope with a look of horror on her face.

'Of course not! Do you think I'd let him take the shot if I knew of him at all? I would have ordered Conchita to eliminate him. No, Conchita did not contact me until the phone call a few minutes ago.'

'What did she do?' asked Kaliope.

'Karagianis had given her a letter addressed to this man Donovan, which confirmed that the mark was to be Alex. She went up to his suite to deliver the message with a plan to let him seduce her so as to give her time while he slept, to tamper with the bullets of his sniper rifle.'

'She's a brave woman,' interjected Chris. 'I've heard all about this man Donovan. I believe he's considered the best assassin in the world and taken over the mantle of the Jackal as assassin supreme. Wasn't he with the Mossad at one time?'

'Yes he was. That's where he learned his tradecraft. He left them and went rogue some ten years ago. Since then he has been hunted high and low by police forces, federal agents, competitors, and his victims' business associates, but he always seems to be able to slip their nets.'

'Why didn't she just kill him when she had access to him?' asked Leonidas.

'She would have blown her cover if she had. Karagianis would have known it could only be her. Her life would have had a span of just a few hours. So she took an executive decision based on risk reward. She reasoned that if she tampered with the bullet casings there was negligible risk of Alex being killed and she would be safe from having her cover blown. That is also the reason we have not apprehended him, Karagianis would know that it was Conchita who had given him away.'

'He only fired one round Yannis. How many bullets did she tamper with?' asked Chris, a look of worry on his face. He knew he would not like the answer.

Now Yannis was worried. Conchita had told him that she had tampered with both bullets. He is a professional and he will check his equipment at some point, even if he has not done it already. Conchita must go to ground for a while.

'Two,' answered Yannis. 'Yes I know, she could be in great danger,' he acknowledged. 'I'll warn her.'

Yannis dialled Conchita's mobile phone. The message he heard *'this phone is out of service please try again later'* didn't calm his nerves much. She could have turned her phone off, he reasoned, so that she couldn't be tracked.

'No joy I'm afraid, she must have her phone off. I'm going to call EKAM headquarters and get an all-points bulletin out for her to be picked up when sighted. Chris and I have to leave for the airport in a few minutes. How long before Alex's doctor gets here?' asked Yannis.

'Should be here any minute now,' said Argi. 'How is Alex Kaliope?'

'I think he is concussed but his pulse is strong and I've manage to stem the bleeding,' said Kaliope.

Just at that moment Alex's secretary buzzed through to the room informing them that the ambulance had arrived. They all looked at each other perplexed. An ambulance had not been called, what was going on?

'Maria, can you go down and see what they want? Tell them we haven't called an ambulance,' instructed Kaliope.

Maria went down to the front entrance of the building where the ambulance was parked. She looked around for the paramedics but could not see them. Deciding that they were probably sitting in the back of the ambulance, she walked round and opened the doors.

Before she passed out she had seen a body lying on the gurney but it wasn't that which caused her to faint. It was what was on the chest of the body that had horrified her. It was a head! A head covered in long dark hair the ends of which were soaking in the blood around the severed neck.

Chapter 32

19th August 2013 – Salonika International Airport – 15:00

Donovan was pacing up and down the British Airways departure lounge, waiting for his flight to London. He was not a happy man – hence the pacing - he was angry with himself. He had never missed a target in his life, his international reputation would be tarnished once it got out that he had botched a job. It wouldn't have been so bad if it were a bad shot, or a sudden gust of wind had affected the trajectory of the shot, but it was his own ill-discipline. He had let himself be taken in by a beautiful woman, something he had never done before. Perhaps he was getting old – no he couldn't accept that. It was plain old arrogance with a touch of flattery which had been his downfall and he would have to accept it.

Donovan looked at his watch – he had one hour to kill before his flight was announced. He switched on the burner phone he had purchased from the airport's mobile shop outlet, just half an hour earlier, and punched in Karagianis's number.

'Dimitris!' Donovan almost shouted down the phone.

'Calm down Donovan,' soothed Karagianis. What the hell does he want now, Karagianis thought. 'What do you want?' he ventured, not really wanting to know, as he knew it would not be good news.

'I want to know where Kalfas is,' said Donovan.

'Why?' asked Karagianis with some trepidation in his voice.

'Because I must finish the job.'

Karagianis gave out a quiet sigh. 'We are paying you anyway so why do you want to finish the job as you put it? You won't get any extra fees for having another go.'

'I don't want another fee. I must finish the job – my reputation depends on me being successful. Now please tell me where Kalfas is today,' said Donovan his exasperation evident.

'Look Donovan I hired you to take out Kalfas. You failed, now that's the end of it. I can't sooth your disappointment at missing the mark, that's not my job is it?' said Karagianis. 'You'll have to deal with that yourself, the responsibility is yours'

'I could make it yours,' retorted Donovan angrily. 'You know I could make life difficult for you.'

'Is that a threat?' said Karagianis.

'No, not a threat, a promise.'

Karagianis shivered as if someone had walked on his grave. If Donovan went through with his threat, which Karagianis knew would be to expose his activities to the wider public, he would be finished.

'Okay, give me an hour to find out where he is. Should I use this number?' asked Karagianis referring to the mobile number showing on his phone screen.

'Yes. I'll wait for your call. Don't let me down.'

After he had disconnected from the call, Donovan decided to stay at the airport. Wherever Kalfas was he wasn't at the airport that's for sure, so Donovan rightly surmised that he would have to take a flight. Probably to Athens. He was thirsty so he headed for the nearest bar where he would wait for Karagianis's call.

Forty-five minutes later Donovan's phone rang. It was Karagianis.

'Well?' he asked gruffly.

'I've managed to find out where he is,' said Karagianis.

'Where?'

'He is in Edessa in Macedonia. He is touring the area which has been devastated by the forest fires,' revealed Karagianis. 'He is staying overnight at The Four Seasons Hotel in Edessa itself.'

'That is wonderful news, thank you Dimitri,' purred Donovan who was now his normal cool suave self. 'I promise you - you will hear some good news tomorrow morning.'

'I don't doubt that,' agreed Karagianis. 'Good luck.'

'Thanks but I won't need it. Kalfas is as good as in the ground.'

With that Donovan shut the call off and hurried towards the domestic airlines ticket desk. As luck would have it there was a flight to Edessa scheduled to depart in twenty minutes. Donovan purchased a single ticket as he had no plans of staying in Greece but intended to hire a car and head for North Macedonia. He checked his luggage in but held onto a carry-on bag in which he had what looked like a hunting rifle. The pieces which turned the rifle into a snipers rifle were safely tucked away in his luggage in the hold, each piece impossible to recognise as components of a powerful rifle. He figured that Greek security wasn't as vigilant as say the USA or the UK and he would get away with it.

Donovan boarded the twin engine turbo-prop Boeing ATR 72 up the steps into the front section of an aircraft which accommodates twenty-six passengers in a single class. As there wasn't a business class, Donovan had requested a seat by the emergency exit to give himself the extra leg room. He looked around watching the flight attendant help the elderly passengers to their seats. Donovan reckoned that except for the pretty flight attendant, he was the youngest person on the plane.

The cabin was almost full and Donovan was grateful no-one had sat next to him. The flight attendant was starting to close the door when there was the sound of someone running up the steps, yelling at the flight to wait. A few seconds later a strikingly beautiful blonde, wearing a blue skirted suit and high heels, burst into the cabin, her attaché case leading the way. She looked around the cabin for an empty seat, then spied the vacant seat next to Donovan.

Perhaps it won't be a boring flight after all she said to herself. What a stunningly handsome man – fit looking too. The woman made her way down the aisle to the empty seat, gave Donovan a smile that would have melted anyone's heart and said, 'Do you mind, this seems to be the only vacant seat on the plane?'

'Be my guest,' said Donovan smiling. 'Here let me take your attaché case.'

'Thanks but no thanks,' said the woman, gripping the handle even tighter.

The woman sat down, putting the case under her seat, before straightening her skirt. Once she had made herself comfortable she turned to Donovan flashing him another bombshell of a smile. Extending her hand, on which, Donovan noted the immaculately manicured nails, and said, 'Hello, my name is Argi.'

Chapter 33
19th August 2013 – Macedonia Air Space – 23:55

Chris and Yannis squirmed as the troop carrier glider hit an air pocket throwing, both and the twenty men accompanying them, back onto the hard cold metallic side of its fuselage. They had taken off from a military airbase west of Salonika forty minutes earlier, pulled by an Airbus C-295M turboprop, which was now circling in ten-mile-wide circles at five thousand feet, above the mountains, thirty miles from the North Macedonian border. Both their thoughts were on what had happened earlier that day.

Earlier that morning the sight of Conchita's headless body lying in the back of the ambulance, had shocked them all. It wasn't until the body was undergoing a post-mortem, that an unspent bullet was found taped to her chest, that they realised how she had been found out. They were correct in assuming that Donovan had detected that the bullet had been tampered with. In fact Donovan had sensed that the shot was not the perfect shot he was used to and instead of taking a second shot decided to check his spare bullet and found the score marks which Conchita had made.

Yannis, on seeing it was Conchita on the gurney, had immediately ordered an Athens wide search for the ambulance drivers, but by the time they had taken off from Salonika, they had not been apprehended. Not even the prints they had taken from the vehicle yielded anything. Donovan too, was being sought by the authorities and all the airports and ports around Greece had his description, although unfortunately a current photograph was not available, but luckily EKAM had managed to obtain an old photograph from his days with the Mossad.

Alex's private physician had visited him a short while after the incident with the ambulance. He treated his wound, declaring that Alex did not have concussion, which was a miracle in itself, and a couple of hours' rest should see him fully fit to be at his desk, albeit maybe with a sore head. Kaliope had been praised for her quickness in stemming the flow of blood and administering the appropriate first aid.

Kaliope had travelled to Edessa in the afternoon to see for herself the damage done by the fire. Against her better judgement both Alex and Gitta had persuaded her to let them come along. Alex wanted to visit the area and publicly show his concern for the damage to the environment and visit the relatives of the couple and child, that had been so cruelly gunned down. Gitta decided to stay in Edessa and rest up, so Kaliope and Alex with their respective bodyguards had gone to meet the families who had fled the fire. To their relief not one of the families they met blamed the Government for the fire; on the contrary they were angry at the arsonists who had set the fire. The damage was very extensive but at five o'clock yesterday afternoon there had been no civilian casualties despite the destruction of three villages which were in the path of the fire.

The other good news was that the wind had dropped and the firefighters together with the army units had managed to slow down the progress of the fire. But, unfortunately it was already the worst case of arson that had ever occurred on mainland Greece. When they got back to The Four Seasons hotel in Edessa, Alex discovered that Gitta was missing. Both he and Kaliope went down to the concierge to check whether she had left a message. She had not, but the concierge told them that she had hired a car, leaving the hotel at four o'clock that afternoon.

'Going back to Athens?' Kaliope asked Alex

'I don't believe so,' said Alex. 'I'm afraid she has gone because she has some unfinished business.'

Kaliope was quick on the uptake even if she hadn't been privy to Gitta's pillow talk with Alex two nights previously. 'Eckersley?'

'I'm afraid so,' said Alex, certain that she was heading for his villa. 'I'm going to take a couple of the EKAM officers who are guarding our floor and head out to his villa.'

Within the hour Alex was sitting in the back of an EKAM SUV heading for Eckersley's villa.

Both Argi and Leonidas had remained in Athens to firefight all the media flack the Government was getting about the hostage situation in North Macedonia and the forest fire.

Leonidas had held a meeting with the heads of some of the most influential business groups, the Bank of Greece, and the Athens Stock Exchange directors. Whatever was said seemed to have worked and when Leonidas appeared on the six o'clock news he was able to announce that the stock exchange had recovered the losses of the previous two days, particularly Hellenic Aluminium, which had lost 15% of its value, but, bullish investors had managed to outmanoeuvre the bearish trend led by Eckersley and the shares had recovered most of their losses.

Argi spent most of the day on the phone discussing the situation with some of her European counterparts, the foreign secretary of North Macedonia and the Secretary-General of the United Nations. Although all imparted sympathy for the plight of the hostages, they all seemed to be in some sort of weird time-warp waiting for the UN to do something. North Macedonia stuck to their line that the hostages had been taken by some obscure mercenary group and as such was not really their responsibility. They too wanted to wait for the UN to negotiate for the release of their delegation. Argi ended the day completely frustrated that she hadn't made any progress, but happy in the knowledge that there would be an attempt to free the hostages later that night. Unable to stand her impatience for some news, she decided at the last minute to fly up to Edessa.

Also earlier that day around nine o'clock in the morning, an anxious Karagianis was pacing his office, as he had heard nothing in the news about Alex being shot, and he had slowly come to the realisation that somehow Donovan had failed. Why he had failed he did not understand. Donovan was supposed to be the best in the business. He attempted to get hold of Conchita in the hope that she knew something, but her phone was switched off. As he was debating what to do next his mobile phone rang.

'Yes.'

'It's Donovan I'll be brief, your girl is working for another agency and she sabotaged my ammunition,' said Donovan quite calmly but with a touch of menace in his voice. 'Kalfas is probably still alive.'

'Oh my god!' exclaimed Karagianis. 'If we don't move fast they will give her sanctuary in a safe house and she will spill all the beans.'

'Not if we find her first. Do you know where she might go?'

'She is probably in the area of Vissis Street where she hangs out with the druggies.'

'Right,' said Donovan. 'I want you to send two men in a highjacked ambulance to meet me in that street. Just tell them to park and keep the engine running. Text me their mobile numbers. Do it quickly!'

'Yes, okay, 'said Karagianis, quite happy to let Donovan clear up the mess. Shame he thought, I quite liked Conchita. Oh well.

Twenty minutes later Donovan was in Vissis Street, a street that was in an area of Athens called Exarcheia, an area that tourists were warned to avoid. The district was controlled by the extreme right wing of the Golden Dawn party. Graffiti decorated buildings whose owners had long gone from the neighbourhood, leaving it to squatters, drug dealers and the Nazi styled gangs.

There was little traffic on Vissi Street; it was not a popular place for motorists or casual pedestrians. If you were in Vissi Street you were there for a purpose and not a good one at that. Donovan strolled down towards the southern end of the street. He was banking on Conchita not being anywhere within the maze of small streets and alleyways leading off Vissi Street but on Vissi itself. He was wearing a baseball cap which he hoped covered most of his dark grey hair, and tatty old jeans with matching shirt, not the colour matching, just the tattiness, which he had bought from a second hand shop a few minutes previously. His regular clothes were in the brown paper carrier bag he carried in his left hand, together with the machete he had just bought from the DIY shop next to the clothes shop.

Donovan marvelled at the style of architecture of the buildings on the street. Take away the graffiti and worn-out look of the facades he could see that these had once been magnificent homes. Whilst admiring the building his eyes continuously scanned the street. His phone bleeped and so as not to attract too much attention he turned into an alleyway to read the text notification. It was from Karagianis, a telephone number of a person called Petros. Donovan called the number and a voice at the other end who assumed was Petros told him that an ambulance had been commandeered and he was now driving it slowly down Vissi Street.

Donovan peered out from the alleyway spotting the ambulance immediately. He described himself and told Petros to pick him up opposite the alleyway. Once in the ambulance they continued along Vissi Street at a slow pace with Donovan scouring the left hand pavement and Petros's sidekick the right hand side.

'There she is!' yelled Donovan, pointing down the road to where a street vendor was selling yogurt with honey and walnuts. Conchita was in a queue, second in line for the yogurt.

'Drop me here,' instructed Donovan, brandishing a hypodermic needle in Petros's face. 'As soon as she hits the deck, roll up to the kiosk and bring out the wheeled stretcher to put her on.'

Donovan alighted from the ambulance some fifty metres from the kiosk. He walked purposely towards Conchita who seemed oblivious to any danger and was intently studying her mobile phone. Donovan passed behind Conchita, plunging the hypodermic needle into her neck, injecting the sleeping agent, then extracting the needle before Conchita could react. Her hand went to the area of the puncture as soon as she felt the prick of the needle entering her flesh. Her thoughts raced as she turned towards Donovan, her right hand reaching for the gun nestled in the small of her back. But before she could draw it out the quick acting agent engulfed her senses and to her the world started to slow down to a crawl. Conchita collapsed onto the pavement. Immediately the ambulance had stopped and the two men had opened the doors. They wheeled the gurney over to where Conchita lay, picked up her motionless body, laid her on the gurney and had her in the back of the ambulance before anyone at the kiosk had realised what had happened.

Donovan who had climbed into the ambulance with the gurney sat beside the still body of Conchita. He searched her, retrieving her gun which he put into her bag. He would get rid of that later. He produced another hypodermic which contained adrenaline and injected the liquid into her arm. Conchita's eyes opened slowly trying to bring the interior of the ambulance into focus. When she laid eyes on Donovan she took a sharp intake of breath. She would not let him see her fear she decided.

'What the fuck do you want?' she yelled at Donovan. She tried to rise from the gurney but her muscles obviously had not woken up yet. She felt around the back of her jeans for her gun.

'Sorry bitch,' apologised Donovan sarcastically. 'I have tucked it away safe and sound in your bag.' He called for the two men up front to stop the ambulance and come and join him.

'You realise you are going to die, unlike your Prime Minister who is alive because of you.'

You bastard,' yelled Conchita and spat into Donovan's face.

Donovan didn't bother to wipe the spittle off but instructed the two men to hold Conchita down face up so she could see what was coming. When she was held fast Donovan produced the machete from the carrier bag and laid the blade along her neck just below her Adams-Apple. Her eyes unflinchingly bore into his, as Donnovan started to saw into her neck. He continued sawing long after Conchita had passed out from the pain and loss of blood. He only stopped sawing when her head was severed from her neck. He produced the second tampered with bullet and placed it on her chest.

'Take her to the front entrance of the Mega Maximo and act as though someone had called an ambulance for Alex Kalfas. Place her head on the bullet, then get out of there,' instructed Donovan

With that, Donovan got out of the ambulance, hailed a taxi, then telling the driver to take him to Salonika International airport, he settled back into seat, closed his eyes, and went to sleep.

Fifteen hours later, in the troop carrier glider circling above Macedonia, Yannis looked at his watch, then said, 'Not long now Chris, we should be releasing soon to start our glide into North Macedonia. The electromagnetic pulse bomb will be deployed in thirty seconds at one o'clock, and then our pilots will release the towrope, and head for the border of North Macedonia.'

At precisely one o'clock the twenty men plus Chris and Yannis felt the tug as tow rope was released. Silence descended on the glider, except for the soft sound of air passing over the wings as it banked, turning towards a heading of ten degrees which would take them just to the north of the farmhouse where the hostages were prisoners. Below them it was completely dark, not a light could be seen. Within a fifty mile radius the pulse bomb had shorted out every electrical component there was, including radar.

Even Edessa would be effected, thought Yannis, even Eckersley's villa would be in darkness.

'I hope the coach driver turned his engine off as instructed,' said Chris. 'Otherwise we will be stuck at the border until a recovery vehicle manages to get there.'

They both laughed at the irony of that scenario and it eased the tension that both were feeling. Both men sat in silence, feelings of excitement combined with apprehension of the unknown pervaded their senses, but above all both of them were looking forward to the firefight that was minutes away.

Chapter 34

20th August 2013 – North Macedonia – 01:30

Both Chris and Yannis braced themselves as the glider touched down three kilometres to the north of the farmhouse in North Macedonia and bumped and twisted its way across the grassy field for close on two-hundred and fifty yards before coming to rest against a small thicket of trees.

'Everyone alright?' yelled Yannis.

Twenty men shouted 'yes' in unison.

'You okay Chris?' asked Yannis.

'Fine,' said Chris. 'Just a little bruised I guess.'

'Right everyone out and remember keep on radio silence. You all know your teams, let's see if we can get this done before the lights come on again. Everyone on me and good luck,' said Yannis reverting to the standard forces and police jargon. Instead of 'follow me,' he used 'on me.'

Initially the men walked south in single file with Yannis on point, - in army-speak leading -, and Chris was tasked with taking up the column's six, which in army-speak means being at the rear of a column. At least it's only until we split into teams thought Chris. He reassured himself with the thought that no-one could have seen them land, therefore he was in no danger of anyone appearing behind him. He was right of course and that was exactly why Yannis had put him in that position – it was the safest spot in the column.

One kilometre out from the farmhouse the men split out into two teams of five, and two teams of six. Chris's team was tasked with entering the farmhouse from the front door. Yannis's team had the hardest job in that they were going to enter the building through the roof. The other two teams would gain access through the windows on the south and north sides of the building.

As the teams approached the farmhouse they could see, silhouetted against the stars -fortunately, there was no moon that night – the lookout posted on the roof of the building. The lookout was sitting on a wooden crate and facing south towards the border with Greece. This was a job for a sniper, and Chris watched as one of the men from Yannis's team detached himself and took up a firing position so that the lookout's back was facing him.

Five minutes later all four teams were in their respective places around the farmhouse, night vision masks on, stun and smoke grenades at the ready, waiting for Yannis's signal to move in. His signal, two clicks on the radio, would also be the signal for the sniper to take down the lookout.

'Click.... click' The lookout slumped forward as the snipers bullet passed through the back of his head and exited through his forehead. Immediately, all four teams moved swiftly and quietly, in unison, towards their respective targets. The operation was over in what Chris felt was the most frightening and most cacophonic twenty seconds he had ever experienced. It seemed as though he had frozen in time - yet he was moving, but his finger never pulled the trigger, and his stun grenade was still clutched in his right hand.

He looked around as the smoke cleared from the stun grenades. There were bodies everywhere he looked. A body in front of him stirred and he turned the muzzle of his Heckler & Koch MP5 machine gun towards the movement.

'Chris, No!' screamed Yannis. 'It's a hostage. All the terrorists are dead. Let's get them to safety before the lights come back on.'

For a second Chris froze, his heart racing at the thought of nearly ending an innocent person's life. He was astonished that the close quarters' sounds and smells of a fire fight had affected him so much. In the past he had never had any qualms about shooting the bad guys. Not that he had shot that many, but all of them had been in one-on-one situations. No, it was definitely the noise of zinging bullets, gunfire, and the smell of - yes that was it – death.

'I know what you're feeling,' said Yannis as he put his arm around Chris's shoulder. 'It happened to me on my first fire fight, it's not an experience that you can shrug off just like that. The second one is much easier.'

'Thanks, Yannis. But I don't want to experience another firefight. Let's get on.'

Yannis realised that Chris didn't want to talk about it anymore. He'd probably want to later, maybe in a few days after he had come to terms with his experience. The hostages had all gathered in a group and were being ushered out by Yannis's men. Yannis spied Aliki Traka and called her over. Alex had asked him to take good care of her. He looked her over. No sign of any injuries but she did look exhausted.

'How are you feeling Aliki?' asked Alex, taking her arm. 'You are safe now, please follow me.'

'Just very tired,' admitted Aliki. 'But I wasn't afraid!' she said defiantly daring Yannis to say otherwise.

'After your exploits in the Greek resistance during WWII I have no doubt you weren't,' said Yannis, giving her a toothy grin.

An hour and three kilometres later, a tired group of twenty six UN delegates were standing on the Greek side of the border waiting for the convoy of three empty army trucks and two light military vehicles, to arrive from a military base near Edessa. Electricity within a fifty kilometre radius of the pulse bomb would start to be repaired after the effects of it had worn off. Yannis was grateful that the army base was just outside the fifty kilometre perimeter.

Roughly half-way between the border and Edessa, at Eckersley's villa, Alkis was finishing repairs to the electrics of Eckersley's Mercedes which, as with all vehicles within the pulse bomb's radius, had all its fuses blown. Initially when the lights had gone out both Eckersley and Alkis had naturally thought that it was a simple power cut. But when the electric generator hadn't kicked in they realised that something more sinister had happened.

'Check the cars Alkis,' said Eckersley. 'I have a sneaky feeling that something is afoot.'

They both went outside, Eckersley checked his Mercedes, Alkis checked his Audi, and some of the staff checked the other vehicles. They were all dead – not one would start.

'Interesting,' mused Eckersley when they had learned that not one car would start.

'What?' asked Alkis.

'I know I have an ultra-suspicious mind but this is no ordinary power cut, in fact it's not a power cut at all. Something caused all the electrics to short out. It looks remarkably like the result of a magnetic pulse.'

'Who would be responsible for that?' asked Alkis.

'We'll find out shall we?' said Eckersley. 'I'm going to use my satellite phone which is in the safe. If I'm correct the pulse cannot penetrate a lead casing.'

'Who will you call?'

'The airbase at Bitola about fifty kilometres west of the farmhouse. I'll ask them to send a reconnaissance drone over the farmhouse.'

'Do you think the blackout has something to do with the hostages?' asked Alkis.

'I don't know but there is a niggling thought in my head that is telling me that something is not right,' confessed Eckersley.

Eckersley hurried to his safe, opened it and took out the satellite phone. Before he had even shut the safe he pressed the 'on' button. He breathed a sigh of relief when he saw the steady green light that signified the phone was working properly. He swiftly dialled the

Bitola and spoke to the air force adjunct of the base commander. After explaining who he was he was put through.

'Good evening commander,' said Eckersley. 'My name is Arthur Eckersley, CEO of Xplore Industries.'

'Yes Mr Eckersley I know who you are,' said the commander with a respectful tone in his voice. 'My superiors in the Ministry of Defence speak very highly of you. What can I do for you?'

Eckersley explained what had happened and was relieved to learn the base hadn't been within the sphere of the black out. He outlined to the commander what he wanted.

'No problem at all,' said the commander eager to help. Particularly as he correctly surmised that going against Eckersley's wishes might be a career breaker. 'Would you like it armed?'

Eckersley thought for a moment before he answered. 'No thank you,' he said. 'But I would like the feed transmitted to this phone.'

'We can do that I'm sure. I'll talk to my engineers about that. Could I have the detail and co-ordinates for the drones area sweep?' Eckersley relayed to the commander what he wanted and where he wanted the drone, thanking him when he was finished, then hung up.

The whole conversation took place in the front garden of Eckersley's villa because to get a satellite signal the phone needed to be outside. He didn't realise that he was being overheard – hiding in the bushes just inside the grounds of the villa crouched a very determined Gitta.

She had been fortunate that it was summer and a warm night because she had been waiting in the shadows for several hours, ever since the ride she had hitched from a local farmer had dropped her off half a kilometre down the road. She had been waiting for everyone to retire to bed before she could enter the main house in relative safety. Once inside, she knew where Eckersley's bedroom was, so would be able to make her way to it in the dark without a problem. Something was going on, probably to do with the operation to extract the hostages and that is why no-one had retired for the night. Now, because of the delay she feared that Alex having seen that she was not in their room, would have realised she was out for revenge and was heading for the villa. In fact she wondered why he had not yet turned up.

But, Alex had turned up, and he was not far away from the entrance of the villa, where, together with two EKAM officers, he was concealed in the trees, almost opposite the front entrance. Alex unknowingly had passed the farmer who had given Gitta a ride, without realising she was in his vehicle. So when he came to the villa he assumed Gitta had not yet arrived, particularly as the grounds were ablaze with light. He and the officers, decided to park-up out of sight of the villa and wait. Not far from the entrance they found a small area where the trees did not quite line the road but left enough room for the SUV to reverse into the gap. Not long after they spied the farmer's vehicle go past and then ten minutes later Gitta walked past, thankfully without so much as a glance in their direction.

Relieved at that point that Gitta had not spotted them, they watched her walk into the trees opposite the entrance. For several hours Gitta waited in the trees but around midnight, when most of the lights in the grounds of the villa had been extinguished, they had seen her slip across the road and enter by the front entrance. An hour later the pulse bomb did its damage and it became pitch black. Alex and the two officers took advantage of the blackness to move through trees until they were opposite the entrance.

From their vantage point they watched as Eckersley spoke animatedly on the satellite phone to the commander of the base. Someone had repaired the generator and the grounds were ablaze with light once again. Gitta squeezed as far back as she could to avoid being spotted. Alkis was working on Eckersley's Mercedes again, no more than five metres from her. She could take him out, she decided. She unsheathed her USN Mark-2 marine utility knife which wasn't standard equipment for a CIA operative, but it was a coveted weapon which had been given to her by her father.

She crept out of the foliage towards Alkis. Then froze! She could see herself in one of the wing mirrors on the Mercedes. She only had two choices, rush at Alkis and hope she can kill him before he raised the alarm or turn tail and run hoping that she could disappear into the blackness of the trees before he reacted. The choice was made for her and it was a choice she hadn't even contemplated. Alkis swivelled around to face her, in his right-hand a Glock which was pointing at her chest.

'Hello my dear. I knew I would get another chance to kill you,' he said menacingly, a nasty smile playing on his lips.

Chapter 35

20th August 2013 – Eckersley's Villa – 04:30

Alex looked on in horror from the cover of the trees as the scene unfolded in front of him. He couldn't shoot because Gitta was in the way. He looked at the two EKAM officers standing in the shadows next to him as if to say, what do I do now. One of the officers said, 'Distract him long enough to allow Gitta to dive for cover and we can deal with him.'

'How?' asked Alex.

'See that large stone over there. Throw it to the other side of Gitta into the bushes.'

Alex nodded his understanding – then nervously picked up the stone. What if I miss and hit Gitta, or worse still hit the metal gate post, the noise will certainly make Alkis jumpy, and if he blazed away with his gun the rest of the staff would be alerted. Taking a deep breath Alex lobbed the stone underarm for better accuracy towards the bushes. Bullseye! Alex thought, the stone landing in the bushes made a rustling sound as if someone were in the foliage.

Alkis involuntarily turned his head in the direction of the noise. In that instance, Gitta's right hand which held the knife shot forward and the knife left her fingers - travelled the two metres separating Gitta from Alkis, before thudding into Alkis's right shoulder. He grabbed his right shoulder, swung his gun hand towards Gitta, but his fingers wouldn't respond to the messages from his brain, as all feeling left his hand and the gun dropped to the ground. Gitta moved fast, she bent down and grabbing the gun, she stepped towards Alkis who was attempting to sit up, but before he was able to shout a warning to Eckersley, she struck him over the head with the gun, knocking him unconscious.

As Alkis slumped back onto the ground, Alex and the two EKAM officers rushed through the villa's gate to Gitta's side. Realising that Alex was a little out of his depth she immediately took control of the situation.

'Take this bastard to your vehicle, we'll be right behind you,' she whispered to the EKAM officers. 'Come on Alex let's get back to the vehicle too. We can't do anymore here for now,' she gave him a quick peck on his lips as she said it. She smiled at Alex. 'Thank you for saving my life.'

Once inside the EKAM SUV they decided to take Alkis to Edessa where they could officially charge him with attempted murder of a Government official, while they developed evidence of the list of crimes he was alleged to have committed. They'd keep him on ice in a cell before transferring him to a black ops terrorist detention centre in Salonika, where he would be interrogated.

Back at the villa, Eckersley was watching the screen on his satellite phone as it came to life. The feed from the drone he had requested was as clear as a bell and he could see quite clearly, courtesy of the night vision lens of the drone, the contours of the terrain below it.

Almost immediately the farmhouse came into view, as the drone began to circle above it. Eckersley peered at the screen looking for any signs of life. Even after the drone had magnified the view, he couldn't see anything moving. Then as the magnification grew larger he began to see evidence of a firefight. Spent cartridge cases, discarded weapons, and a couple of bodies, one lying in a doorway and the other hanging from a windowsill.

'Are you still there Commander?' said Eckersley.

'Yes sir.'

'It looks to me like a firefight occurred at the farmhouse, what do you think?'

'I concur sir, no sign of hostages either,' said the Commander.

'No and that could be a problem. Did your radar pick up any aircraft traffic in the last hours?'

'We don't have a radar on the base. We get a feed from Prilep to the north. That base has our southernmost Early Warning System.'

'Did they see anything?' questioned Eckersley.

'No sir, they went off-line about three hours ago and haven't come back yet.'

'A bit of a coincidence that your EWS base goes offline just about the time the farmhouse came under attack, isn't it Commander?'

'I don't believe in coincidences sir,' said the Commander. 'If I was a betting man, which I'm not, I would wager some sort of tactical weapon has been deployed.'

'Something that knocked out electrics within a certain radius?' asked Eckersley.

'Precisely sir, I believe we are talking about a small pulse bomb.'

'A pulse bomb!' exclaimed Eckersley. 'I doubt if Greece possesses one of those, nor does it have the technology to make one.'

'But the Americans have the technology,' confirmed the Commander. 'Greece has remarkably close relations with the Americans. It's not out of the question they borrowed one or asked the Americans for a favour.'

'Would you let the drone cross the border into Greece?' asked Eckersley.

But before the commander could answer Eckersley heard the sound of several vehicles approaching the villa from the north. He rushed towards the front gate and was just in time to see a convoy of army vehicles, three army trucks and two EKAM light military vehicles speed by. But not before he spied non-military personnel in the back of the trucks.

Damn it, cursed Eckersley to himself, *they had taken the hostages from under my nose.*

'I take my request back Commander. The people that freed the hostages have just passed my villa. I won't need your drone now. At least not an unarmed one,' said Eckersley, laughing at his own joke.

'Goodbye Commander.'

'Goodbye sir,' said the Commander.

Eckersley looked around the gardens. He was wondering where Alkis had got to. He should be fixing the cars thought Eckersley, but he wasn't where the cars were. He noticed that the bonnet of his Mercedes was up and went over to see if Alkis was doing some repair under the car. He walked to the car and peered under the chassis. Not a sign of Alkis. Eckersley then walked around the car. When he reached the front he froze. There on the ground was a red patch, he bent down, drew his finger along the almost dry patch and smelled it. Definitely blood, the pungent smell of rust filled his nostrils.

Eckersley needed help. He called out Gregori his recently acquired personal minder, an ex-boxer from North Macedonia. Since the escape of Gitta from the villa he had been actively looking for a minder to replace the incompetent one who had allowed himself to be trussed up like a turkey by Gitta.

'Gregori, bring the men to the parking bays, quickly!' shouted Eckersley. He was glad he had pulled twelve of the mercenaries from the farmhouse a few days as extra security for the villa.

The men gathered around Eckersley.

'Alkis is missing,' he said. 'There is blood on the driveway, possibly there are more blood stains indicating which direction he may have gone. He could be gravely injured, possibly bleeding to death, so we need to find him fast. Go!'

The men dispersed to all points of the compass, looking for the apparently injured Alkis. Eckersley went back to the main house, pouring himself a strong coffee, while he waited impatiently for some news. Thirty minutes later all the men had returned and reported their findings. None of them had any idea of where Alkis was, it was as if he had disappeared. Only Gregori who took on the role as leader of the men, could offer up a solution to Alkis's disappearance.

'Boss,' there is only one blood stain on the grounds – the one you spotted in front of your car. It was a big stain which probably means that Alkis was bleeding out from a wound. Unless he found help he would have collapsed from loss of blood. As we haven't found him he couldn't have collapsed, therefore he was taken, kidnaped probably as I doubt there were any passers-by to play the good Samaritan. No, almost certainly Alkis is in the hands our enemies,' Gregori sat down as if the effort of speaking was too much for him.

It was by all accounts more words spoken than Eckersley and the men had heard out of Gregori's mouth in one go. Eckersley told the men to stay vigilant, then dismissed them, keeping Gregori at his side. He was worried, a concern he shared with Gregori. Afterwards, having sent Gregori on his way on a mission to Edessa, he mulled over all the options he had shared. There seemed to be only one viable option left if he were to own those bauxite mines. Drastic yes, but not impossible, but he would have to have a lot of help from his friends in the North Macedonian Government. The only elephant in the room would be their unwillingness to commit resources to what was essentially tantamount to covertly declaring war on Greece.

Chapter 36

20th August 2013 – Edessa 08:00

Gitta and Alex on returning to Edessa with their prisoner, together with their two EKAM escorts, immediately headed for the EKAM headquarters for the Macedonian region. They had contacted Yannis and Chris on the way arranging to meet them there. After the necessary protocols, they notified Alkis of his rights, then formally charged him with attempted murder of a public servant.

By nine o'clock that morning Alkis had been taken blindfolded, to one of EKAM's black ops sites ten kilometres outside of the town. The building was originally a majestic villa built in the sixties and owned for many years by a woman who became notorious for her wild parties, which were in reality an innovative way to promote her brothel and her girls. The villa was auctioned and picked up by the government when the unfortunate Madame was killed in a traffic accident several years ago.

Alkis was put into what used to be the basement storeroom, when the brothel was a working enterprise. But now it was cold and damp, except for a metal table and chair, both fixed to the floor, a single springless bed, also fixed to the floor, and a small, barred window without any glass.

Alkis was shackled to the chair when Yannis walked into the room and sat down opposite him. He looked Alkis in the eye and said with a trace of a sardonic smile, 'How do you like your accommodation?'

'Fuck off,' spat Alkis with all the venom he could muster, staring at Yannis with his piercing cold eyes.

Yannis sighed. 'Let me tell you a few of the rules around here. Rules which if you follow them will allow you to stay in this room. If you don't the consequences for you will be unbearable. We won't kill you but we are experts in keeping prisoners alive but close to death. Do you understand this?'

Alkis said nothing. He just stared at a spot somewhere above Yannis's head.

Yannis leaned forward, 'There are few rules and none of them is onerous. Rule number one requires you to answer every question asked. If you don't we will keep on asking the same question until you answer to our satisfaction. Oh yes! I almost forgot. In between repeated questions you will experience a variety of very unpleasant sensations. Do you understand?

Alkis again said nothing.

Yannis leaned forward and pressed a button situated below the edge of the table. Alkis's body began to jerk as his muscles spasmed with twenty thousand volts of electricity coursing through his body. The voltage increased every five seconds by ten thousand volts until it reached fifty thousand volts, the voltage of a taser, then it levelled off. Alkis's body slumped forward his muscles stopping their contractions.

'Don't worry,' said Yannis laughing. 'The current is around a quarter of an amp – not enough to kill you. But that is the lowest dose we offer our guests. Imagine what double that dose could do for you.'

After five minutes Alkis was able to struggle upright in the chair. His wrists were red raw from the manacles rubbing violently against them.

Yannis pulled a sheet of paper from a file he had brought into the room earlier and handed it to Alkis. 'Those are a list of the charges against you. I, or someone else will be asking you about those later. Bear in mind the rules. Now, back to my original question. How do you like your accommodation?'

Alkis stared defiantly at Yannis.

'As you wish,' said Yannis as he left the room.

Two minutes later the door of the room burst open and a figure with its head covered in a hood came into the room holding a high pressure hose, its nozzle pointing at Alkis. Then, a stream of ice cold water exploded out of the nozzle, pummelling a helpless Alkis who tried in vain to escape the jet of water.

Chapter 37

20th August 2013 – Four Seasons - Edessa
08:00

Meanwhile, in Argi's suite in the Four Seasons Hotel in Edessa, Argi and Donovan were stirring from their sleep. Argi turned towards Donovan and kissed him on his lips.

'Good morning darling,' she whispered.

'Good morning,' said Donovan. 'Coffee?'

'Mm, please.'

Donovan threw the sheet to one side and lightly slipped out of the bed, heading for the coffeemaker. Argi watched him move across the room. She was fascinated by the way his muscles expanded and contracted as he walked and it took all her self-discipline to stop herself from going after him to run her hands over his toned body.

She thought back to the previous evening after they had agreed το share her limousine from the airport. On the plane Argi had been a little annoyed that she was not able to sit by the emergency exit where she would have had nobody next to her, but on the other hand, also pleased that she was sitting next to an incredibly good looking fit man. She played it cool, not seeming to be too enthusiastic. So when Donovan tried to strike up a conversation with her, she used the excuse that she needed to work, while fishing out of her briefcase a paper to supposedly work on.

Unfortunately for Argi the paper she pulled from her briefcase was a Government paper. She realised too late what she had done and even though she had quickly turned the paper over, it was not quick enough for Donovan's keen eyes.

'You work for the Greek Government I see,' said Donovan, awarding Argi with his best smile. 'What department are you in?'

It was a fait-accompli, Argi couldn't duck the question now.

'I'm a cabinet minister,' answered Argi. 'In the foreign office.'

Donovan feigned amazement. 'Wow, don't tell me you are the foreign minister of this great country?'

'I'm afraid so,' admitted Argi. 'But if I told you what I'm working on, I would have to kill you,' she said giving Donovan a flirty smile.

Donovan laughed, leaning towards her he put his hand on her thigh and said, 'Now you have really scared me.' Donovan's mind was racing. He could see that Argi was attracted to him – he had to admit that he too was fascinated by her. But the uppermost thought in his mind was the knowledge that Argi could lead him to Alex Kalfas.

The two of them talked and flirted throughout the short twenty minute flight to Edessa. After the plane had landed they cleared security without any hitches, the security guard only making a cursory inspection of Donovan's hunting rifle. Once outside the terminal Argi announced that a limousine was being sent to pick her up.

'Where are you staying?' asked Donovan.

'The Four Seasons,' said Argi. 'You?'

'The same.'

'In that case I can give you a lift,' said Argi enthusiastically, happy that she had avoided a potentially awkward moment by not having to ask Donovan anything which would make her seem too forward. She could sense that he was attracted to her but due to her station in life or simply that he was a shy man, he might be nervous about being too familiar. At least now that they were booked into the same hotel she could make some suggestions which might embolden him to want to see her again.

'I'm starving,' announced Argi once they had settled into the back seat of the limousine.

Donovan saw his chance. 'Me too,' he said. 'Would you like company over dinner?'

Argi's took a sharp intake of breath at the sound of his words. Her instinct warned her that she should make this a little more difficult for him. 'We can't be seen having dinner in the hotel restaurant. Some of my colleagues are staying at the hotel too.'

'How about I meet you at a taverna in another part of Edessa then,' suggested Donovan.

'That's a good idea, so yes I would love to have dinner with you. I know a family run taverna on the outskirts of Edessa. I could meet you there later, say at nine o'clock. Would that be a good time?'

'Perfect,' agreed Donovan.

So it was agreed that once at the hotel, Donovan should go straight to the bar before checking in, giving time for Argi to check in and disappear up to her suite. The limousine dropped Donovan one hundred metres from the front entrance of the hotel before taking Argi to the main entrance. Argi checked in and went up to her suite. It was just after seven o'clock so she had time to find out which of her colleagues were around. As it turned out none of them. Alex was going after Gitta and Kaliope was with the forensic teams at the scene of the forest fire.

In a way she was glad no-one was around because it enabled her to get ready in peace. She was going to make herself irresistible tonight she vowed.

And she was! When Donovan saw her walk into the tavern the sight of her took his breath away. She wore a pure white dress which had a slit up each side, so as she walked her toned thighs were in clear view. The dress set off her tan, and extenuated her green eyes framed in a cascade of blonde hair. He had to remind himself that this was work and he should not get emotionally involved. Particularly as he might be forced to kill her.

'You look stunning,' said Donovan, flashing a smile as he complimented her. He lightly held her bare shoulders as he bent down and kissed her on both cheeks. Argi's heart skipped as he kissed her. Was it the kiss or was it the gentle touch on her shoulders she wondered.

Over the three hours or so they were at the taverna they managed to consume three bottles of wine, four liquors and two coffees between them. They were both extremely tipsy perhaps Argi a little more so than Donovan, so just after midnight they both tumbled into a taxi and headed back to the Four Seasons hotel. Their luck held out and they weren't spotted by anyone who knew Argi as they crossed the foyer and asked the desk clerk for their respective card keys. They of course knew that only one bedroom would be occupied that night.

As they entered the lift Argi said to Donovan. 'My room not yours. 'A flush of awareness and excitement on her face, her body inclined towards him. Donovan said nothing, instead he pulled her to him and kissed her passionately on her lips. When the lift finally arrived at her floor, Donovan had already found out that Argi wasn't wearing any underwear. And soon after entering her suite she lost her dress to Donovan's deft fingers.

Not bothering to go for the bed or even the settee they rolled around on the floor with Donovan kissing every bit of her flesh he could find while at the same time helping her tear his clothes off.

'Stop!' said Argi when the last piece of clothing was off Donovan and he was completely naked. 'Stand up!' she commanded. Donovan stood up.

'You have an amazing body,' she said breathlessly as she ran her fingers of both hands down his back, then along his arms, feeling the muscle tensions as she went. Donovan took a sharp intake of breath as Argi ran her hands down his thighs, down his lower limbs to his feet. She felt her blood rise in a wave of heat through her body.

'Turn around!' she commanded again. She stayed kneeling as she stretched upwards bringing her hands down on his chest and over his stomach. His manhood was aroused now, so she cupped his balls in her hands and flicked her tongue against his now upright penis. She played with it with her tongue until Donovan began to breathe a little harder and make small moaning sounds.

Sliding her hand behind his scrotum she found his G-spot and began stroking it as she slid her lips over his penis until it was at the back of her throat and her tongue was working on the base of his erection. She felt that Donovan was close to orgasm – she grabbed his buttocks with both hands, pulling then pushing, simulating fucking her mouth as the full length of his penis filled her mouth momentarily, then was sliding out. Donovan could not restrain himself any longer and emptied his juices into her welcoming throat.

Argi smiled up at him showing him the sperm on her tongue, then she took him by the hand and said, 'Your turn darling.' Before leading him to her bed. What followed was several hours of passionate love making which left them both exhausted.

These recalled thoughts raced through Argi's mind while Donovan brewed the coffee and brought a cup over for Argi before announcing he was heading for the shower. He could see that she was slightly disappointed he was not coming back to bed, but he had some thinking and planning to do, and the shower was the best place to do it.

Chapter 38

20th August 2013 – Eckersley's Villa - 10:00

'Damn it! Dimitri. What the hell is going on?' Eckersley almost screamed down the phone. He was rattled, Alkis had disappeared, the hostages had been freed and the share price of Hellenic Aluminium was moving up, making his intended purchase more expensive. Although ever the optimist, he had a nasty knot in his stomach which was nagging him - he felt as if his control of the situation was slipping away. He needed Dimitri Karagianis as a sounding board.

'What is the public's mood today Dimitri?' said Eckersley.

'Support for the right is beginning to slip away I'm afraid. A newspaper leaked that the forest fire was arson by a group of North Macedonian activists. The leak came from the Home Office initially. Also news that an attempt to assassinate Kalfas had been thwarted by EKAM agents, and that the culprit had been apprehended in Edessa, attempting to flee the country into North Macedonia, angered the public,' explained Karagianis.

'I told you that attempting to kill Kalfas was a mistake. You should have consulted with me before you ordered the hit. They obviously think Alkis is the assassin and that's why they took him,' complained Eckersley.

'I had to try it. The public mood was in my favour because they were disillusioned by the violence in the streets and the destruction of iconic monuments. With Kalfas out of the way, the forthcoming general election would have been brought forward. We would have stood a good chance of winning or forming a coalition. We were only a couple of points behind his party before the assassination attempt, 'explained Karagianis.

'And now?' questioned Eckersley impatiently.

'And now Donovan the would be assassin, has become a loose cannon and is looking to finish the job.'

'Bugger,' said Eckersley. 'That won't improve the public mood now, will it?'

'No, now that the hostages are freed and the forest fire culprit is in custody, Kalfas's death will only boost the public's support for his party. I'm pretty certain he is in the Edessa area, he is a cunning devil and would certainly have found out where Kalfas is,' said Karagianis, not wanting to admit he was the whistle-blower on Alex.'

'Look, I need those Bauxite mines. If I can't buy them because the remaining shareholders won't sell, particularly with the price rising as it is, then I'll have to take them by force,' said Eckersley in a resigned voice, as a flicker of irritation and impatience shone in his eyes.

'That would be madness,' said Karagianis his eyes taking on a bleak look. 'That is tantamount to war.'

'Yes, indeed. But once they are taken it would be damn difficult to take them back without destroying them.'

'I hope you know what you are doing Arthur,' said Karagianis. He was now beginning to think that maybe Eckersley was quite mad. However, his main worry was Donovan. He could not let him assassinate Alex; it was too much to hope that he would fail again.

'What I do know is that I want those mines – no, I need those mines,' emphasised Eckersley, a hint of anger in his voice. 'The only thing I need you to do Dimitri is get rid of the Kalfas threat. Goodbye!'

Karagianis looked at his phone in disgust after Eckersley had disconnected the call. He was thinking on how rude Eckersley could be. But he wasn't going to do anything about Kalfas just because Eckersley wanted it. The Golden Dawn's, and thereby his own standing, would be far better served if Donovan were dead and he distanced himself from Eckersley.

If Donovan was still travelling around Greece immune from danger, it was because nobody was able to identify him. But if somehow Donovan's photo were to get into the public domain, there would be nowhere for him to go. Karagiannis racked his grey cells. Donovan had been adept at avoiding traffic cams and street cams but he might have overlooked or not noticed one. Then, Karagianis remembered that the kiosk where Conchita had been abducted had a security camera just to the side of the serving window. So perhaps because he was so busy with Conchita, Donovan hadn't noticed the camera.

Twenty minutes later Karagianis was sitting inside the kiosk looking through video footage from the day that Conchita had been taken from in front of the kiosk. It was going to be another scorcher of a day with the weather forecast predicting forty degrees Celsius for the tenth day running. Sitting in the cramped space of the kiosk Karagianis was soon sweating like a pig.

'Eureka,' yelled Karagianis as he came across the section of the video he had been hoping against hope to find. He looked around to see if anyone had heard him. Not even the kiosk owner had turned around. The video clearly showed for a few seconds Donovan's face full on. Got you now, thought Karagianis, a full face still photo is going to be circulating all over Greece in a few hours. Karagianis smiled for the first time in days as he hit the buttons on the video recorder that would produce stills from the video.

As Karagianis got into his car, he felt the ground tremor. Another earthquake. There had been several small earthquakes already that summer, none of them more than 5.6 on the Richter scale. Enough to cause older structures' brickwork to crumble a little, or cracks to appear on the walls, but not sufficient to cause alarm to the population who were used to such tremors. Greece sat astride several active fault lines and it is these along with plate movements which produce the regions earthquake risk.

Karagianis settled back into the back seat of his car after telling his driver to head for the Ministry of Home Affairs, the ministry that was headed up by Kaliope the Home Secretary. He would drop one of the static shots he had extracted from the video at the Home Office, and another shot of Donovan he would take to the right wing newspaper The Freedom Times.

At three o'clock that afternoon Kaliope, who was sitting with Argi in the ground floor bar of the Four Seasons Hotel enjoying a cup of Greek coffee, heard her mobile phone ping. Argi had been telling her about the lovely man she had met on the plane on the way to Edessa. Kaliope could tell by the way Argi was gushing and animated that she was madly in love with this man.

Kaliope reached for her mobile which was on the table in front of her. Instinct telling her that it was business and not personal.

Kaliope said, 'So, you haven't told me his name yet.'

Oh, sorry Kaliope, it's Donovan.'

'He's Irish?

'You would think so, but he has no trace of an Irish accent. He said he was - well come to think of it he didn't say where he was from.'

Kaliope laughed, a contagious laugh that those around her adored. 'You are smitten,' she said as she fondly took Argi's hand. 'When are we going to meet him?'

'Any moment now. He is coming down for a coffee.'

As another earthquake tremor shook the hotel slopping the contents of full glasses over drinkers and tables alike, Kaliope pressed the notification tab on her phone and saw that her office had sent her an urgent message with a photo attached. She opened it. The message read *Urgent: Front facial of suspected assassin. Awaiting further instructions.*

'Wow, my office has sent the first photograph we have of Alex's would be assassin. He is a good looking man in a dangerous sort of way,' said Kaliope as she passed her phone to Argi. 'Here have a look.'

Argi took one look at the photograph, then froze. All the blood drained from her face as she sat staring at the face of the man she had just spent the night with.

'Are you alright Argi?' asked Kaliope on seeing Argi's ashen features. 'What's the matter?'

'I'm going to be sick,' moaned Argi. 'That's the man about whom I've been talking. He's here in the hotel,' Argi's voice was beginning to reach a hysterical volume.

'Calm down!' said Kaliope forcefully and took both of Argis' hands in hers. 'Look at me! Now take deep breaths, slowly. Keep looking at me.'

Kaliope was frantically thinking. She had to calm Argi down before that man appeared for his date with her. Where were Yannis and Chris when I need them. Or, Gitta for that matter. Well, she knew where Gitta was. She was with Alex. Argi seemed calmer now so Kaliope released one of her hands and deftly retransmitted the photo on her phone to the WhatsApp group of Alex, Gitta, Chris and Yannis. At the same time she pressed the red button in the centre of her phone which sent a signal to both Yannis and Chris indicating she was in danger.

'We should leave now,' suggested Argi.

'No!' said Kaliope rather too forcefully. 'If he comes down and you are not here he might become suspicious that something is wrong and disappear. You have to brazen it out.'

'Okay,' Argi agreed reluctantly.

'Hello Argi,' said Donovan as he pulled up a chair and sat down. He pretended not to notice how agitated Argi was, instead he turned his attention to Kaliope.

'And you are?' he enquired.

'I am one of Argi's colleagues,' said Kaliope looking Donovan in the eye without flinching. Which ministry are you in then,' asked Donovan, giving Kaliope his most wholesome smile.

'I'm afraid if I told you I would have to kill you,' said Kaliope giving Donovan an equally wholesome smile.

Donovan looked at Argi but she wasn't about to help him. She could not even meet his eyes and that made Donovan suspicious. This other one is brazen, thought Donovan. He remembered that as he sat down she had hurriedly put her mobile phone away. Why he thought. They can't possibly know who I am. I made sure not to expose my face to any traffic cams or security cameras.

His mind raced, recalling his movements of yesterday. He would bet on the fact he hadn't been exposed to any traffic cams or security cameras, then how he asked himself. The only other possibility would be someone photographed him. Who though? Conchita? Had he missed a camera inside her bag when he searched it? He was sure he hadn't.

Had she taken a photo with the mobile phone? He ruled that out at once because he had confiscated her phone from the bag. Unless of course, she took a photo while he was asleep but then if she had, he would have been picked up at the airport in Salonika. No, he'd missed something.

Then he had it. Shit he thought, the kiosk, it would have had a security camera. Karagianis has done the dirty on me and my face is now circulating around Greece.

While he had been thinking Donovan had slipped his right hand into the big front pocket of his Cargo shorts and pulled out his Beretta.

'If you don't tell me who you are I will kill both of you,' he calmly stated, holding the gun out of sight under the table, pointing it at Kaliope's midriff.

Chapter 39

20th August 2013 – EKAM Black Ops Site - 15:00

Alkis slumped over the metal table waiting for the inevitable interrogation. This is how it had been since early morning - an electric shock followed by a cold water dousing from a high pressure hose – followed by interrogation. Yannis always administered the electric shock treatment and unknown to Alkis, a hooded Chris handled the high pressure hose.

The door of Alkis's holding cell opened. He steeled himself with what more was to come. He could feel his determination and the fight draining bit by bit from him. He watched as Yannis and Chris sat down. Yannis put the large jug he had been carrying down on the floor along with a muslin cloth. Alkis's heart sank, he was to be water-boarded!

'Hello Alkis,' said Yannis. 'Are you ready to talk?'

Alkis said nothing as he tried to steel himself against the fear of being water boarded.

'Look we know you tried on the Prime Ministers life. All we want from you is who put you up to the attempted assassination. What you did is treason, which means the death penalty in Greece as you know. But if you give us the information we want we will be able to help you get it commuted to life imprisonment. Isn't that so Chris?'

'Yes, indeed,' confirmed Chris.

Still Alkis said nothing.

Yannis picked up the jug and cloth and moved round behind Alkis. Chris took the cloth, pulled Alkis back in his seat making sure his face was looking up to the ceiling, then placed the cloth over his nose and mouth. Yannis started pouring the water over the cloth while Chris held his nose. Alkis squirmed and struggled as he tried to drink the water but with his nose pinched he had to breathe through his mouth - and that was where the water was. Alkis started to choke as the water entered his windpipe, he tried to cry out but it just made his lungs fill with more water. He felt he was drowning.

Yannis stopped pouring the water while Chris let go of Alkis's nose, pulling the cloth away at the same time. They sat Alkis forward so he could cough up the water and clear his lungs. He was heaving with the effort and both Yannis and Chris feared he was going to have a heart attack. When Yannis felt that Alkis's breathing was back to normal, he signalled to Chris and picked up the jug.

'No stop!' yelled Alkis. 'I'll give you what you want, but please no more.' There was desperation in his voice, he had obviously had enough.

Yannis smiled at Chris. 'Let's get him freshened up and into a clean interrogation room. Someone will come and escort you to the showers and give you clean clothing Alkis, maybe something to eat. You will be given a paper and pen where you can write your statement. Make it comprehensive. We'll talk later.'

An hour later, Yannis and Chris were sitting opposite Alkis who was handcuffed to the table they were sitting around.

'For the benefit of the recorder I am Yannis Spanos, with Chris Horsman and we are interrogating Alkis Eleftheradou in connection with his statement. Chris why don't you start?'

'Thank you,' said Chris. Then turning to face Alkis he said. 'Your statement was thorough I'll give you that. You've been a naughty boy haven't you? Most of what you confessed to us we knew about already...woah.'

Chris was interrupted by another tremor which lasted ten seconds. The building struggled, as this time instead of a horizontal movement, the tremor produced a vertical movement, which was far more dangerous for the integrity of buildings.

'That was the strongest to date. Go on Chris,' said Yannis.

'Where was I? Ah yes. What we don't know is what plans and resources Eckersley has for taking the bauxite mines in Macedonia. I'm sure as his right hand man you have knowledge of what he intends.'

Alkis sat for a moment thinking. How far could he go to avoid another session of extreme pain. He supposed whatever degree of confession he made it would make no difference to how long he stayed in prison but it just might help to avoid the death penalty for treason.

'Eckersley is desperate for both alumina and aluminium which the bauxite mines have in abundance particularly the two coming on-line soon. His company have recently successfully built and tested a new commercial airliner which will compete with both Airbus and Boeing. It is a two decker just like the Airbus 380 but it can carry more passengers, is quieter due to its Xplore Whispering engines and lighter than any commercial jet on the market today. So he needs those mines,' said Alkis.

'And how does he propose to get them?' questioned Chris.

'If he can't buy them he will take them by force.'

'We destroyed his mercenary army which had taken the UN delegation hostages at the farmhouse,' said Yannis. 'So he can't use them anymore, can he?'

'He doesn't need them because he had already extracted a dozen of the best men from the farmhouse before it was taken by you. He will use those to take the mines by force. Then in order to keep to hold on to them he has a pledge from the North Macedonian government to supply him with the arms and men needed to hold them.'

'But that is tantamount to war!,' exclaimed Yannis.

'Yes,' said Alkis.

At that moment, the screens of both Yannis's and Chris's phones displayed the notification that Kaliope was in danger, along with a photograph.

'Donovan!' said Yannis. 'Let's go!'

Two minutes later a hooded figure holding a gun, stepped into the interrogation room where Alkis was, calmly walked up to him, then shot him in the head.

Chapter 40

20th August 2013 – Four Seasons Hotel - 16:00

Yannis and Chris bundled into an EKAM SUV telling the driver to get them to the Four Seasons hotel as fast as possible, and if that meant breaking the speed limit so be it.

'You can remove your hood now Chris,' said Yannis.

'What? Oh, yes, didn't realise it was still on.'

'I'm calling for a drone to monitor the area around Eckersley's villa,' said Yannis. 'We need to know if and when his band of soldiers leave the villa.'

'Good call,' agreed Chris. 'It feels as though we are almost at the end game now. What's your plan when we get to the hotel?

'I don't know yet but we need a ploy that gets us near to Donovan so we can take him out without endangering the guests or Kaliope. I've told the driver to take us to the tradesman's entrance.'

'ETA six minutes,' said the driver as he passed a truck and only just managed to squeeze in front of it to avoid the oncoming vehicle, whilst leaving a cacophony of angry horns in his wake.

Meanwhile, back at the Four Seasons hotel bar, Kaliope was wondering if Donovan's patience would run out before Yannis turned up. She had been forced to call Alex when she had realised that the danger to Argi's life was not an idle threat. She couldn't let Argi become a victim of a mad terrorist, for that was what Donovan was. But of course it was also a risk that saving Argi's life could put Alex in grave danger too.

She had spoken to Alex just five minutes previous, inviting him down for coffee and the opportunity to mingle with some of the guests. 'It was good PR,' she said. Fortunately, Alex could not come down at once so there was no immediate danger to him from Donovan. Kaliope was praying that Yannis would turn up before Alex showed up.

Suddenly, Donovan noticed a waiter heading for their table.

'Get rid of him,' hissed Donovan.

Kaliope saw that it was Yannis dressed as a waiter carrying a tray with three glasses on it.

'Θελεται ποτα, καφεδακι μιπος;'said Yannis to Donovan, asking him if he would like a drink or a coffee.

'I don't want anything, now go away,' said Donovan not understanding a word of what Yannis had said.

Yannis turned to Chris who was dressed as a waiter too and was carrying some delicious looking cakes on his tray. 'Ελλα να με βοηθησες,'shouted Yannis, asking for help.

Chris walked over. 'What can I help you with Yannis?' said Chris in passable English. Yannis repeated what he had said before. Chris turned to Donovan and said, 'This waiter does not speak English. He asked if you would like an alcoholic drink or a coffee.'

'And I told him that I don't want anything, neither do my two friends here,' said Donovan in an agitated voice, whilst at the same time acknowledging the two women at his table..

Kaliope and Argi were transfixed at the surreal conversation taking place in front of them. They were separately thinking how the hell were Yannis and Chris going to subdue Donovan before he gets to fire the gun he was holding under the table.

They didn't have to wait long before they had their answer. Chris turned towards Yannis who, as they had rehearsed just the once a few minutes ago, turned quickly towards Chris. Their trays smashed together with a loud crash, and the cakes, with the help of Chris, flew up in the air before falling around Donovan's head.

Donovan barely noticed as he concentrated on keeping his gun steady, pointing it at Kaliope's midriff. He didn't even notice when

Chris, with a deft sleight of hand, produced a small syringe filled with Midazolam.

'So sorry sir,' apologised Chris as he feverishly started to clear the crumbs and bits of cake from Donovan's shoulders and hair. Whilst doing this Chris made sure that the needle of the syringe, broke the skin at the back of Donovan's neck. As both Yannis and Chris had hoped, the faint scratch did not register with Donovan at all, his concentration blocking out any physical senses. His body too, didn't register that a powerful debilitating poison was now coursing through his blood stream.

'We'll bring something to clean up the glass from the floor sir. And once again sorry for the mess,' apologised Chris, as he and Yannis hurried away.

'How long for the poison to work?' asked Yannis when they were out of earshot.

'Should begin to work any moment now,' said Chris.

Kaliope watched as two men disguised as waiters left the area. She hadn't a clue what had gone on, so she was puzzled as to why they had not tried to disarm Donovan. Just then another earthquake tremor shook the hotel sending a few glasses crashing from tables. It lasted twenty seconds. Kaliope and Argi braced themselves by holding onto the edges of the table.

Donovan too felt the tremor. He tried to bring his free hand up to support himself as both Kaliope and Argi had, but his arm would not do as his brain commanded, so he swayed in his chair to the rhythm of the earthquakes movement instead. He felt a pang of fear as he was not used to not being in charge of his body. The gun in his hand felt extraordinarily heavy. His brain sent a command to his trigger finger to pull it, but it wouldn't. he couldn't even remember why he was holding a gun or what he was doing sitting with two beautiful women.

In fact, those were his last thoughts, he had no knowledge of his gun falling from his lifeless fingers, then dropping to the floor, and he never heard the loud thud of his head hitting the edge of the table, as he fell off his chair onto the floor.

Chapter 41

20th August 2013 – Four Seasons Hotel - 21:00

Alex listened with astonishment as Yannis, Chris, and Kaliope gave him a run-down of everything that had happened since the arrest of Alkis. He was particularly pleased that Donovan had been neutralised, splitting his sides with laughter at Kaliope's description of Chris's distracting cake-throwing antics.

Argi was feeling sorry for herself and didn't contribute much to the story, even though they all told her that none of it was her fault as there was no way she could have known that Donovan was the assassin. Once Alex was up to date they turned their attention to what to do about Eckersley and his small army of mercenaries.

'Do you think that Alkis was telling the truth?' Alex asked Yannis.

'There is no way of being certain of course but the fifty- odd passes that our reconnaissance drone has done in the last two hours, has indicated that there definitely are more men at the villa than the few that Gitta saw.'

'But we don't know exactly how many?'

'Not exactly but a good guesstimate would be close to the number that Alkis stated,' said Yannis.

Just then another tremor shook the hotel. When it had stopped Chris laughingly said. 'With a little luck these tremors will cause the villa to collapse and bury Eckersley.'

Everyone chortled at his comment. Argi's mobile phone buzzed. Looking at the screen she said, 'It's Leonidas.'

'Take it on speaker,' said Alex.

'You're on speaker Leonidas,' said Argi. 'We are all here. What have you got for us?'

'Good evening everyone. In the last half hour the shares of Texon have shot through the roof because there is a strong rumour that Simon Millar is planning a hostile takeover for Xplore Industries. Millar wants to join the commercial space race and fears the others such as Origin etc, are too far ahead for him to catch up and get a decent piece of the action.'

'Won't Xplore Industries shares go through the roof?' asked Kaliope.

'You would think so under normal circumstances however Millar apparently is not a fan of Eckersley or North Macedonia. He is a Grecophile and believes they are going too far in their belief that Greece's Macedonian province belongs to them. So he is planning to break Xplore Industries up into little chunks and sell off the parts he doesn't want. Because of this fear investors are selling the stock off.'

'Eckersley won't like that,' said Alex.

'No he won't,' agreed Leonidas. 'But there's more. Many investors have been spooked by Xplore Industries connection with North Macedonia. Skilfully leaked information from an unknown source has underscored the fact that the company is woefully short of aluminium and alumina resources and that they are having trouble sourcing the metal. This too has given the sell-off a lot of momentum.'

'That's wonderful news Leonidas,' praised Alex. 'How are Hellenic Aluminium shares doing?'

'Since the Millar rumour they have been on the rise. Investors are betting that Millar will also try to get a majority holding because he will need aluminium and alumina to clad the space vehicles which he hopes he will have, after acquiring Xplore Industries.'

'Question is, what will Eckersley do when he hears all this? He is bound to do so very quickly or he's even heard it already,' said

Yannis, his forehead wrinkled as if he was in deep thought. 'He's still a dangerous man.'

Gitta's body gave an involuntary shudder at Yannis's remarks, her mind racing back to her ordeal in Eckersley's villa. Alex who was sitting next to her noticed and placed a comforting hand on her thigh. She gave him a reassuring smile, letting him know that she was all right.

'Yes, I agree with Yannis,' said Chris, looking around the table. 'I believe he will act immediately he hears the rumours regarding Millar. We should be vigilant tonight and make sure we can anticipate his every move. I suggest we get an EKAM platoon on standby all night as well as beef up the drone passes over his villa. If he moves it will be at night. Do you agree Yannis?'

'I'll get onto it right away if Alex agrees,' said Yannis.

Alex nodded his assent.

'Argi, what's the latest from the UN regarding our veto on the North Macedonian name?' asked Alex.

'Our people have been working hard canvassing the delegates in the UN. Preliminary estimates are showing that we probably have enough votes to win the day.'

'When is the vote?'

'This evening at eight o'clock eastern standard time in the United States.'

Alex looked at his watch. 'In four hours' time then,' he said.

To Alex, it felt like the end game was fast approaching and the God's seem to be favouring us for once. Perhaps it will all be over by the morning and they could all go back to Athens to take up their normal routines.

He was looking forward to meeting his son, whom Gitta had promised to bring to Athens as soon as this was all over. Perhaps he and Gitta should get married, he was sure the public would be overjoyed. Argi had confirmed that he, Alex, was now more popular than he had been for six months, and his party was ahead in the polls, with the Golden Dawn was losing ground. He was confident that the election in five months' time, not far away now, would give him a workable majority.

While Alex was having happy thoughts in the Four Seasons hotel, Arthur Eckersley definitely was not. In fact he was having very nasty thoughts. The news that Millar was after Xplore Industries distressed him. He needed to head the potential takeover bid full on. He had to do something to push up Xplore's share price and make it more difficult for Millar.

Earlier, Eckersley had spoken to the company's finance officer about the rumoured Millar takeover. The finance officer had suggested that they should buy back a large amount of their own shares. This would have the effect of giving shareholders an extra dividend while at the same time increasing the value of the company.

As the current market capitalisation of Xplore Industries was ninety-five billion sterling, Millar would probably have to offer another 10%. The finance officer also suggested that taking over Hellenic Aluminium would help stave off Millar too.

On hearing this, Eckersley had given his finance officer the go ahead to buy-back twelve billion pounds worth of Xplore shares.

But, it wasn't enough for Eckersley. He was an impatient man, who was angry and who therefore was not thinking very clearly. This had been the first time in his business life that he had felt vulnerable, and he didn't like it. His arrogance had always helped him brush aside any problems that came up. He had to act decisively, so he ordered Gregori, who had earlier returned from Edessa with the news that Alkis was a prisoner of the Edessa EKAM unit, to get the men to fully arm themselves.

Back in the Four Seasons, a naked Kaliope was lying on her back on her bed, eyes closed, while Yannis was giving her an oily sensual massage. Her phone buzzed breaking the erotic mood.

'Oh bum!' she uttered.

Yannis stopped the massage, pinched one of her nipples and said, 'You had better get that, it might be one of the drone pilots.'

Kaliope poked he tongue out at Yannis then reluctantly picked up her phone. 'Yes?' she said.

'Ma'am it's Tatoi drone control here, I'm patching through the video feed from the drone circling over co-ordinates 40.80.17 and 22.04.40.'

'Thank you, I'll let you know what to do as soon as I can.'

'Check this out Yannis,' said Kaliope showing him the video feed. '

As they both watched the screen, they could see twelve well-armed men dressed in fatigues were sitting in three open top four-by-fours, moving away from the villa on the Edessa road. Eckersley had taken up the point position at the rear of the men, in a jeep.

'They must be heading for the bauxite mines of Hellenic Aluminium. I'm going to get the men ready,' said Yannis as he struggled to get his clothes on whilst attempting to still look at the screen. 'Call Chris, Alex and Gitta could you darling, and get them to meet me in front of the hotel.'

Once dressed Yannis gave Kaliope a long lingering kiss before heading for the door. He turned to her saying, 'I love you. We'll continue where we left off later.'

'Be careful darling,' said Kaliope blowing him a kiss. 'Come back safely.'

Once in the hotel lobby Yannis called the EKAM base and told his No. 2 to pick twenty-five men and meet him on the outskirts of Edessa on the road to the bauxite mines. Before long, the others joined him in the lobby and as they walked to the hotel car park where Yannis's EKAM SUV was parked he updated them on what the drone had seen.

'Kaliope has allowed my phone to access the drone video feed so we have real-time information.' Turning to Alex he said, 'You don't have to come Alex. There is going to be a firefight and it's dangerous, you could get badly hurt. Don't forget you are the Prime Minister, not a soldier, nor an agent like Gitta.'

'I've debated this with Gitta already Yannis. I want to be there when it's done and dusted.'

'Okay but my report will say that we warned you and that we reluctantly yielded to your wishes.'

Alex nodded his understanding of the situation, assuring them that whatever happened to him it was on his own head and his responsibility alone.

Five minutes later they had joined the rest of Yannis's men on the road to the mines.

Chapter 42

21st August 2013 – Road to Bauxite Mines – 03:00

Yannis had cast the video link from the drone from his phone to the screen on the dashboard of their SUV. They could see that the four vehicles carrying Eckersley and his men were moving quite slowly because for security reasons they were travelling without lights.

'I've calculated that we will reach the turn-off to the mines fifteen minutes before Eckersley does. That's assuming of course that they continue at their current speed.'

'What's the plan?' asked Chris.

'Well, before they reach the turn-off there is a long left hand bend, so they won't see the turn-off until the last minute. We can take the turn-off and park the SUVs and then set up a couple of traps back on the main road just before the turn-off.'

'I take it we'll hide in the trees either side of the main road and when their vehicles have been disabled, open up with guns blazing. Do we want to take any prisoners?' asked Chris.

'No, let's make this clean. Not even Eckersley should survive this.'

Suddenly, Yannis who was driving, wrenched on the steering wheel as some unknown force pushed the SUV towards the side of the road. At the same time they saw the vehicles in front swerving over the road too. The SUV started to bounce up and down as it travelled over cracks in the road.

'Earthquake!' yelled Yannis. 'A big one this time. There are old underground mines around here so there's a danger of large fissures opening up.'

The tremor lasted a good thirty seconds with the motion being up and down as opposed to the previous tremors being side to side.

All the vehicles had stopped moving as they waited for the tremor waves to subside.

'I wonder if that was the big one,' mused Chris to no-one in particular.

'Let's go!' Yannis barked into his helmet mic, ordering his men to move forward.

Five minutes later they approached the turn-off - they followed the lead vehicle as it turned right onto the road leading to the bauxite mines and parked up. The men alighted from their vehicles and gathered around Yannis.

'Listen up lads, we have ten minutes till Eckersley and his men arrive at this turn-off. String a wire across the road between two trees, attach grenades either end, so that when their lead vehicle trips the wire the grenades will blow. As they are without lights we can lay down a spike strip just beyond the trip wire, just to make sure no vehicle tries to make a run for it.'

With two minutes in hand the traps were set and the men were stationed on either side of the road ready to shoot the hell out of Eckersley's men.

'Quiet lads,' whispered Yannis into his helmet mic. 'Here they come.'

They heard, rather than saw the enemy vehicles as they came around the bend approaching the trip wire. As the lead vehicle tripped the wire the grenades exploded causing the vehicles to screech to a halt, but not before the lead vehicles tyres blew as they hit the spike strip.

'Now!' yelled Yannis into his helmet mic. The men, hidden in the trees, either side of the road, raked the three SUV's with over a thousand rounds of ammunition. As they did, another earthquake occurred, this time it was the big one they had been waiting for. It only lasted twenty seconds but it was much stronger than all the previous ones over the last few days. Several fissures opened up along the road, one large one claiming a vehicle. A number of trees crashed to the ground but amazingly no-one was hurt.

When Yannis was certain that no-one could have survived the onslaught of fire power he told his men to stop firing. An eerie silence descended on the road as the smell of cordite wafted over the men and the swirls of smoke from the machine guns swayed in the breeze.

'Anyone hurt?' Yannis shouted not bothering with his mic. Miraculously nobody was injured.

'Okay, excellent job men. Let's clean this mess up and head back to Edessa.'

'I'm going to check on Eckersley,' announced Gitta.

'I'll come with you,' said Alex.

'Me too,' echoed both Chris and Yannis. 'But let's be careful,' warned Yannis. 'It's too dark to see much back there.'

The four of them walked to the back of the convoy, clambering over pieces of metal, bodies, and avoiding large cracks in the surface of the road. As they neared where they estimated Eckersley's jeep should be, they heard a low groaning sound somewhere in front of them.

The ambient light, the light from their collective torches and the vehicle's headlights started to reveal the scene in front of them, they saw that Eckersley's jeep was on its side with one of its wheels lodged in a two metre wide fissure.

As the foursome carefully approached the fissure they realised that the groaning was coming from the fissure itself. Standing on the edge they saw that it was Eckersley who was lying at the bottom of the fissure some four metres below the level of the road's surface. He had obviously been thrown out of the jeep when it had overturned onto its side.

'Help!' yelled Eckersley the moment he saw their faces looking down at him. 'Get me out of here, I think my leg is broken and it's trapped by a rock.'

Gitta smiled down at him as she remembered the pain that he had inflicted on her while she was a prisoner in his villa. 'I should shoot you where you lie,' she shouted down at him. 'Give me one good reason why we should spare your life?'

Just then an aftershock rumbled through the area and the fissure began to close inch by inch.

'It's too dangerous to go down and attempt a rescue,' said Alex as Eckersley screamed with the pain of the pressure on his leg.

'I know this sounds callous, maybe inhuman even, but this is a golden opportunity to let him die and avoid legal trials, cost consuming evidence gathering and astronomical legal fees paid by the taxpayers,' said Yannis.

The others nodded in agreement as another aftershock hit the area. The fissure closed a few more inches, which triggered even shriller Eckersley screams as his leg was crushed even more.

Without any sense of guilt or remorse Yannis, Chris, Alex and Gitta, turned away from the fissure. As they walked towards their SUV Gitta took Alex's arm and said, 'I'm glad it's over at last darling.' Alex squeezed her arm affectionately and smiled at her in response.

Up ahead Yannis put his arm around Chris's shoulder. 'Thanks for your support Chris, it's a good feeling knowing that America is our strongest ally.'

'No worries Yannis, c'mon let's get back, the beers are on me.'

Article Extracts from The Hellenic News

22/08/2013 – The United Nations vote on the validity of the name North Macedonia, found that it was not appropriate and no other country should use the name Macedonia as part of their name.

23/08/2013 – An autopsy on the body of Arthur Eckersley the CEO of Xplore Industries found that he had died of loss of blood due to a severely damaged leg.

29/08/2013 – Simon Millar the CEO of Texon completed the acquisition of Xplore Industries and became a major stakeholder in Hellenic Aluminium.

16/09/2013 – The cabinet office was pleased to announce the engagement of Alex Kalfas to Gitta Lehrer. Here they are pictured with their son Alex JR.

07/10/2013 – Alex Kalfas was returned to Government in a landslide victory in the general election. The Golden Dawn party lost all but one of their seats.

About the Author

Educated in the United Kingdom Philip had a successful career in investment banking working for Citibank and Chase Manhattan in Europe and the Lebanon in Treasury, before transferring to London as Head of Learning and Development for Union Bank of Switzerland.

He was later appointed to their New York office as Head of Learning and Development for North America. He then set up a successful financial training company in New York City. In 1999 he returned to London where he worked as a training consultant to financial services institutions and the Ministry of Défense.

He then went to Greece where he built educational databases for several on-line brokerage houses and wrote several book teaching English as a second language.

Since retiring and returning to England he has published two books on investment instruments (Mastering Options and Competing In The Financial Markets) targeting university graduates. His fictional works include The Gladio Protocol his first Alex Kalfas thriller, If I could Paint Your Picture, an anthology of poems, and Smokescreen, the second in the Alex Kalfas thriller series.

Don't miss out!

Visit the website below and you can sign up to receive emails whenever Philip Cooper publishes a new book. There's no charge and no obligation.

https://books2read.com/r/B-A-SHGM-NVZHC

BOOKS 2 READ

Connecting independent readers to independent writers.

Also by Philip Cooper

Alex Kalfas Series
The Gladio Protocol
Smokescreen